THE FARM STAND

AN AMISH MARKETPLACE NOVEL

Amy Clipston

ZONDERVAN

The Farm Stand

Copyright © 2020 by Amy Clipston

This title is also available as a Zondervan ebook.
This title is also available as a Zondervan audio book.

Requests for information should be addressed to:
Zondervan, *3900 Sparks Dr. SE, Grand Rapids, Michigan 49546*

ISBN 978-0-310-35647-9 (softcover)
ISBN 978-0-310-35646-2 (e-book)
ISBN 978-0-310-35648-6 (audio download)
ISBN 978-0-310-36148-0 (library edition)
ISBN 978-0-310-36665-2 (mass market)

Library of Congress Cataloging-in-Publication
CIP data is available upon request.

Printed in the United States of America

21 22 23 24 25 / CWM / 10 9 8 7 6 5 4 3 2 1

For my wonderful literary agent,
Natasha Kern, with love

GLOSSARY

ach: oh
aenti: aunt
appeditlich: delicious
bedauerlich: sad
boppli: baby
bopplin: babies
bruder: brother
bu: boy
buwe: boys
daadi: granddad
daed: father
danki: thank you
dat: dad
dochder: daughter
dochdern: daughters
Englisher: a non-Amish person
fraa: wife
freind: friend
freinden: friends
froh: happy
gegisch: silly
gern gschehne: you're welcome
Gude mariye: Good morning
gut: good
Gut nacht: Good night
haus: house
Ich liebe dich: I love you

kaffi: coffee
kapp: prayer covering or cap
kichli: cookie
kichlin: cookies
kind: child
kinner: children
krank: sick
kuche: cake
kumm: come
liewe: love, a term of endearment
maed: young women, girls
maedel: young woman
mamm: mom
mammi: grandma
mei: my
naerfich: nervous
narrisch: crazy
onkel: uncle
Ordnung: The oral tradition of practices required and forbidden in the Amish faith
schee: pretty
schmaert: smart
schtupp: family room
schweschder: sister
schweschdere: sisters
sohn: son
Was iss letz?: What's wrong?
Wie geht's: How do you do? or Good day!
wunderbaar: wonderful
ya: yes
zwillingbopplin: twins

The Amish Marketplace Series Family Trees

GRANDPARENTS
Erma m. Sylvan Gingerich
|
Lynn m. Freeman Kurtz
Mary m. Lamar Petersheim
Walter m. Rachelle
Harvey m. Darlene

SECOND GENERATION PARENTS AND CHILDREN
Lynn m. Freeman Kurtz
Christiana __|__ Phoebe

Mary m. Lamar Petersheim
Cornelius (Neil) __|__ Salina

Ellen m. Neil Petersheim
Betsy Kay __|__ Jayne

Darlene m. Harvey Gingerich
Bethany __|__ Anthony

Rachelle m. Walter Gingerich
|
Leanna

Leanna m. Marlin Wengerd (deceased)
|
Chester

Joyce m. Merle Stoltzfus
Jeffrey ⌐ Nicholas

Jean m. Ira Yoder
Josiah ⌐ Lizzie

Shirley m. Gary Zimmerman
Irvin ⌐ William ⌐ Roger

Karen m. Irvin Zimmerman
|
Heather

Loretta m. Robert Horst
Caroline ⌐ Irene

NOTE TO THE READER

While this novel is set against the real backdrop of Lancaster County, Pennsylvania, the characters are fictional. There is no intended resemblance between the characters in this book and any real members of the Amish and Mennonite communities. As with any work of fiction, I've taken license in some areas of research as a means of creating the necessary circumstances for my characters. My research was thorough; however, it would be impossible to be completely accurate in details and description, since each and every community differs. Therefore, any inaccuracies in the Amish and Mennonite lifestyles portrayed in this book are completely due to fictional license.

CHAPTER 1

Salina Petersheim huffed as she pulled two wagons piled high with boxes of fresh fruit and vegetables across the parking lot at the Bird-in-Hand marketplace. The hot Pennsylvania morning air felt like a smothering, wet blanket, and perspiration pooled at the base of her neck as she blew out a puff of air to push the ties of her prayer covering out of her face.

Customers' cars already filled nearly all the spaces in the lot, a sign that it would be another busy day in July. She looked toward the front of the building, where people already stood in line waiting for the market to open.

Her shoulders tightened with frustration, and she silently scolded herself. Why hadn't she set her alarm before she climbed into bed last night? She was running nearly thirty minutes behind, which meant she'd not only made her driver wait but she would still be stocking the shelves in her Farm Stand booth when all those customers spilled in through the front doors. The market was open only Thursday through Saturday each week, and since today was Thursday, she had to set up all her produce at once.

If only Josiah and his family hadn't stayed so late after supper last night, she might not have been so tired that she forgot to set her alarm.

Ashamed to be placing blame on her boyfriend, she pushed the thought away. Then she heaved and yanked as the wheels of the two wagons hit the ramp. She pulled them to the top and halted, hoping they would stay in place as she pulled her key card from her pocket to unlock the back door reserved for vendors. Once the door was open, she managed to pull the wagons through without help and then start her journey to her booth, grateful it was near the back of the building.

Her arms and shoulders ached as she maneuvered down the short aisle to the Farm Stand, the wagon wheels scraping along the worn oak floors as she trekked past the Unique Leather and Wood Gifts booth, run by Jeff Stoltzfus, her cousin Christiana Kurtz's boyfriend.

"Salina! There you are!" Christiana, who was also her best friend, appeared as Salina moved past her Bake Shop, located across from Salina's booth. Her cousin grabbed the handle of one of the wagons and pulled.

"Hey, Christiana," Salina responded as she switched to using both hands to pull the second wagon. She considered her cousin's concerned expression. She'd always thought Christiana, who was twenty-six and only six months older than Salina, was her prettiest cousin—although she kept that opinion to herself. Christiana had fiery red hair and blue-green eyes, coloring unique among the cousins. Salina had inherited dark-brown hair and baby-blue eyes from her mother.

"I was so worried about you," Christiana said. "You're normally already here when I arrive. I even called your *dat*'s phone, and he told me you were running late."

One reason Salina enjoyed running a booth in the marketplace was that it gave her the opportunity to spend time not just with Christiana but with all her favorite cousins. Bethany and Leanna ran booths there as well, and they all looked out for one another.

Salina lowered her gaze and sighed. "*Ya*, I was late this morning. I don't like starting the market weekend like this. You know I always do my best to be organized and ready for my customers."

Jeff sidled up to Salina and took over pulling her wagon. "Let me get this for you."

"*Danki*, Jeff."

She was grateful the couple met when Christiana opened her Bake Shop last spring. Their booths were next to each other, so they'd had plenty of opportunities to talk, and soon they were dating. Jeff was a kind and thoughtful man, handsome with dark eyes and matching dark, curly hair. He was also twenty-nine, a few years older than Christiana. Salina wondered if he was ready for marriage and would propose to her cousin soon.

The thought brought both excitement and anxiety. Would she be ready to get married if Josiah asked? Would she be ready to join the Yoder family?

She couldn't think about that now. She had so much to do, and the market was opening in five minutes. As she entered her booth, she cringed. She'd never get even half her inventory organized in time. What would her customers think if her space was disheveled? They might consider buying their produce at a more presentable market—although hers was the only booth here that sold such a variety from a garden. She turned toward the empty shelves and pressed her lips together.

"We'll help you. Put us to work." Christiana seemed to have read Salina's mind.

"But you have to get your own booths ready." Salina gestured across the aisle.

"We are ready," Jeff said.

"*Danki*, then." Salina's shoulders sagged as humiliation set in. Her tardiness wasn't affecting only her day. It was affecting Christiana and Jeff's, too, and she hated that.

She set out a box of corn on the cob and then unloaded plastic containers of blackberries. Soon the hum of customers' conversations danced from the aisle as she turned to arrange a display of cucumbers.

"Excuse me."

Salina spun to look up into the face of a man with golden-blond hair and striking blue eyes. He looked to be in his late twenties, and she could tell by his clothes that he was Mennonite and not Amish. He wore a blue plaid, button-down shirt and jeans, along with suspenders that clipped to his waistband. He also held a hat in his hand. It was similar to the straw hats her father and brother wore, but its rim wasn't quite as broad. And he was tall—just as tall as her father and brother, if not taller.

"*Gude mariye.*" He was also clean-shaven, but unlike Amish men, a Mennonite man without a beard could be single or married.

"Hello." Salina stood straighter and swiped her hands down her apron, hoping she looked acceptable for her first customer.

"How much for all your cherry tomatoes?" He jammed his thumb toward the display Christiana had just set out.

Salina blinked. Had she heard him correctly? "You want all of them?"

"Please." He gestured widely. "I'd also like all your cucumbers, carrots, and butterhead lettuce."

Salina tilted her head and studied his face. She wasn't in the mood for humor this morning. "Is this some kind of joke?"

He chuckled. "No, it's not. I own the restaurant across the street. Zimmerman's Family Restaurant? You may have noticed it. We've been open for about a year, and I want to add some dishes with local ingredients to my menu and upgrade my salad bar. I'm not just the owner. I'm the chef too."

"Oh."

"You'll have to stop by for a meal sometime."

She nodded and looked past him as customers filed in and out of nearby booths. How would she make it through the day if this man wiped out so much of what she had to offer?

Christiana and Jeff came over, and her cousin's eyes sparkled with what was no doubt curiosity as she looked back and forth between Salina and her customer. "We're going to head back to our booths now."

"*Danki* for your help." Salina touched Christiana's arm. "I'll talk to you later."

"*Gern gschehne.*" Christiana nodded at the man, who smiled at her, and then she and Jeff hurried off.

The man looked down at the floor as Daisy, the resident marketplace cat, brushed against his leg. Then he grinned as he squatted and rubbed her chin. "Hello there. What's your name?"

"That's Daisy," Salina said. "She lives here and likes to visit with the vendors and customers."

"Nice to make your acquaintance, Daisy," he told the gray tabby before he stood and gave Salina two palms up. "What do you say, then? How much for everything I need?"

"Let me work up a price for you."

"Fantastic." He rubbed his hands together. "You have a great selection. Where do you get your produce?"

"I have a large garden." She walked to the counter at the back of her booth, and he followed.

"You grow all this?" He glanced around, taking in all her displays.

"*Ya.*" She pulled a calculator from a shelf under the counter.

"This is impressive. How long have you been gardening?"

"Ever since I could walk, I suppose." She began pushing buttons.

"*Gude mariye,* Salina!" one of her regular customers called as she entered the booth, causing her to look up.

"Hi, Salina!" Another Amish woman waved at her.

Salina smiled at them both before one perused her cucumbers and the other her corn. Then she finished her task and gave the man her price.

"That's fair." He pulled out his wallet and counted out a stack of bills. "I can tell you're popular around here."

Her cheeks heated as she took his money. "*I'm* not popular, but my produce sells well."

"I'm not surprised you stay busy." He slipped his wallet back into his jeans pocket and then held out his hand. "I'm Will Zimmerman, by the way."

She shook his hand. "Salina Petersheim."

"Nice to meet you."

"How are you going to transport all this produce to your restaurant?"

He looked at her with a sheepish expression. "I was just wondering the same thing. I wasn't expecting to find everything I need here." He gestured toward her wagons sitting at the back of the booth. "Any chance I could use one of those?"

When she hesitated, he grinned.

He put his hand over his heart. "I promise I'll bring it back soon. You know where I work, so you can come after me if I don't."

She couldn't stop a smile from forming. "Okay. I'll trust you."

"*Danki.*" He claimed the wagon and then loaded his purchases. "I'll see you soon, Salina." He nodded and then pulled his borrowed conveyance into motion.

"Salina," her customer near the green peppers called, "your vegetables are beautiful today!"

"*Danki*, Martha." Salina glanced toward the far end of the booth as Will pulled the wagon into the aisle.

"Just look at these blackberries!" the other woman said. "The Lord has blessed you with a bountiful garden, Salina."

"*Ya*, he has." Salina watched Will and the wagon disappear into the aisle before turning toward the customer admiring her blackberries. "How is your family, Sylvia?"

. . .

"Who was that tall Mennonite man who came to your booth this morning?" Christiana asked Salina as they sat at a high-top table in their cousin Bethany's Coffee Corner booth at lunchtime. Jeff was there too. They were counting on Sara Ann King to keep an eye on their booths while they took a break to eat, which she'd done before when the crowds had thinned out enough. None of them were thrilled with Sara Ann's habit of playing the marketplace gossip, but her quilt booth was next to Salina's, and they knew they could trust her with their businesses.

The aroma of Bethany's almond-flavored coffee filled Salina's senses as customers at nearby tables drank the fabulous special of the day.

"His name is Will Zimmerman, and he owns the restaurant across the street." Salina took a bite of her turkey sandwich and then placed it back on her paper plate.

"What did he buy?" Bethany grinned as she pushed the ribbons from her prayer covering behind her slight shoulders. Her light-blue eyes seemed to sparkle in the fluorescent lights humming above them. Her Gingerich cousin was younger than Salina at twenty-three, and once again Salina marveled at how Bethany always seemed to be upbeat with unfailing energy and that constant, pretty smile.

"He bought all my cherry tomatoes, cucumbers, carrots, and butterhead lettuce." Salina checked off the items on her fingers as she listed them.

"What? He bought them all?" Leanna asked. Leanna was her oldest cousin as well as the shortest. She had the same shade of dark-brown hair Salina had. But unlike Salina's eyes, hers were a beautiful brown that resembled chocolate milk. Her eyes weren't what Salina most admired about Leanna, though. Her cousin had been only thirty-one when she lost her husband, Marlin Wengerd, in an accident, and now, four years later, she was still raising her son alone—although they did live with her parents. Yet with an unwavering positivity, she consistently counted her blessings, including the success of her Jam and Jelly Nook booth at the marketplace.

Salina nodded as she took a sip from her bottle of water, then said, "*Ya*, he bought them all. He also borrowed one of my wagons to take everything back to his restaurant."

"I hope he returned it," Leanna said with a pointed look.

"He did." Salina fingered her bottle as she recalled Will's wide smile when he returned. Something about him struck her, but she couldn't put her finger on it. He wasn't a flirt, but he was outgoing, almost to the point of it feeling familiar to her. "He also said he'll see me soon."

"Sounds like he was *froh* with what you had to offer, then. This will be great for your business." Bethany grinned.

"*Ya*," Jeff said. "Helping to stock his restaurant with local produce should be profitable for you, especially if he lets his customers know you're his supplier."

Salina nodded. "That's true. My booth stays busy, but a consistent customer like Will would be *gut*. He said he wants to make a point of adding local produce to his menu."

Christiana swiped a chip off Jeff's plate and grinned at him before turning back to Salina. "You said something about being late this morning because Josiah came over last night and stayed late. Did he come for supper?"

"*Ya*, he did. His family came too."

"Why did they stay so late?" Leanna asked.

Salina swallowed a sigh. "You know how our *dats* get when they start talking. I thought they were never going to finish their conversation. Next thing I knew, it was after eight, and I hadn't finished packing my produce yet. *Mamm* helped me, but I didn't get to bed until almost eleven—and I forgot to set my alarm. You know I always work in the garden before I head to the market. And then I was running late . . ." She sighed and took another bite of her sandwich.

"How long have you and Josiah been together now?" A smile twitched on Bethany's lips.

"Almost a year," Christiana answered as she grinned at Jeff. "Salina and Josiah started dating in August, which is when we started dating." She gave Jeff an elbow in the side, and he smiled at her.

Salina looked down at her half-eaten sandwich. Christiana

and Jeff seemed to easily show their affection for each other, but Salina couldn't remember if Josiah had kissed her cheek last night when she walked him to his buggy. Had he even held her hand? Salina liked Josiah very much, and she enjoyed his company. He was funny and sweet, and he always brightened her day when he stopped by to visit. But if their relationship was solid, why did showing affection seem so difficult for them?

Or maybe not difficult but an afterthought.

"Has he said anything about getting married?"

Salina's eyes snapped up to meet Bethany's. Then she looked at Jeff, sure her cheeks were turning red. Didn't Bethany realize how embarrassing that question was—especially in front of Christiana's boyfriend?

Bethany's eyes rounded, and she cleared her throat before turning to Leanna. "How's business at the Jam and Jelly Nook today?"

Thankfully, Leanna didn't miss a beat when she responded. "*Gut.* A tour group came in and bought nearly all my cranberry and apple jam."

As Leanna shared more about her morning customers, Salina finished her sandwich and more thoughts about Josiah filtered through her mind. She was grateful she'd managed to dodge the question Bethany asked, because her response would have been no. Josiah had never mentioned marriage. The subject had never even come up once since they'd started dating. Did that mean they didn't have a solid relationship after all? Maybe with most couples, marriage would be discussed after dating for eleven months.

Salina further contemplated their relationship as she munched on her pretzels. It seemed right when Josiah asked her to be his girlfriend last year. After all, they'd been friends for their whole lives, and he was handsome with his dark hair, dark eyes, and warm smile. He also worked hard and made a good living as a foreman in his father's roofing company. His parents had been close friends with hers since before she and Josiah were born. To no one's surprise, her father not only approved of the relationship but encouraged it. *Strongly* encouraged it. It made sense that Josiah would ask her to date him—and, of course, Salina had said yes.

She looked up just as Christiana leaned close to Jeff's ear and whispered something. When he laughed and then whispered something in return, Salina's stomach twisted. Suddenly she craved a warm and romantic relationship like the one Christiana enjoyed with Jeff. But that wasn't what she had with Josiah. Would she ever? Did they just need more time to develop those feelings?

This wasn't the first time she'd asked herself such questions. Doubt had been a near constant companion lately, but she'd just pushed it away.

"Oh my goodness," Leanna announced when she glanced at the clock on the wall. "Look at the time. I need to get back to my booth."

Salina gathered her belongings and then started toward the Coffee Corner exit. "See you later," she called back to everyone.

Christiana caught up to her with Jeff close behind. "Wait, Salina. Are you okay?"

Salina kept walking. "*Ya*. Why?"

"You seem upset about something."

"I'm fine." Salina forced a smile and gave them a little wave. "Have *gut* sales." Then she waved her thanks to Sara Ann as she hurried into her booth and stowed her lunch bag and purse in the back.

Christiana walked up behind her. "You know I can read you like a book. Something is bothering you. You're always quiet, but today you're even quieter than usual." She paused. "You can trust me."

Salina closed her eyes for a moment and then turned to face her cousin. "I'm fine. I was just thinking about everything I have to do when I get home tonight. You know I can't stand it when I get behind on my chores in the garden. I'm just frustrated with myself. I started today on the wrong foot, and now I'm trying to catch up."

While that was true, it wasn't what was heavily weighing on her mind. And it wasn't that she didn't want Christiana's help. She did. She longed to ask her if she loved Jeff. And if so, how did she know she did? She also wanted to know if Christiana and Jeff had discussed marriage, and if Christiana wanted to marry him.

She needed to know if her relationship with Josiah measured up to what Christiana and Jeff had together—or could. Again, they seemed to have something she and Josiah didn't. But the conversation was too personal to have in the market. Customers were walking into the Farm Stand.

"You're too much of a perfectionist." Christiana wagged a finger at her. "Last year you kept telling me to give Jeff grace when I was frustrated with him. I think you need to give *yourself* some grace."

Salina snorted. "It's easy for you to say that when your *dat* isn't the bishop."

"Excuse me. Do you have any more cherry tomatoes?"

Salina looked over her shoulder. Two women dressed in shorts and T-shirts stood next to her display of tomatoes. One of them was pointing to her empty shelf.

"I'm sorry, but I sold out of them this morning."

"Too bad." The other woman snapped her fingers and then gestured toward the display of figs. "Your figs look fantastic, though. Those are hard to find!"

Salina turned back to her cousin. "I need to take care of my customers."

Christiana gave her a warm smile. "I know. Me too. Talk to you later." She glanced down at Daisy as the gray tabby sauntered over and brushed against her leg. "Have you noticed Daisy seems hungrier lately? She even looks like she's gaining some weight. But then, I know we all feed her—probably too much." She leaned down and rubbed the cat's ear.

Salina shrugged. "Now that you say that, she does look a little fluffier than usual."

"Come on, Daisy. I'll give you a snack anyway." Christiana beckoned for the cat to follow her and then walked out of the booth with Daisy jogging behind.

Salina smiled as she made her way to her customers, but she mentally shook her head before greeting them. Perhaps she was too focused on her feelings for Josiah. After all, he was a good Christian man, and God had blessed her when he brought him into her life. Josiah was just busy with his work, and so was she.

Surely the warmer relationship she craved with him would come. She'd just have to wait a little longer.

CHAPTER 2

"The customers are raving about the salad bar," Danielle said as she walked into the restaurant's kitchen later that afternoon. "I think it's that *appeditlich* butterhead lettuce and those ripe cherry tomatoes."

Will grinned as he grabbed another head of lettuce from the counter and began to wash it in the sink. "I told you I found a *wunderbaar* new source."

"Did you say you went to the marketplace across the street?"

"*Ya.* I decided I wanted to start featuring local produce, and when I checked out the booths over there, I found an Amish *maedel* who grows all her own vegetables and fruit. Her prices are fair, and you can see the produce is fantastic." Will separated the lettuce leaves and started laying them on a paper towel. "If you look at the specials list on the chalkboard out front, you'll see I added a note that says we now feature locally grown produce."

"Sounds like you found a *gut* vendor. I'm going to need that lettuce. The salad bar is almost out."

"I'm working on it." Will held up one of the large, green petals. "I'll bring it as soon as I have it ready." He nodded toward one of the stoves. "Check out my stuffing over there. I'm serving turkey tomorrow, and I'm trying something different with the stuffing."

Danielle took a clean spoon from the counter next to the stove and put a bit of the stuffing into her mouth. She swallowed it and then gagged. "Ugh. Is that sage?"

"*Ya.*" Will pointed to the pan. "I added more than the recipe said to give it extra flavor. Not *gut*?"

"No." She shook her head. "Not to me. Too much."

"Hmm." He rubbed his chin. "I'll try again." His mind immediately spun with ideas to improve the recipe, and he was grateful his staff felt comfortable enough to offer opinions. Danielle Hoover was just one among his great hires.

Danielle dropped her spoon into the sink and then leaned against the long counter as she pushed the ties from her Old Order Mennonite prayer covering over her shoulders. Then she smoothed her hands down the gray apron that covered her pink dress decorated with small white flowers, which Will knew was her favorite. It seemed like she'd been wearing it even more than usual lately.

"We need more lasagna for the buffet too," she said. "It's been going fast."

"We have another pan ready to go."

His brother Roger walked into the kitchen from the small room in the back and then grabbed two pot holders before picking up the pan Will had just taken out of one of the large ovens. "I don't know how you find anything in that office, Will. It's a mess. Don't you lose things?"

"I know where everything is," Will muttered, and that was mostly true. He loved his kid brother, but he didn't need criticism from him. Four years younger than Will, Roger was twenty-six and just slightly shorter than Will's six foot three. Their grandmother liked to refer to them and their older brother, Irvin, as "three peas in a pod," not only because of their height but because of their almost identical blond hair and blue eyes. Will had to admit the family resemblance was uncanny. Even Irvin's wife often commented on how much alike the three of them looked.

Will noticed Danielle's bright smile as she looked at Roger. And when she straightened her name tag, she seemed to stand a little taller.

"I'll walk with you out to the buffet," Roger said as he carried the pan toward the double kitchen doors leading to the dining room. He was smiling too.

"I'll get the door," Danielle said. Then she pushed open the door on the right and held it while Roger went through.

"I'll bring out the lettuce," Will called after them, but they seemed to ignore him.

Will grinned as he shook his head. Lately he'd noticed a spark between Roger and Danielle, which might account for seeing that favorite dress of hers more often. When Will hired Danielle as one of his waitresses last year, she seemed to be all smiles whenever Roger was in the room. And lately his brother seemed to smile whenever he saw Danielle. Perhaps he would ask her out soon.

Will turned his attention to chopping lettuce and dropping it into a container, and then he sliced mushrooms, green peppers, cucumbers, and carrots before chopping onions. He might as well replenish everything on the salad bar. After grabbing more cherry tomatoes, he placed all the ingredients into separate containers and set them on a tray. Then he hefted it onto his shoulder, pushed through the kitchen door, and stepped into the dining area, where patrons' voices buzzed in his ears.

He smiled as he glanced around at all the people eating

plates full of the selections he and Roger had placed on today's lunch buffet—lasagna, garlic bread, green beans, and corn, along with their usual variety of sandwiches and desserts. Happiness radiated through his body as he took in the restaurant he and his brother ran together—the large dining room, the oak tables and chairs, and the large windows where bright early-afternoon sunlight spilled in.

This was Will's dream, the fruition of all he'd strived for since he was nineteen and spent the summer working at his uncle Eddie's restaurant in upstate New York. That had been eleven years ago, when he'd arrived at his uncle's home spiritually bewildered. But he left there with a calling that felt as though it had come straight from God.

If only Uncle Eddie were alive to see what he'd accomplished through hard work and prayer.

"We're low on just about everything on the salad bar," Valerie said, rushing past Will, the skirt of her dress fluttering as she carried a tray of drinks to a nearby table. She was another one of his waitresses, just as dependable as Danielle was.

"I'm on it," Will called back to her. Then grateful to see a brief lull in customers helping themselves to the salad bar, he quickly set the tray on a nearby cart and started switching out the nearly empty containers with his full ones.

As he worked, he recalled how when his usual produce supplier had run low on a few items last week, he'd decided it was a good time to improve the selections he and Roger offered. Then he'd asked his staff for recommendations for a new supplier. Minerva Martin, a waitress who'd become like a surrogate grandmother to him, Roger, and the rest of the staff, had recommended the marketplace across the street. Will had been convinced the cost there would be too high for his budget, but Salina Petersheim's prices were reasonable, and her produce was impressive.

He chuckled to himself as he recalled her confused expression when he'd asked to buy so much of her stock. Her brow had puckered, and her blue eyes had narrowed. She stared up at him as if he were completely crazy—or at least as if she was trying to figure out if he was teasing her.

When he returned her wagon, he'd observed her while she was deep in conversation with an older Amish woman. They were talking about the vast number of herbs Salina's booth offered. Her attention to detail came across in her tidy display, and their discussion had been quick and to the point. She seemed to be a serious if not a shy young woman. He guessed she was only in her early to midtwenties and yet was a shrewd and mature businesswoman.

Also apparent was that she loved her produce. She'd been meticulously arranging her cucumbers when he'd first arrived that morning. He could imagine her spending hours in her garden, weeding and caring for the plants as if they were her precious children.

He tried to envision how large her garden would be for such a vast variety of produce. Was it many acres like his father's pasture at his dairy farm? Did she tend to all the plants and trees by herself, or did she have a houseful of siblings helping her?

A strong hand on Will's shoulder startled him from his thoughts. Turning, he found two of his regular customers smiling at him.

"You've outdone yourself today, Will," Don Bradford said as he withdrew his hand. "That lasagna is superb."

His wife, Pam, placed one hand on her chest and briefly

closed her eyes. "Oh yes. And that cheesecake is out of this world!"

"Thank you. I'm so glad you liked them both." As the couple walked away, Will made a mental note to ask Salina about her blackberries. He could make some delicious desserts with them. His mind ticked off a list of recipes. Blackberry cream pie, chocolate blackberry tart, blackberry cobbler—

"Will?"

He glanced over his shoulder to find his girlfriend smiling up at him. "Caroline. Hi. I didn't expect to see you here today."

"We're going to run errands this afternoon, and we thought we'd surprise you by having lunch here first." Caroline turned and grinned at her younger sister, Irene. Although the Horst siblings were four years apart, they looked almost as much alike as Will and his brothers did. The two women had the same sunshine-kissed blond hair under their Old Order Mennonite prayer coverings, a shade inherited from their mother, Loretta, and the same honey-brown eyes, inherited from their father, Robert.

Will recalled how quickly he'd fallen for Caroline's beautiful smile and adorable laugh when a friend introduced them. That was four years ago, when her family was visiting his church, one of two Mennonite churches in their general area. Then, after getting to know her for about six months, he'd asked her to be his girlfriend.

"That's great." He tucked the now-empty tray under one arm. "You get off work early?"

Caroline nodded. "*Ya*, we did. The bookstore wasn't busy all morning, so we got a lot of our work done, and *Mamm* and *Dat* said we could both leave." She turned toward the salad bar. "Oh my. Doesn't that look fantastic, Irene?"

"*Ya.* The lettuce is so green."

Will nodded toward the stack of bowls. "Help yourselves. Also, I have a surprise for you, Caroline." It was a good thing he'd made her favorite cream pie that morning instead of waiting for the lull between the lunch and supper crowds.

"You do?" Caroline set her hand on his forearm as her smile brightened. "I can't wait to find out what it is. By the way, I was wondering if you'd like me to come back and help you clean up tonight."

"That's not necessary, but *danki.*"

Her smile grew coy. "Well, someday we're going to be husband and *fraa*, and then I'll be here to help with cleanup all the time. Why not start now, right?"

Will swallowed against his suddenly dry throat, and he had to work to keep his eyes from widening as he took in Caroline's hopeful expression. Her comments about marriage seemed to come more often lately, and each time he fought back anxiety. He cared about her very much, yet every time marriage came up, doubts about their relationship rose to the surface. He wasn't sure why. He should be excited by the idea of marrying his sweet and beautiful girlfriend.

He forced his lips into a cordial smile. "Well, okay. If you'd like to. But right now I need to see if the next pan of lasagna is ready to come out of the oven. Please help yourself to the buffet. I'll bring out your surprise in a little while."

He nodded greetings to several customers as he made his way back to the kitchen, and once there, he set the tray on a counter and the empty containers in the large sink. Then he checked the timer on the oven with the lasagna.

"I saw Caroline and Irene out there," Roger commented as he walked up behind him.

"I just spoke to them."

"When are you going to propose?"

Will glanced over his shoulder at him. "Not you too."

"What does that mean?"

Will sighed as he opened the oven door and pulled out the pan. "Caroline has been making a lot of not-so-subtle comments about us getting married. She just asked about coming back here to help clean up when we close tonight, since, she said, she'll be doing it when we're married."

"Can you blame her, Will?" Roger pulled a tray of garlic bread out of the second oven. "After all, you've been together three years, and neither of you is getting any younger. You're thirty, and she's twenty-seven. She's probably ready to start a family."

That was the last thing he wanted to hear. How could he be ready to be a father when he wasn't even certain he was ready to be a husband? *At least not Caroline's husband.*

He cringed at the thought. He'd choose Caroline when he was ready to marry, wouldn't he? Just not yet. First he had to wrestle with the doubts that had run rampant for weeks now.

"What are you afraid of?"

Will faced his brother. "I'm not afraid. I'm just not ready."

"But you're in your thirties now. When *will* you be ready?"

"I don't know."

Roger shrugged as he slid the bread onto a tray. "You'd better figure it out before Caroline gets tired of waiting."

. . .

"*Danki* for coming back to help us clean up." Will held Caroline's hand as he walked her up her parents' driveway later that night.

"You're welcome. And *danki* for my delicious cream pie! It was just perfect, as usual." She looked back at his van, where Roger was waiting for him, and then smiled. "I appreciate your having your driver give me a ride home."

"*Gern gschehne.*"

"*Ich liebe dich*, Will."

Her eyes were full of her love. But he couldn't echo the meaning in them and her sugary sweet tone by repeating her words. It would feel like telling a fib. Something had to be wrong with him!

He leaned down and kissed her cheek. "Sleep well."

She placed her hand on his arm. "You too."

"*Gut nacht.*" Will felt tense, but he gave her hand a gentle squeeze. Then when she turned to wave at him from the top of her porch steps, he waved back before she entered the house.

As he climbed into the front passenger seat of the van, renewed guilt sloshed in his stomach. Caroline was perfect for him, but he was so confused. Shouldn't his feelings for her have grown into love by now? Perhaps they still would—over time. He just had to be patient and continue to appreciate her. After all, he did care for her, and he was always happy with her around. But all this talk of marriage . . .

"So is tomorrow's lunch special still chicken potpie?" Roger's question broke through Will's thoughts as the van rolled toward their house in Lititz.

Will's body finally relaxed. Concentrating on the menu was a welcome relief to this suffocating guilt. Cooking and talking about cooking were always a balm to his soul. It was what kept him sane when anxiety plagued him.

"*Ya.* Chicken potpie is still the plan." Will twisted around so he could see his brother in the back seat.

"Good." Roger held up an index finger. "It's one of our most popular items. And we'll still have the sandwich area and chicken fingers for kids. We'll also have our vegetable and chicken noodle soups. And, of course, our burger bar."

Will turned back around and looked at passing traffic as he considered the recipes he'd use the next day. Salina's succulent produce came to mind, just as it had throughout the day. He already had to go back to her booth for more salad makings, and he also wanted to try her corn. He'd go first thing tomorrow.

"Well, we're here," Austin Helms announced as he steered into the driveway of the house Will and Roger shared. "You two have a nice evening."

"Thank you." Will shook Austin's hand. Old Order Mennonites weren't permitted to drive cars, and the trip from Lititz to Bird-in-Hand was too long for a horse and buggy. Will not only appreciated Austin's service but his flexibility too.

"See you in the morning," Roger told Austin before climbing out of the back seat.

The brothers walked up their driveway to the two-story, dark-red brick house their grandparents had owned for a few decades. It was divided into two apartments, one upstairs and one downstairs. When he and Roger started working at local restaurants two years ago, they moved out of their parents' home and rented the units. Then when Will had finally saved enough money to start his own restaurant, he and Roger became business partners, opening the restaurant in their family's name.

"*Gut nacht.*" Roger yawned as he unlocked the door that led to the second floor.

"Get some rest." Will grinned as his brother yawned again before disappearing inside.

Will stepped into his downstairs apartment, flipped on the lights, and hung his keys and hat on the peg on the wall above an end table in his small family room. He'd furnished the room with a worn blue sofa and matching love seat his older brother passed down to him along with another end table and two old brass lamps. Caroline and Irene had dropped by with some soup not long ago when he was down with a head cold. Even then Caroline had assumed marriage, telling him how she'd love to decorate the place.

He would never bring a bride to a place like this, but he didn't want to think about that now.

He shuffled through the small kitchen and down the short hallway, passing his second bedroom. When he'd moved in, that room had immediately become a home office. But soon it was just as cluttered as his office at the restaurant was now, and that clutter nagged him as he made his way to the master bedroom. One of these days he'd clean up the mess in both spaces. At least that's what he kept telling himself.

He flipped on the light in the bedroom, which was also plainly furnished. Against its white walls were a king-size bed, two matching cherrywood nightstands—hand-me-downs from his grandparents—and two matching dressers. He undressed and climbed into the bathroom shower. He stood under the hot water, allowing it to flow over his aching muscles, sore from another day of working in his beloved restaurant.

After his shower, he pulled on his favorite nightclothes—a worn-out pair of sweatpants and a black T-shirt—and then returned to the kitchen. He poured himself a glass of iced tea and then gazed at his bookcase in the corner.

The bookcase held his most valued cookbooks. Most of them were worn and weathered, but he rarely took them to the restaurant. He liked to look through them at home. He'd bought some at yard sales and picked up others at used bookstores. Still others had been gifts from relatives and friends. Each of his cookbooks held at least one favorite recipe that had brought him closer to his dream of owning a restaurant.

Will ran his finger over some of the bindings and stopped when he reached the cookbook his uncle Eddie had given him. He pulled it out and sank into one of the two chairs at his small, round table.

He smiled as he flipped through the recipes and imagined working in his kitchen the next morning. But first he'd visit Salina Petersheim's booth to buy more of her stellar produce. He'd do whatever he could to make his customers happy.

CHAPTER 3

"Bethany makes the most *appeditlich kaffi*," Salina said as she hurried past the used books booth beside Christiana and Jeff. She always liked exploring that booth when she had time, but the doors to the marketplace were just about to open.

Jeff nodded as they all headed toward their businesses. "She sure does. This mocha flavor is amazing."

Salina had just noticed the delicious scent of Christiana's Bake Shop goodies was already wafting through the area when she halted. So did Jeff and Christiana. Will Zimmerman was looking at her display of cherry tomatoes, and two large carts sat beside him.

"Your *freind* is back," Christiana sang close to Salina's ear. "And with *two* carts."

Salina spun toward her and hissed, "He's not *mei freind*."

Her cousin gave her a little shove. "Go sell all your tomatoes. Maybe you can close up early and go home if he buys everything you've got." She giggled before she and Jeff slipped into her Bake Shop across the aisle.

Salina squared her shoulders as she walked into her booth.

Will looked up and smiled, and his intelligent, sky-blue eyes seemed to twinkle in the bright fluorescent lights. "*Gude mariye.*"

"Hi." She stared up at him. "The market isn't open yet. How did you convince the security guard to let you in?"

His smile seemed a little sheepish. "I just explained that I own the restaurant across the street and that I need to get supplies before I have to start preparations. He let me in." He paused, and his smile faded. "I hope this is okay with you, though. I suppose I should have considered your time."

"It's fine." She shrugged and set her cup of coffee by the cash register and then stepped behind the counter. "How may I help you today?"

Will pushed his carts over and then leaned against the counter. "Your produce was a hit yesterday. I had to refill the salad bar four times, twice for lunch and twice for the supper crowd."

"I'm *froh* to hear it." She glanced down at the cash register to avoid his intense gaze. Why did this man she didn't even know make her feel so self-conscious? And was his smile always so bright?

"How was your evening after work?" he asked her.

Her eyes slid to his, and she took in his easy expression. Was he just making small talk? Or was he flirting with her? But his expression seemed genuine, so maybe he was just being friendly. "Fine."

"*Gut.* Mine was too." He looked over his shoulder at her produce. "I'd like to buy more of your butterhead lettuce, cherry tomatoes, and carrots." He tapped his chin. "Could I also get some of your green beans and corn?"

Salina blinked at him for the second time in two days. Was he really going to buy so much of her inventory again? Perhaps she *would* get home early, just like Christiana joked she might.

"I brought my own carts today." He pointed at them. "Now

I won't have to use your wagon." Then he tapped his forehead. "But I didn't think to bring boxes. I knew I had forgotten something, but I couldn't figure out what it was."

"I have some plastic crates. How many do you need?"

He rubbed his chin again. "Maybe four?"

She retrieved four plastic crates from the pile at the back of the booth. Then she found a handful of plastic bags and set the crates and bags on his carts. "Here you go."

"Danki." He pushed the first cart over to the lettuce and began filling a crate.

Salina straightened the items on her counter and then watched Will move from the lettuce to the carrots. She took in how his gray shirt complemented his blue eyes. Curiosity took over. Was he married? Did he live near his restaurant? Was he a good chef?

She dismissed her questions. This man's life wasn't her business. He was only a customer.

Salina looked into the aisle just in time to see Sara Ann King saunter past with an armload of quilts. She looked at Salina and smiled, and Salina responded with a smile she had to force. Salina didn't want to be caught up in any gossip this morning. She released the breath she'd been holding when Sara Ann disappeared, no doubt into her booth next door.

Salina pulled out her record book and began making a list of what produce she needed to replenish the next day. She had just finished when Will appeared in front of her, his two carts full. He beamed as he pulled his wallet from his trouser pocket.

"All this looks so *gut*. What do I owe you?"

"Let me see . . ." She took out her calculator again, heat rising up her neck because she could feel him gazing at her. Why was he doing that?

When she looked up, he was still looking at her. She gave him the amount and stilled as she waited for his response.

"*Danki* for another fair price." He took out his wallet and handed her a stack of bills. As he slipped his wallet back into his pocket, he nodded toward her display of blackberries. "Do you happen to have a recipe for blackberry pie?"

"I would have to check *mei mamm*'s cookbooks, but I'm sure my cousin does." She pointed across the aisle. "She runs the Bake Shop across the way. I could ask her for you."

His light eyebrows rose. "Your cousin has a booth here?"

"*Ya.* Three of them do, actually. My cousin Bethany runs the Coffee Corner, and Leanna runs the Jam and Jelly Nook. Then Christiana has the Bake Shop over there."

"Do you like working with your cousins?"

"I do," she told him as she pulled out his receipt. "We usually meet for *kaffi* in Bethany's booth before we start our day. I consider them *schweschdere* since I don't have any. I only have an older *bruder*." She pressed her lips together. Why did she feel compelled to share so much personal information with this stranger?

"I'm the middle child. I have an older *bruder* and a younger *bruder*. My kid *bruder* is in business with me."

"Oh." She felt stuck on that detail for a moment. She had to change the subject before she shared any more. "I can ask Christiana for a recipe. But don't you have one? You're a chef, after all."

"I have plenty of cookbooks, but I'm always looking for new recipes to try."

"Okay. And like I said, I'll also ask *mei mamm* if she has one. She's a much better cook than I am."

He shook his head. "I find that hard to believe. I can see the care you take with your produce, and I'm certain you take care with all areas of your life. But I would like to try her recipe if she has one. Your cousin's too."

"Okay." She studied his eyes, not knowing how to react to the compliment he'd given her.

"Do you ever take a lunch?"

She froze. Maybe he *was* flirting! She wasn't sure how to react. "Sometimes. If we're not too busy. Why?"

"You should come to the restaurant sometime. I'm sure you'd like seeing how our customers are enjoying the food you've grown."

"Oh." When her cheeks began to heat, she looked down at the cash register and realized she hadn't given him his receipt. She ripped it off and handed it to him. "I almost forgot."

"*Danki.*"

"*Gern gschehne.*"

"I'll bring back your crates soon."

She shook her head. "There's no hurry. I have plenty of extras."

"Have a great day, Salina." He nodded at her and then pushed his carts toward the aisle.

Sara Ann appeared at the entrance to the booth. She nodded at Will, who nodded in response and left.

"Oh no," Salina muttered to herself as Sara Ann pranced inside.

"Who was that?" Sara Ann asked.

"His name is Will. He runs the restaurant across the street." Salina folded her arms over her black apron.

"He's so handsome, and he bought so much from you!" Sara Ann said with a simper. "You must be so excited to have a customer like that."

"*Ya*, I'm blessed that he chose to buy produce for his restaurant here." Salina glanced toward the clock on the far wall. "The doors will be opening soon. Don't you need to set up your booth?"

"We have a few minutes. How's Josiah?" Sara Ann's lovely eyes glinted as she smiled. Salina had always considered her to be pretty with her dark hair and striking gray eyes. Her tendency to gossip wasn't pretty, though.

"He's fine." Salina longed for one of her cousins to pop into her booth and save her. Last year, when Christiana and Jeff had a disagreement over Christiana's long customer line blocking Jeff's booth, Sara Ann told the other booth owners about their squabble. Salina didn't want any details about her life to be fodder for Sara Ann's gossip at the market or her quilting bee.

"Has he proposed yet?"

Salina fiddled with the hem of her apron, willing herself not to groan. "No."

"I'm certain he will soon. You've been together about a year now, right?"

"We have." Salina looked back at the clock. The doors should open any second now . . .

"Aren't you ready to get married?" Why was Sara Ann pressing her on this?

"I don't know—" Thank goodness Salina's words were cut off by the whoosh and loud voices of customers as the marketplace opened for the day.

"Oh! Time to go. I'll see you later." Sara Ann waved and then hurried out.

Salina felt something brush against her legs and glanced down as Daisy blinked up at her. "Are you ready for another busy day at the market?"

Daisy meowed.

"I'm ready, too, Daisy. Let's sell some produce—at least what I have left to sell."

. . .

Will whistled to himself as he pushed his carts through the back door and into the kitchen. Then he steered them up to the longest counter and rubbed his hands together. This was his favorite time of day—prepping for the lunch crowd.

The swinging door from the dining room opened with a whoosh, and Roger and Danielle came in together, laughing.

"You're back." Roger walked over to the carts. "Wow. You got some great produce."

"*Ya*, I did." Will pulled out a bag of green beans. "I'm going to use these and the corn in the chicken potpies today."

Danielle pointed to the carrots. "You should use those too. They look fantastic."

"I agree with Danielle." Roger smiled at her.

Will hid a grin. His brother obviously liked Danielle as much as she liked him.

Danielle's dark eyes focused on Roger as if Will weren't even in the room. "I'm going to start putting the utensils and plates out on the buffet."

"Okay. I'll come out and check on . . . everything later." Roger winked at her, and Will turned his attention to unloading the purchases he wouldn't need until he was preparing for the supper menu.

A few minutes later Will focused on his favorite chicken potpie recipe. "I might change this up a bit. You know I like to experiment."

"Uh-oh," Roger said. "As long as you have time to make more if your experiment doesn't work out!" He grinned. "I'll start washing the vegetables."

They worked in silence for several minutes, then once Will had the counter organized with everything he needed, he said, "What do you think of blackberry pie as a dessert next week?"

Roger looked up at him, then paused before shrugging. "Blackberry pie sounds *gut* to me. Why?"

"Salina has the most succulent-looking blackberries. I also asked her for a recipe for blackberry pie."

"Wait a minute." Roger held up a hand. "Who's Salina?"

"She's the Amish *maedel* who runs the booth where I bought all this produce."

"Oh." Roger seemed to study him. "You have close to a hundred cookbooks and you asked her for a recipe?"

Will laughed at his brother's confusion. Although Roger was eager to go into business with him, he didn't share Will's obsession with the culinary arts. "I know you can't understand my fascination with recipes, but I'm always looking for new ones. I thought she might have one that's better than what any of my cookbooks have to offer. You should see her booth. It's well organized, and all her produce is ripe and perfect. I thought she might have a *gut* recipe since she seems to take both her gardening and business so seriously."

"Okay." Roger seemed satisfied with that response and returned to washing.

Will sorted through the ingredients for the potpie crusts. "When are you going to ask her out?" If Roger could ask him when he was going to propose to Caroline, he could ask him when he was going to date Danielle.

"Who?" Roger's head popped up.

"Come on now. Do you think I'm blind?"

Roger bit his lower lip and glanced toward the doors to the dining room. "Do you think she likes me?"

"It's quite obvious that she does—and I think she has for a long time. You should ask her out."

"Maybe I will."

"I hope you do." Will turned his focus to crust making, but his mind wandered from potpies to images of the blackberry pies he wanted to make next week. He hoped Salina would have a good recipe. If so, he'd try it and maybe add it to his collection.

CHAPTER 4

Later that afternoon Salina finished counting her money and closing out her register. Then she stowed her remaining produce before pulling her two wagons into the aisle, where she met Christiana and Jeff.

"How was your afternoon?" Christiana asked.

Salina adjusted her tote bag on her shoulder. "*Gut.* I ran out of quite a few items."

"Thanks to your Mennonite *freind*?" Jeff asked.

"Actually, *ya*. That reminds me." Salina looked at Christiana. "Do you have a recipe for blackberry pie?"

"Probably. Why?"

"Will asked me if I had one, and I told him I would ask you. He says he wants to buy some of my blackberries for pies."

"Oh." Christiana began pushing one of her rolling baker's carts toward the back exit while Jeff pushed the other. "I'm certain I have a recipe. I'll check my cookbooks tonight. But if he owns a restaurant, wouldn't he already have a recipe?"

"He said he enjoys finding new ones. But it was still kind of strange."

Jeff pushed the button next to the door, and it automatically swung open. They exited and then moved down the ramp toward the parking lot. The humid air hit Salina like a wall after working in the cool, air-conditioned market all day.

She scanned the parking lot and spotted her driver's van sitting at the back, in front of a row of tall oak trees and a few picnic tables.

"Have a *gut* evening. I'll try to find a recipe tonight," Christiana said as she and Jeff headed to his waiting horse and buggy. Salina had seen Jeff head outside periodically throughout the day, no doubt to tend to his horse.

"*Danki. Gut nacht!*" Salina waved to them and then hurried off.

. . .

"What are you looking for?" *Mamm* asked Salina as she sat down across from her at the kitchen table that evening. They'd just finished cleaning up after supper.

"A recipe for blackberry pie." Salina scanned the list of pies in her mother's favorite cookbook.

"I'm sure there's one in there. I believe I made it years ago. Would you like me to look?"

"I found it." Salina had just turned to a new page, and she smiled as she popped up from the table and found a notepad and pen. Then she sat back down and began writing.

"Did Christiana ask you for my recipe?"

"No." Salina shook her head as she continued to write. "One of my customers did. I told him I would try to find one for him."

"Him?" *Mamm* leaned toward her. "A man asked you for a pie recipe?"

"*Ya*, that's right." Salina glanced at her mother, who was watching her with eyes full of curiosity.

"He's Old Order Mennonite, and he owns the restaurant across the street from the marketplace. He came in yesterday and today and bought a lot of my produce. He also asked me if I had a recipe for blackberry pie. He's interested in my blackberries too."

"Huh. What's the name of the restaurant?"

"Zimmerman's Family Restaurant. His name is Will Zimmerman."

"I suppose he was impressed with your produce if he came back a second day."

"He said he had to refill his salad bar four times." Salina grimaced at her words. Had she just sounded prideful? If so, it was a good thing *Dat* hadn't heard her. She was certain he'd lecture her about how the Amish are supposed to be humble.

"That's *wunderbaar*." *Mamm* tapped Salina's hand. "Have you ever eaten at his restaurant?"

"No, but he suggested I stop by for lunch sometime and see how the customers are enjoying my produce." She pushed back her chair and stood. "I should go through my pantry and make sure I have enough for tomorrow."

"Do you want help?" *Mamm* asked.

"No, *danki*. You rest." Salina smiled at her mother and then walked down to the basement. Her father had built a second kitchen and pantry down there for her three years ago—when she first opened her booth at the market. The large room had a sink, a table for sorting and canning, a propane-powered refrigerator and freezer, a row of shelves, and storage containers. She enjoyed working down there, where she could get lost in thoughts and prayer—and love of her produce. The only place better was her garden.

She was checking her inventory of lettuce when she heard her father call down the stairs for her.

"Coming!"

When she entered the kitchen, *Dat* was sitting at the table with *Mamm*.

"Here she is," *Mamm* said before turning to Salina. "I was just telling your *dat* about the Mennonite man at your booth. I told him you might get more business since the customers at his restaurant are so impressed with your produce."

Dat nodded, but *he* didn't seem impressed. "It's *wunderbaar* that you might have more customers because of this opportunity. But remember you won't have your booth when you and Josiah are married. You'll have too many responsibilities as a *fraa*. Josiah will carry the burden of taking care of you, just as a husband should. He's doing well with his father's roofing company, and I think he'll be ready to support you soon."

Salina's back and shoulders stiffened.

"You'll have plenty to do at home," *Dat* said, continuing his lecture. "And when *kinner* come, you'll be even busier, so you might have to give up so much gardening too. You know how busy Ellen is with your nieces. Just imagine when you and Josiah have *kinner*."

Salina nodded out of habit, but she felt a hot jolt of frustration. How she tired of her father comparing her to her brother and his wife! Just because Neil married at twenty-five didn't mean Salina was ready to be married.

And why did her family assume she would marry Josiah? Of course they didn't know she was having doubts about her relationship with him. She'd kept those to herself.

Dat looked at *Mamm*. "Mary, I meant to tell you that Neil did a great job balancing the books last night. I think he's going to do just fine when he takes over the business."

"Oh, I'm certain he will. He's learned so much from you, Lamar."

Salina looked down at the toes of her black shoes as a familiar pang of jealousy washed over her, adding to her frustration. It was a sin to be jealous of her older brother, but she grew tired of living in Neil's shadow. She'd never live up to his perfection. After all, her father was the bishop for their district, and Neil was the deacon. Salina's light would never shine as bright as theirs.

"Are you ready for devotions?" *Dat* asked Salina as he held up his Bible.

"Of course." She sank into a chair beside her mother. Only God could help her sort out her feelings.

"*Gut.* I'd like to read from the book of John."

As her father opened their devotional time with prayer, Salina bowed her head and opened her heart.

Please, God, help me be the dochder *my parents want me to be. And please help me sort out my confusing feelings for Josiah. Help me feel the way I should if you want me to marry him someday.*

. . .

Will pushed his carts to the marketplace the next morning and found Salina arranging a display of figs in her booth. He took in her profile and noticed how her blue eyes were a beautiful contrast to the dark-brown hair peeking out from under her prayer covering. Today she wore a green dress and a black apron, and she looked very pretty.

Wait. Not only was Salina an Amish woman who would never be interested in a Mennonite man, but he was with Caroline. Having thoughts like that about another woman was completely inappropriate! He might be having doubts about their relationship, but he would never want to hurt Caroline that way.

Salina turned toward him, and a shy smile overtook her lips. *"Gude mariye."*

"Gude mariye."

"How was your evening?"

Her question caught him off guard. She hadn't seemed interested in small talk before.

"It was pretty *gut*. I stayed at the restaurant a little later than usual to make sure I was organized for today, and then I just went home and crashed. I was too exhausted to do anything at the *haus*. How about yours?"

She leaned back on the counter behind her. "It was okay." She pulled two pieces of paper from her apron pocket. "I have two recipes for you. I found one in *mei mamm*'s cookbook, and Christiana also found one for you."

"That's fantastic." He smiled as she handed the papers to him. *"Danki* so much." He glanced over the recipes, taking in each handwriting. Which one was Salina's? Then he looked up at her expression, which seemed . . . eager? "Which recipe is your favorite?"

She glanced past him as if making sure no one could hear her. Then she leaned in closer and pointed to the recipe in his right hand. "This one is from *mei mamm*'s cookbook. It sounds the most *appeditlich* to me. But don't tell Christiana I said that."

He laughed, and she grinned. Suddenly he felt as if something between them had changed. It was as if they might become friends, and the feeling warmed his heart.

"Let me know what you think," she said.

"I will." He nodded toward the blackberries, displayed to her right. "How many boxes of those will you let me buy?"

"You're going to buy them now?" Her brow pinched.

"I'll need to if I want to make the pies on Monday. You're not open again until next Thursday."

"Oh. Right." She gave a little laugh, and he enjoyed the sound. "You may buy as many as you'd like."

"Great." He began loading one cart with the little plastic containers of fruit. "I already told *mei bruder* we're going to make blackberry pies next week."

"You said he runs the restaurant with you. Not your other *bruder*?"

"No. Irvin works in construction."

"Really?" She handed him more containers. "*Mei dat* is a carpenter. He owns a cabinet-making business, and *mei bruder* works with him. Neil is going to take over the business someday soon. *Mei dat* likes to remind me of that often." Her eyes widened, and she looked away as if realizing she'd said too much.

"And that bothers you?" He hoped she would finish that thought.

She looked up at him and then waved off the comment. "It's nothing." She pointed to the display of berries. "Would you like more?"

"I would if that's okay."

"Of course."

They worked without talking for several moments, and he hoped she'd break the silence. He wanted to know more about her father and how he seemed to favor her brother. But when she didn't speak, he searched for something else to say.

"These pies are going to be *wunderbaar*. You should come by next week to taste them. Bring your cousins. I'll be sure to save a few slices for you."

She gave him a smile. "I'll see if I can. *Danki*." Then she hesitated with the last container of berries in her hand. "You're going to buy all my berries?"

"I will if you'll let me."

She laughed. "I don't think I have a choice." She handed him the container and then gestured around the booth. "Do you need anything else?"

"You know I do." He pulled out the list he'd made during his ride to the restaurant that morning.

"What can I help you find?"

For the next several minutes, they loaded his carts with almost every kind of vegetable she had. Then Salina worked up his price, and he paid her.

"We don't have church tomorrow. Do you?" she asked as she handed him the receipt.

"No, we don't, but I'm going to spend the day with my girl-friend and her family."

"That sounds nice. I hope you have a *gut* day with them."

"Danki." He stuck the receipt in his pocket. "I hope you have a great day too. And don't forget to stop by for pie next week."

"I'll try."

"I'll see you next Thursday, though."

"I'll be here." She gave him a little wave, and then he pushed his carts out of the Farm Stand.

Will nodded at the redhead in the Bake Shop as he moved into the aisle. He now knew her name was Christiana. A smile overtook his lips as he recalled Salina's adorable expression when she admitted she liked her mother's recipe more than her cousin's.

He'd never reveal that secret, but he had to stop thinking about her adorable expression.

CHAPTER 5

Salina sipped from a water bottle as she sat at a picnic table between Bethany and Christiana and across from Josiah and Jeff on Sunday afternoon. The hot sun beat down on her neck and back as she looked out toward a lush, green area where other youth group members played volleyball on the grass, their laughs and yells sounding through the humid air.

"How was your week?"

Salina's gaze snapped to Josiah's as he pushed his hair off his tan forehead. She marveled at how his long hours working as a roofer in the summer sun had turned his skin almost golden brown, making his eyes seem like a deeper shade of their usual mocha brown.

His eyebrows rose as a frown overtook his face. "Are you all right, Salina?"

"*Ya*, of course." She chuckled as she began to peel the label off the plastic bottle in her hands. "I was just thinking."

"Oh." He took on an apologetic expression. "I'm sorry I didn't get by to see you. We've been so busy with all these big roofing projects." He leaned toward her. "How were your sales at the market?"

"*Gut*. A new customer bought nearly all my produce each day."

"Really? Who is she?"

"It's a he, actually." Continuing to pull at the label, she told him about Will and how he'd purchased produce for his restaurant. "He wiped out my supply of blackberries yesterday so he can make blackberry pies this week. He suggested I stop by for a slice."

"We should do that."

"You think so?" She looked up at him.

"Why not?"

"I don't know." She hedged as she imagined showing up at Will's restaurant. Wouldn't it be awkward? They hardly knew each other.

"Bethany," Josiah said.

"*Ya?*" Bethany turned from talking to Christiana and faced him.

"Don't you think Salina should go to the restaurant owned by that Mennonite man and taste the pie he's going to make with her blackberries?"

"That sounds *appeditlich* to me." Bethany turned to Salina. "You don't want to go?"

"I don't know," she repeated. Having already successfully removed the label from her bottle, Salina fingered a loose piece of wood on the tabletop. "Wouldn't it be strange to just walk into his restaurant?"

Bethany chuckled. "Why would that be strange? Don't you normally just walk into a restaurant? And then you sit down, order food, eat it, pay the bill, and leave, right?"

Salina looked down at the table, wishing she'd never brought up the subject.

"We should go there for supper this week," Josiah said as though he were insisting more than suggesting. "Salina, you work so hard. You should enjoy the fruits of your labor." He grinned. "Get it? Fruits!"

Bethany snorted. "You're so *gegisch*, Josiah."

"That's why Salina likes me, right?" Josiah waggled his eyebrows.

Salina laughed.

Jeff stood. "Who wants to play volleyball?"

Josiah looked at Salina. "Want to join them?"

"Come on." Bethany tapped Salina's shoulder. "Let's show these guys we know how to play."

Christiana winked. "Exactly."

Jeff smirked. "That sounds like a challenge, right, Josiah?"

"*Ya*. Let's go."

Salina smiled as she followed her cousins to the volleyball court. How she enjoyed these afternoons!

. . .

"Did you have fun today?" Josiah asked as he guided his horse toward Salina's home.

"*Ya*. Did you?"

He gave her a sideways glance and smiled. "Of course I did."

She took in his profile as he trained his eyes on the road again. With his long, thin nose and strong jaw, Josiah was an attractive man. But that wasn't the only thing she admired about him. He was kind, funny, and thoughtful. He also supported both her passion for gardening and her work at the marketplace.

She crossed her arms and stifled a yawn as she looked out the windshield, her thoughts wandering to her father's comments about giving up her booth when she was married. Why did thoughts of marriage to Josiah send her pulse galloping with fear? Wouldn't they love and cherish each other forever?

She swallowed as the familiar doubts crashed around in her head. She recalled Neil being excited about proposing to Ellen, and she knew Ellen was excited when he did. Shouldn't she feel the same way when she thought about Josiah proposing to her?

"What's on your mind?" Josiah's question broke through her thoughts as he steered his horse onto her street.

"Nothing." Her answer came a little too quickly, but Josiah didn't seem to notice. "I was just thinking about all the chores I have for tomorrow. It's laundry day. And I need to weed my garden and harvest my produce, of course. I also need to can so I have items to sell during the winter season."

"Like I said, you work hard. I think we should have supper at that Zimmerman restaurant Tuesday night."

She still wasn't sure that was a good idea. "You don't have to take me out."

"I want to." His smile was warm—genuine. "Let's celebrate how successful your booth is. Besides, I'll be finishing a big project on Tuesday, so we can finally spend some time together. Is five thirty a *gut* time to pick you up?"

"*Ya*, it is."

Josiah guided the horse up the driveway to her family's white, two-story home.

"I look forward to seeing you then," she said as he halted the horse.

He turned toward her and smiled. *"Gut nacht."*

She hesitated, waiting to see if he would lean over and touch her hand. Or hug her. Or maybe even kiss her. But when he did nothing, she picked up her bag. "I'll see you in a couple of days, then. Be safe going home."

She climbed out of the buggy and hurried up the front porch steps before turning to wave.

As Josiah's horse trotted down her driveway, a familiar disappointment overcame her. Why did their relationship seem so . . . platonic?

Then a new thought hit her. *Does Josiah have the same doubts I do?*

. . .

"What a *schee* sky." Caroline pushed the glider into motion before sipping from her glass of iced tea. "It's the perfect Sunday evening."

"*Ya*, it is." Will glanced at her beside him and smiled, then settled back and looked out toward her father's red barn and the pasture beyond. Lightning bugs made their presence known in the glow of the orange-and-red sunset as if welcoming the night, and the sweet aroma of summer filled his senses.

"*Danki* for the beautiful flowers you brought me today," Caroline said.

"*Gern gschehne.*" Will patted her arm. "I saw those daisies in *mei mamm*'s garden, and I thought of you. I know they're your favorites."

"You know me so well. And they look so *schee* on the table." She gave his hand a gentle squeeze. "What do you have planned for your menus this week?"

"I told you about my new supplier, right?"

"You did. An Amish *maedel* at the marketplace? At a booth called the Farm Stand."

"That's right. I bought all her blackberries, and I'm going to make blackberry pies for one of our desserts."

"Oh my! That sounds fantastic." She angled her body toward his, and her smile seemed to glow in the light of the porch lamps. "Did you find the recipe in your *onkel* Eddie's cookbook?"

"No, actually, I didn't. Salina gave me a recipe."

Caroline's smile wobbled. "Who's Salina?"

"She's the *maedel* who runs the Farm Stand."

"Oh." Caroline's eyes seemed to search his. "Does she run it alone?"

"*Ya.* She grows everything too. You should see her booth. Her produce is incredible."

"You seem to know her pretty well. Is she married?"

Will took in Caroline's hesitant expression and thin lips. Was she jealous of Salina? Did she truly believe he would hurt her by deliberately spending time with another *maedel*?

"I don't think she's married, but I don't know her well. I've only talked to her when I've bought produce from her. That's all."

"Oh." Caroline nodded, but her smile seemed forced. "Well, I'm sure the pies will be amazing, and I can't wait to sample a piece." Then her expression grew coy again, and she tilted her head. "When we're married, will you do all the cooking? Or will you at least let me make you breakfast before you head to the restaurant?"

Will opened his mouth to respond but then closed it. Why did she have to constantly push the marriage issue? Couldn't they have one conversation without discussing it?

Her smile flattened, and she laughed awkwardly. "I was just kidding. I'll do all the cooking at home. And, of course, at least until we have *kinner*, I'll be working at the restaurant with you six days a week."

The screen door opened and then clicked shut as her father stepped onto the porch.

Will's jaw relaxed. Robert had saved the day! "Hello there," Will said as he looked up at him.

"May I join you?" the older man asked. Somehow he'd managed to unlatch the door when he was carrying both a glass of iced tea and a plate of cookies. "I brought chocolate chip *kichlin*."

"Of course, *Dat*." Caroline pointed to the rocker beside their glider. "Sit."

Robert sat down and held out the plate to his daughter. "Would you like one?"

"*Ya*." Caroline took two cookies and handed one to Will.

"How are things at the restaurant?" Robert asked him.

"*Gut*. I have a new produce supplier, and that's already improved not only my salad bar but some of my recipes." As Will told Robert about finding the Farm Stand, he noticed Caroline's posture relax. "I already have some new items planned for this week."

"He's going to make blackberry pies," Caroline announced with enthusiasm.

"Who's making blackberry pie?" Irene asked as she came out of the house.

"I want a piece," Loretta chimed in as she joined the group.

"Will is going to make them at the restaurant this week," Caroline told her mother.

"That sounds fantastic." Loretta sat down on a rocker beside Robert, and Irene sank into the last rocker beside her.

"And has the bookstore stayed busy?" Will asked.

"It has," Robert said. "Tourists always seem to enjoy visiting an authentic Mennonite store."

Irene nodded as she took a cookie from the plate her father had placed on the small table that sat between them all. "And they love to ask questions about the differences between Amish and Mennonite. They just don't understand why we use electricity when the Amish don't."

"I'm certain you get similar questions," Robert said to Will. He smiled as he took another cookie. "I do."

"Tell us more about this blackberry pie," Loretta said. "Will we be able to sample a piece? If not, we're never going to invite you back for Sunday supper."

Will laughed, and everyone joined in. He glanced around the porch and took in this wonderful family. When he was with them, he felt as if he were home. Why, then, was he so confused whenever he thought about marrying Caroline? She was such a good friend to him, and surely God not only approved of their relationship but blessed it.

He just needed to count his blessings.

. . .

Will walked into his home office later that evening and surveyed the mess. A mountain of paperwork on the desk leaned precariously, containers overflowed with old receipts, and the stapler, hole puncher, calculator, and tape dispenser he knew he owned sat lost among the random folders and books scattered around. More stacks of books lined the narrow pathway to the door. He didn't even have time to read them—especially since opening the restaurant, most of his reading required cookbooks, not the biographies he favored.

Roger was right when he said Will needed to get organized, but who had the time? He spent long hours at the restaurant, and when he was home, he was preparing for the next day. Someday he would get both his offices in shape, but it wouldn't happen today. It was Sunday, the day of rest.

Will closed the office door to prevent the disaster from glaring at him, and then he strode to the family room, where he sat down on the sofa and picked up his favorite devotional. He flipped through the pages as thoughts of Caroline and her family overtook his mind. He had enjoyed visiting with the Horst family, but the familiar confusion and doubt had warred within him when once again Caroline mentioned marriage. It was obvious she was ready for him to propose, but he wasn't ready. Worse, he wasn't sure he ever would be. That bothered him more than he cared to admit even to himself.

Suddenly his life seemed almost as messy as his offices.

Then he spotted a Scripture verse from Romans that had always spoken to him. *May the God of hope fill you with all joy and peace as you trust in him, so that you may overflow with hope by the power of the Holy Spirit.*

Closing his eyes, Will whispered a prayer. "Lord, *danki* for my family, my girlfriend, my community, and my restaurant. I'm so very grateful for all the blessings in my life. But I'm confused about my relationship with Caroline. I care for her, but I have so many doubts. I'm not sure I see her as more than a precious *freind*. She's *wunderbaar*, loyal, and special, and I know I should cherish her. Is something wrong with me? Why don't I love her? I trust you, God—with my life, as messy as it seems right now. Please lead me down the path you've chosen for me. My heart is open to hearing you, and I will listen for your guidance."

CHAPTER 6

"A re you ready to go?"

Salina gasped as she turned toward the kitchen doorway to find Josiah standing there. She put her hand to her chest and breathed in deep puffs of air, trying to calm her racing heart.

Josiah grinned as he walked toward her. "Did you not hear me come in through the mudroom? The screen door slammed behind me."

"I'm so sorry. What time is it?" She looked at the clock on the wall.

"Five thirty."

"*Ach*. No! I've been so busy harvesting my produce . . ." She pointed to the bucket of cherry tomatoes she'd planned to take to the basement.

"Don't you want to go out to supper?" Josiah seemed to study her. "I took a shorter lunch today and worked as fast as I could to get here on time."

"*Ya*, of course I want to go. I'm so sorry. I've just been focused on getting ready for the market on Thursday."

Mamm stepped into the kitchen, and her gaze bounced back and forth between them. "Hi, Josiah. What's going on?"

"I forgot to tell you, *Mamm*. We're going to have supper at Zimmerman's Family Restaurant. Remember I told you Will Zimmerman said he was going to make pies with the blackberries he bought from me and suggested I come by? Josiah invited me to go tonight, but I lost all track of time." Salina looked down at the garden dirt peppering both her black apron and blue dress. "I need to get changed."

Mamm crossed the floor and pointed to the large bucket of cherry tomatoes on the counter. "I'll take care of these for you. Go on upstairs and get ready."

"I'll be right back," Salina told Josiah.

As she hurried up the stairs to her bedroom, the pair's voices floated up the stairwell behind her.

"You know how Salina gets when she's focused on her work," *Mamm* said. "She has to make sure all the produce is perfect for her customers."

Salina slowed her steps and listened.

"I know. It just seems like I'm always waiting for her."

Salina pressed her lips together as a memory filled her mind. She was sixteen, and her family was ready to leave for church. But Salina had overslept and was scurrying around. She could still hear her brother yelling up the stairs, "We're ready to go, Salina! Why aren't you ready? The bishop's family should arrive early, not late! Don't embarrass us in front of the whole district!"

Closing her eyes, she huffed out a deep breath. She was always disappointing someone. Usually it was her parents or Neil, but this time it was Josiah. And apparently, although she'd never meant to, she'd disappointed him more than she'd ever realized. Did that have anything to do with the lack of romance in their relationship?

Perhaps more to the point, would either her family or Josiah ever be happy with her? Never had she been more relieved to know her cousins might challenge her but never judge her.

She continued up the steps and then down the hallway to the bathroom. After washing her hands and face, she went into her bedroom and changed into a plum-colored dress and fresh black apron. Then she checked her prayer covering in the mirror before grabbing her purse and hurrying back down the stairs.

She slowed again when she heard her father's voice coming from the kitchen.

"It's so *gut* to see you, Josiah. How are your folks?"

"They're *gut. Danki* for asking."

"And how's the roofing business? Busy?"

"*Ya.* We got a big project done today, but we're still repairing roofs after those storms we had back in June."

"I guess that's why we haven't seen as much of you as we'd like—although it was great having your whole family here for supper that evening. We just like having you around. Don't we, Mary?"

"*Ya*, we do!"

Salina entered the kitchen. "I'm ready to go, Josiah." Then she looked at her mother. "*Danki* for taking care of the tomatoes, *Mamm.*"

"*Gern gschehne.*" Her mother waved her off. "Go have fun. But bring us back a piece of blackberry pie."

"Blackberry pie?" *Dat* asked. "I want some too."

"I'll see what I can do," Salina told him.

"We won't be out too late," Josiah said as they headed toward the back door.

"Have a *gut* time," *Dat* called after them.

Outside Salina climbed into the passenger side of Josiah's buggy, and then he guided his horse down the driveway.

"Did you work in your garden all day?" Josiah asked as they traveled down Beechdale Road.

"I did. I had a lot of weeding to do before I could harvest. I need to replenish more of my stock than usual since Will Zimmerman bought so much of it last week." She turned toward him. "How was your day? You said you finished up that big roofing job?"

"We did. On a senior living center in Lancaster." He told her more about the project as they made their way onto Old Philadelphia Pike.

When they arrived at the restaurant, Salina glanced around the parking lot. It was full of cars, and a line of horses and buggies sat at the hitching posts near the back of the lot.

"This place is popular," Josiah muttered.

"I was just thinking the same thing."

Josiah steered his horse to an empty hitching post, where he hopped out and secured the reins. Then they walked to the front of the building, where a sign with the name of the restaurant hung above a large picture window. Colorful potted flowers greeted them as they made their way up the steps, next to a ramp.

Josiah held open the door as Salina stepped into the lobby. A chalkboard on the wall featured colorful block writing with the words "Welcome to Zimmerman's Family Restaurant! Today's specials are: Baked Chicken, Roast Beef, and Blackberry Pie." At the bottom it said, "We feature locally grown produce." Salina smiled at the words.

Next to the chalkboard was a podium where two Mennonite women stood across from four benches. One of the women looked to be in her sixties, silver hair and wrinkles lining her bright-hazel eyes. She wore an Old Order Mennonite prayer covering, a blue-and-white-patterned dress, and a gray apron. Attached to her apron was a name tag that told them her name was Minerva, and she seemed busy as she looked over some kind of notebook. Maybe they took reservations?

The other Mennonite woman was dressed similarly, but she was younger. Salina guessed she was in her early twenties. Her name tag said she was Danielle.

No one was waiting on the benches, and Josiah walked up to the podium. "Hello," he said to Danielle, who smiled at them. She had dark hair and eyes, and Salina noticed her pink-and-white-checkered dress paired with a gray apron.

"Wie geht's?" she said as she looked at Josiah, then Salina.

"We're well. I hope you are too," Salina said.

Danielle picked up two menus. "I am, *danki*. Would you like to follow me to a table?"

"Ya," Josiah said.

Salina scanned the large dining room as they followed her. Most of the tables were full, with Amish, Mennonite, and *Englisher* customers all eating from plates piled high with food. The aromas coming from the buffet smelled so good. She took in the long line there and smiled as she imagined Will working in his kitchen to create such sumptuous dishes. His restaurant was obviously a great success, and she was happy for him and his brother.

She spotted a line at the salad bar, too, and she felt pride when she saw her produce being scooped up. But pride was a sin, and she dismissed the thought. Then she looked to her right and found a row of desserts on a separate counter, with slices of what looked like blackberry pie prominently displayed on one end.

Danielle made a sweeping gesture at a table. "How's this one?"

"Perfect," Josiah said.

"Would you like to order from these"—she held out the

two menus she'd brought with her—"Or would you like the buffet?"

"We'd like the buffet." He turned to Salina. "Right? It smells too *gut* to pass up."

"Absolutely."

"Great. What can I get you to drink?" Danielle tucked the menus under one arm and pulled a notepad and pen from the pocket of her apron.

"Water, please," Salina said.

"Water is fine for me too." Josiah jammed his thumb toward the desserts. "We're most excited to try the blackberry pie." He gestured toward Salina. "She grew the blackberries."

Danielle smiled. "You must be Salina, then. I've heard so much about you."

Embarrassed, Salina shifted her weight on her feet.

"I have to tell Will you're here," Danielle added.

Salina shook her head. "No, no, no. I'm certain he's busy, and I don't want to bother him."

"Nonsense. He'd be angry with me if I didn't tell him." Danielle pointed toward the buffet. "Please go help yourselves."

"Danki." Josiah rubbed his hands together as Danielle stepped away. "Let's get some food."

Salina placed her purse on one of the chairs, and then he followed her to the main buffet. They each took a warm plate and walked down the line behind the other customers. Salina scooped up a pile of macaroni and cheese before placing a piece of baked chicken and a large spoonful of green beans on her plate. She also took a dinner roll and then made her way to the salad bar.

Placing her plate on the counter, she set a bed of lettuce in a bowl and then added cucumber, tomatoes, green peppers, and mushrooms. She topped it off with cheese and Thousand Island dressing before returning to their table, where in a couple of minutes Josiah arrived and sat down across from her. Then they bowed their heads in silent prayer.

"Everything looks *appeditlich*," he said as he cut his roast beef.

"*Ya*, it does."

A hum of conversation floated around them as they ate in silence. Then Salina looked up just in time to see Will coming toward their table. A big smile lit his face as he carried a tray with two glasses of water and two slices of what she assumed was his blackberry pie.

She sat up straighter. "Hi," she said.

"Hi! I'm so glad you came." He set the tray on the table and turned to Josiah, holding out his hand. "Hi. I'm Will."

"This is Josiah Yoder, my boyfriend," Salina said.

Josiah stood and shook Will's hand. "It's nice to meet you." He pointed to his plate. "The food here is fabulous."

"*Danki*."

Salina couldn't help comparing the two men as they stood side by side. Will was at least seven inches taller than Josiah, and his eyes seemed somehow bluer today. Maybe it was the blue plaid shirt he wore under his white apron. Or maybe it was the bright lights above them. He just seemed different, almost larger than life. His smile was even brighter, and his happiness was palpable. Perhaps it was because he was standing in his favorite environment, the successful restaurant he'd built. She wasn't sure why he seemed different, but she couldn't pull her eyes away from him for a moment.

Will pointed to the plates on the tray. "I brought you some blackberry pie fresh from the oven."

"Do you have a minute to sit down with us?" Josiah said.

"Of course I do. I'm the boss." Will laughed, and Salina smiled at the wonderful sound.

"How is your day going?" Salina asked as Will and Josiah sat down.

"*Gut.*" Will pointed to the pie again. "But you have to tell me what you think about this pie. I changed the recipe you recommended, but only a little bit."

"You don't have to ask me twice." Josiah dug his fork into one of the pieces and took a bite. He closed his eyes for a moment and then nodded. "It's amazing," he said after he swallowed.

"I'm so glad you like it." Will turned toward Salina and raised his eyebrows. "Will you try it too?"

His expression seemed to be almost pleading with her, as if he wanted her approval. But why would her approval matter to him?

"Of course." She tried a bite from the other piece, and the sweet flavor made her taste buds dance. "This is superb."

"You think so?"

She was almost certain she found humility and self-doubt in his expression, not pride.

"*Ya,* I do."

"*Gut.*" Will gestured toward the desserts. "The pie has been a huge hit. *Danki* for the recipe."

"I'm so glad it turned out well." She pointed to her plate. "Everything is fantastic. I can see why it's so busy here."

"*Danki.* We're running low on all your produce, though. I'd like to come to your booth again on Thursday. Would that be all right?"

"Of course."

"I want to get some of your raspberries and make raspberry cheesecake." He tapped his chin. "I have some other ideas too."

She smiled. "You're always thinking about recipes, aren't you?"

Will sighed. "*Ya*, I am. It's like a curse, I guess. Sometimes it's hard to think about anything else."

Salina studied his face, realizing she wanted to know more about him. Not just what he'd meant by that, but what had inspired him to learn to cook. Did his mother teach him? Or his grandmother? An aunt?

"Will, Roger is looking for you." A blond, middle-aged Mennonite woman swept by the table. Salina caught a glimpse of her name tag—Valerie.

Will's smile faded. "I'll be right there."

Then he turned back to them. "Roger is *mei bruder*, my partner. And boss or no boss, my break is over. Duty calls." He stood and gestured toward a set of double doors. "Please drop by the kitchen before you leave." Then he gave them a wide smile and started across the dining room, pausing to greet a customer on his way.

"This pie is out of this world," Josiah said when he'd finished the last of his piece. "It is easy to see why this place is so popular."

Salina glanced around the restaurant again, taking in the crowd and the hustle and bustle of the waitresses. Will said Roger was his brother. Were the employees all members of Will's family? Danielle didn't seem to be. Maybe she was from his church.

As Salina and Josiah returned to their meal, another silence fell between them. When Josiah left the table to get seconds, Salina looked around and spotted several couples talking. Did they ever run out of things to say? Was it unusual that she and Josiah seemed to sit in silence for long stretches?

Danielle appeared at the table with a tray just as Salina and Josiah finished eating. "How was everything?"

"Amazing." Josiah leaned back and rubbed his flat abdomen. "And I'm stuffed."

"That pie is especially *gut*, isn't it?" Danielle said, gushing. "I had to take some home to my parents." She collected their plates and set them on the tray.

"I need to do that too," Salina said. "May I get a to-go box with two pieces?"

"Sure."

"Also, could we please have the check?" Josiah asked.

"Oh no." Danielle waved off his question. "Will said your meals are on the *haus*."

"But I'll be glad to pay . . ."

"No. Will means what he says. He also told me he asked you to come to the kitchen before you leave so he can say good-bye. Go through the double doors behind me. But just remember the right door is in, and the left door is out. You don't want to knock anyone over." She grinned.

"Okay. But we don't want to be in the way," Salina said.

"You'll be fine." Danielle added their glasses and utensils to her tray. "Let me get that to-go box ready for you. I'll be right back."

After Danielle brought the box, Salina and Josiah weaved through the sea of tables to the double doors. Salina pushed through the one on the right and stepped into a large kitchen. She immediately took in several counters, two large stoves, two large ovens, and an industrial sink and dishwasher.

Will stood at the counter chopping celery as another man— slightly shorter than him but with the same golden hair and blue eyes—pulled a pan of chicken from one of the large ovens.

Cookware and ingredients littered the counters like remnants from a storm that had just blown through the place.

She'd been right. They were busy.

Will looked up, and a smile broke out on his face. "How was the rest of your supper?" He wiped his hands on a cloth as he walked over to them.

"It's was great," Salina said.

"You need to let me pay for our meal, though," Josiah added.

"No, I can't do that." Will looked over his shoulder. "Roger, come here for a minute." When the other man had joined them, he said, "This is Salina Petersheim and Josiah Yoder." Then he looked at Salina and Josiah. "Roger is my baby *bruder.*"

Roger gave Will a look. "Baby?" But then he smiled as he shook Salina's hand and then Josiah's. "Nice to meet you."

"This is the Salina who owns the Farm Stand," Will said.

"Oh. Your produce has been a great blessing to us," Roger said. "I'm so glad *mei bruder* found your booth. The customers love locally grown ingredients. A few of them have asked me where we buy them, and I told them about your place."

"*Danki,*" Salina said.

Roger pointed toward a doorway behind them. "I also heard your booth is neat and tidy. Maybe you can help Will with his office. It's a mess." He held up a finger. "No, *mess* isn't the right word. It's a catastrophe."

Roger had been grinning, but Will grimaced and glanced down at the floor as if he were embarrassed.

Ignoring his brother's comment, she said, "We should let you both get back to work."

"I'm so glad you came this evening." Will shook Josiah's hand. "It was great to meet you."

Josiah nodded. "Nice to meet you too. *Danki* again for supper."

Will looked at Salina, and his smile and the intensity in his eyes seemed to hold something special just for her. It sent an unfamiliar but thrilling tremor through her body.

"I'll see you Thursday," he told her. "Be sure to have enough produce for me."

"I'll do my best."

Salina and Josiah left the kitchen and said good-bye to Danielle on their way out.

As Salina climbed into the buggy, she recalled Will's expression before she and Josiah left him. He was just a friendly and satisfied *Mennonite* customer, with a girlfriend. And she had Josiah. The thrill she'd felt was probably just a result of being appreciated for her work.

"*Danki* for taking me to supper," Salina told Josiah as they headed back to her house.

"*Gern gschehne.*"

Josiah smiled at her and then turned back toward the road ahead as the familiar silence fell between them. Salina looked out at the passing traffic, and a question suddenly overtook her thoughts.

Do Will and his girlfriend run out of things to talk about?

CHAPTER 7

Salina sat at their usual high-top table in the Coffee Corner with her cousins and Jeff on Thursday morning. She sipped Bethany's chocolate raspberry coffee and watched Christiana and Jeff shift their chairs closer together. Then they smiled at each other before taking a sip of the other's coffee. They'd chosen two different flavors to sample.

Salina had grown used to the affection Jeff and Christiana shared, but it irritated her today.

"Have you seen Daisy this morning?" Bethany's question pulled Salina from her thoughts.

Leanna looked out into the aisle. "No, I haven't."

"I haven't either," Christiana said as Jeff shook his head.

Salina shook her head too.

Bethany frowned. "She's normally here meowing while I set up my *kaffi* makers and then feed her some kibble and give her fresh water. But she hasn't come around today. I hope she's okay."

Salina looked up at the clock. "I should get back to my booth. Will Zimmerman said he was coming for supplies today, and he seems to come before the market opens."

"Will is becoming a regular customer, huh?" Bethany grinned.

"What do you mean by that?" Salina regretted her snippy tone as soon as she asked the question.

"I didn't mean anything by it." Bethany tilted her head. "Are you okay?"

"I'm fine." Salina jumped down from her stool. "I'll see you all later."

Before her cousins could stop her, she walked swiftly into the aisle and to her booth. She had to shake her foul mood. She'd been on edge all morning. Even the market's creaky floors annoyed her.

She'd spent all day yesterday preparing for today. She even worked in the basement until bedtime, washing and bundling her produce, trying to anticipate how much Will would purchase from her. She hoped she had enough of whatever he needed. He was counting on her.

She'd thought about Will himself most of the day too— recalling his smile as he greeted them at the restaurant, his laugh as he joked with them, his concern when she tasted the pie, and his embarrassment when his brother teased him about his messy office. Despite her efforts to put that thrill she'd felt aside, she'd thought about it too.

She finally admitted to herself that she was looking forward to seeing the man today. Yet the realization that he'd somehow become that important to her made her tense. She'd never had a friendship with a man who made her feel such a riot of emotions—happiness, yes, but also anxiety and self-doubt. For some reason, Will Zimmerman had burrowed under her skin, and she wondered if he treasured their budding friendship as much as she did.

As she hurried past the candy booth, Salina forced a smile and nodded at the two young women who ran it. Then she stepped into the Farm Stand and noticed how lopsided her display of raspberries was. She walked to the shelf and began rearranging the containers in even rows. After all, what would *Dat* say if he saw it? Her booth reflected not just her but her bishop father—at least to Amish customers from his district.

"I don't think you brought me enough."

Salina gasped, and then the air whooshed out of her as she spun around. Will had been standing right behind her. "You startled me."

"I'm sorry. I was sure you heard me come in." His grin said otherwise.

She lifted her chin. "I beg to differ. And I think your stealthy entrance was deliberate." Then she laughed.

He pointed at her. "There's that smile. How are you today?" The way his eyes seemed to study her made her skin practically itch.

"I'm *gut*. How are you?"

"Fine." He pointed to the two carts behind him, one holding the plastic crates she'd loaned him. "I've brought back your crates, but I'm going to need them again today."

"I'll make you a deal. You can keep the crates as long as you keep filling them with produce from my booth."

"I'll take that deal." He leaned back against the counter that held her display of figs. "I'm so glad you and Josiah came by the restaurant earlier this week. He seems like a great guy."

"He is."

"How did you meet?"

"I've known him my whole life. Our parents are close *freinden*, and we grew up together. We're in the same church district, and we went to the same school, same youth group."

She shrugged. "It just seemed natural when he asked me out and then asked me to be his girlfriend."

"What does he do?"

"He's a roofer. His *dat* owns a roofing company, and Josiah is a foreman there."

"How long have you been dating?" he asked.

"About a year."

"It's serious between you, then?"

She hesitated. "I guess so."

"I'm sorry." He held up his hands. "That question was too personal."

"It's okay." Now was her chance to ask the questions that had been burning through her mind. "Tell me about your restaurant. What inspired you to open it? Who taught you how to cook?" She pressed her lips together as embarrassment caused warmth to creep up her neck. She'd probably just scared him off with her nosiness.

But Will didn't flinch. Instead, he crossed his arms over his wide chest. "It's a long story, but I spent a summer with *mei onkel* Eddie in New York State when I was a teenager. He owned a restaurant, and he taught me just about everything I know."

"Really?" She took a step toward him, intrigued.

"*Ya.*"

Sara Ann stepped into the booth, and Salina barely stopped an eye roll. Why did she have to ruin this perfect chance to talk to Will alone?

"*Gude mariye!*" Sara Ann sang. Her eyes openly assessed Will, looking him up and down as if she'd never seen him before. But of course, she had. Then she stuck out her hand. "Hi. I'm Sara Ann King, but you can call me simply Sara Ann."

"Nice to meet you. I'm Will Zimmerman." He nodded at Salina. "I'm Salina's best customer."

"I've noticed. You've been buying most of her produce these days." Sara Ann smirked at Salina.

Salina bit her lower lip to stop herself from asking the woman to leave.

"I own the restaurant across the street," Will told her.

Sara Ann snapped her fingers. "Zimmerman's! Of course. I've eaten there a few times. Great food."

Why was Sara Ann acting as though Salina hadn't already told her Will owned the place?

"*Danki*. It's even better now that I've discovered Salina's produce." Will glanced at Salina and then back at Sara Ann.

"Is that so?" Sara Ann's smile took on the devious characteristic Salina had seen too often, and her stomach soured. She could just imagine the rumors Simply Sara Ann would spread about her and Will. What would happen if they got back to Josiah? Or to Will's girlfriend?

She heard the whoosh of the market's front doors, and then a multitude of voices announced the arrival of customers.

"Well, it's time to make some sales." Sara Ann gave them a little wave. "It was nice meeting you, Will. Don't be a stranger. Maybe you'd like to buy one of my quilts sometime." She looked at him coyly, and then turned to Salina. "Have a *gut* day."

Salina tried to suppress the frown that threatened to overtake her face as she watched Simply Sara Ann flutter toward her own booth.

"I should get my order together." Will pointed at the raspberries behind her. "Will you still be my *mei freind* if I buy all those?"

"I'll always be your *freind*." The words flowed from her lips without her having any idea they were going to.

"That truly is a relief."

At first she thought he was joking, but his expression was genuine, and his warm smile wrapped around her heart. What was it about this man that made her so happy? Was she imagining this invisible force that seemed to pull her toward him?

"I'm going to buy most of your butternut squash too," he added. "Have you ever had cinnamon roasted butternut squash?"

"No, but it sounds *wunderbaar.*"

"*Gude mariye*, Salina!" Alma Beiler called as she came into the booth.

Salina glanced over her shoulder as several of her regular customers filed inside, and then she looked back at Will. Oh, how she longed for more time to talk to him!

"Take care of your other customers," he told her. "I'll gather what I need and then let you tell me how much I owe you when you have a minute."

"Salina." Alma held out a withered hand as she came closer. "How are your folks?"

Salina smoothed her black apron and then shook hands with the woman. "They're both well, Alma. How are your knees?"

"They just ache and ache when it rains. And my back gives me fits too. It seems like something in my body always hurts. Oh, it's tough to get old."

Salina glanced past Alma and found Will grinning at her. She bit her lower lip to stop a smile from forming. "I'm so sorry to hear that. Would you like your usual order of tomatoes and onions?"

"*Ya. Danki.*"

Salina helped Alma and then took care of three more

customers. As she spoke to them, she somehow knew Will was watching her. She did her best not to give in to the urge to meet his gaze.

Will pushed his two full carts to the counter when her other customers had left. "What do I owe you?"

Salina took in the plastic crates full of his usual items along with most of her butternut squash and what remained of her raspberries. Then she gave her best attempt at looking solemn. "I don't think you'll be able to afford this. You should just put it all back."

His eyebrows lifted as he leaned forward, resting his hands palms down on the counter. "Do you think you're funny?"

She shook her head and then deadpanned, "No, I think I'm hilarious."

He snorted as a laugh escaped his lips, and she joined in.

"Now, what's the damage for real?" he asked.

She gave him a total, and he paid her before slipping his wallet into the back pocket of his jeans. "I know I've already suggested this, but you really should come for lunch sometime."

"I just take a short lunch break. And sometimes it's so busy that I have to eat here in the booth."

"But you need to make the time." He pointed to the butternut squash. "My squash is worth it."

She laughed. "Is that so?"

"It is." He winked at her, and her heart seemed to flip-flop. "I'll see you soon," he said.

Salina watched him walk away. Her heart had returned to normal, however, and she reminded herself to keep her attraction to this man in check. He was a customer and a friend. That was it.

That had to be it.

CHAPTER 8

"Will!"

Will looked toward the kitchen's back door to see Caroline walking in. "How was your day?" she asked.

"Busy. Yours?"

"The same. We had a steady stream of customers at the bookstore most of the day. It was kind of tiring, but we also sold quite a bit." She crossed the kitchen floor and then stood on her tiptoes to kiss his cheek. "I missed you. *Mei dat* said I could come help you close up and then call his driver for a ride home."

"I'm glad you're here." He smiled down at her and touched the tip of her nose. "You can load the dishwasher."

She groaned but then laughed, her pretty face lighting up.

"You're just making her do that because you don't want to," Roger grumbled as he walked past them. "Hi, Caroline. Don't let him make you deal with dirty dishes unless he's willing to clean up that pigsty he calls an office."

"Stay out of it, Rog," Will called after him.

Caroline just smiled as she headed to the dishwasher. "I don't mind dealing with messes."

Will sighed and shook his head. He couldn't remember a single time Caroline had pushed back or argued with him. She always went along with anything he asked her to do. Sometimes he longed for her to stand up to him when he was bossy. But she never did.

Yet what would she do if she knew the truth about his doubts?

And would Salina stand up to Josiah if she disagreed with him?

The last question caught him off guard. Why was he thinking about Salina again? Caroline was the woman who had stood by his side for three years now. She'd been with him through thick and thin, especially as he struggled to make his dream come true and open his restaurant. She'd comforted him when he was turned down for loans, and she encouraged him when renting the first building he'd hoped for fell through. She'd been his rock. But here he was thinking about an Amish *maedel* he'd met at the market.

For the next several minutes, he felt pummeled by shame as he put away supplies, but he deserved to feel shame. He didn't deserve Caroline.

"Should I mop the floor next?"

Will craned his neck to look at her. Hadn't she just said she'd had a tiring day? "No, *danki*. I'll do it."

"I don't mind." She flipped on the dishwasher and then moved to the supply closet and opened the door.

Will had to stifle a groan. He really was a horrible person for not appreciating Caroline enough. Worse, thoughts of Salina had lingered at the back of his mind all day. He kept recalling her beautiful smile, her sweet laugh, and the way she'd teased him in her booth that morning. The truth was he couldn't wait to talk to her again.

But here was Caroline, eager to please him. No, he didn't deserve her. He probably deserved to be alone for the rest of his life.

The roar of the vacuum cleaner sounded from beyond the

double doors, indicating that Roger and Danielle were almost finished cleaning the dining room. The other waitstaff had all gone home. He was wiping down the last counter, the smell of bleach attacking his senses, when he heard the whoosh of the kitchen door opening.

Roger stepped into the room. "Will, Danielle and I finished vacuuming, and she just left. Should I call for our ride now?"

"Not for Will," Caroline said.

Will spun to look at her. "Why not?"

"Is it okay if my driver takes you home instead?" She seemed almost anxious for him to agree. "I'd like for us to talk."

Will swallowed hard as a feeling of foreboding came over him, but of course he'd talk with her. "Sure."

"*Danki.*" She nodded and started mopping again.

Will turned to Roger, who lifted his eyebrows with obvious curiosity. "Go ahead and call Austin for yourself," he told him. "I'll be home later."

"Okay." Roger lingered for a moment, then took a step back toward the dining room. "I'll call on the office phone, and then I'll wait out back since it's such a nice night." He turned and disappeared into the office.

When the mopping was done and Roger had left, Will helped Caroline stow the mop and bucket. Then he made sure everything else had been put away too. His office might be a disaster, but his uncle had taught him the importance of a clean and tidy kitchen. Besides, every restaurant owner could expect surprise inspections.

"Should we call your driver now?" he asked Caroline.

"I was hoping we could talk here first." She walked toward the closed office door, and he took long strides to beat her to it. But then he realized she'd see inside the room eventually.

"Uh, there really isn't any place to talk in here." He opened the door and felt heat creeping up his neck as she took in the mess.

"Wow. Roger wasn't kidding all those times he said this was bad." She gingerly stepped over a cardboard box. "We could get this organized together."

"Not today." He beckoned her to come out. "Let's go talk in the dining room."

He chose a table in the middle of the room and then sat down across from her. "What's on your mind?"

"So . . ." She cleared her throat and then took a deep breath as she set her purse on the floor. "I want to discuss . . . us."

Uh-oh. Will sat straighter. Talk about a surprise inspection. If he wasn't careful, Caroline would see the mess he'd been keeping inside, not just the one in his office. But he didn't want to hurt her. He had to be cautious.

"I want to know how you feel about . . . me," she said. She sounded shaky. "Where do you see our relationship going, Will?"

He'd tell her the truth. "Caroline, I care about you. You know that. You're *schee*, sweet, kind, and thoughtful. You're everything a man could pray for in a *maedel*. You're a blessing to me." He searched her eyes. "Where's this coming from?"

She stared down at her lap, and when she looked up, her eyes were glassy. Then tears started streaming down her crumpled face, and dread wrapped around his chest and squeezed. What was happening?

"Lorene got engaged last night," she said, referring to her best friend. "When I realized she and Randy have been dating for only a year, I started wondering what's wrong with me. Why haven't you asked me to marry you?"

His stomach bottomed out as he reached across the table

for her hand. Then, after taking a deep breath, he said, "Nothing is wrong with you, and I care deeply for you. You're very important to me."

"But not important enough to marry me." Her voice faltered as tears continued to fall.

"*Ach*, no." He came around the table and gently pulled her to a standing position. She leaned against his chest as a sob escaped. "I'm just not ready," he said.

"When will you be?" Her voice was muffled against his shirt.

He'd tell her what he'd told himself for a long time. "When I have enough money for a *haus*."

She looked up at him. "But you already have a *haus*."

He shook his head. "A rented apartment isn't *gut* enough for you."

She stared at him. "You think I'm a snob?" Her chin quivered as more tears flowed.

"No. That's not what I mean." He cupped his hand to her cheek. "What I'm trying to say is I want to save enough money to build you a proper *haus*. I can't have *mei fraa* living in a small apartment when she deserves better." And that really was the truth. He would never feel ready to marry until he could be a better provider.

Caroline took a napkin from the holder in the center of the table and wiped her eyes and nose. "Are you saying you haven't given up on me?"

"Are you kidding?" He put his finger under her chin and angled her face toward his. "I wouldn't give up on you. You haven't given up on me."

"I love you with my whole heart, Will, but I can't wait forever. I want to be a *mamm*. I want *kinner*."

"I understand." He paused for a moment as she looked down at her feet. He was grateful for the chance to avoid her eyes. The hurt there was almost too much to bear. "What can I do to make you feel better?"

She looked up again. "I want to be more involved in the restaurant."

He blinked. She'd put some thought into this. "You do?"

"*Ya.* When are you going back to the marketplace for more produce?"

"Probably not until Saturday since I was just there this morning. Why?"

"I want to go with you. I want to meet this Amish *maedel* and see what her booth is like for myself."

"Okay. I've been thinking of getting some of her kale for a new recipe or two." He recalled recipes he'd perused in a cookbook—kale chips, stir-fried kale, kale and feta salad . . .

"*Gut.* Why don't we call my driver, and then you can tell me about your recipes using kale." She lifted her purse from the floor and slung it over her shoulder.

As they walked through the kitchen to use the phone in his office, Will tried to imagine how Caroline would react when she met Salina. He just wasn't sure which woman he was concerned about. Caroline? Or Salina?

• • •

"Hello!" a familiar voice said.

Salina looked up from organizing her display of onions and froze. Will had just walked in—with a Mennonite woman who was both beautiful and young.

"Hi," she said, recovering enough to greet them.

"Salina, this is my girlfriend, Caroline." Will divided a look between them. "Caroline, this is *mei* new *freind* Salina."

Caroline rushed to Salina and shook her hand. "It's so nice to meet you. I've heard so much about you."

They stood eye to eye at the same height, Caroline dressed in a pretty blue-and-white dress covered with a gray apron. With her blond hair and gorgeous golden-brown eyes, she reminded Salina of a painting of an angel she'd once seen in a tourist gift shop. She was stunningly beautiful with a perfect nose, high cheekbones, and full, pink lips. No wonder Will had chosen to date her.

"It's *wunderbaar* to meet you too," Salina said, grateful to find the words. Then she looked at Will. "How are you?"

"I'm fine." His smile was warm and friendly, as usual.

"How did the raspberry cheesecake turn out?"

"It's been a hit," Caroline answered for him. "The customers love it. I even took one home for my parents. Didn't I, Will?"

He smiled down at her. "You did."

The way he looked at Caroline made Salina's back stiffen. Why was she jealous of this woman when Will was nothing more than her friend and customer? Was she losing her mind?

"We want to buy some kale because Will found some fabulous recipes for it," Caroline said. "We also need more salad ingredients."

"*Wunderbaar.*" Salina pointed toward the lettuce. "Please help yourself."

Caroline scanned the booth. "Wow. Your produce is superb, Salina. I see why Will keeps coming back. I'll start loading up." She pushed one of the carts to the tomatoes.

Salina stared after her. Will and Caroline were obviously happy, and Caroline was obviously a big part of Will's business.

She'd said *our* several times. But why did she feel so off-kilter with this woman in her booth?

"*Was iss letz?*" Will's voice was next to her ear, and his nearness sent a jolt through her veins.

"What?" Salina jumped and stepped away from him.

Will gave a low, rumbly laugh that sent her nerves jangling to life. "I always seem to startle you."

"*Ya*, you do." She folded her arms over her apron and looked at Caroline again. "You should go help her before she leaves you broke."

"Are you going to double charge me today?"

Salina looked up at him, and his smile faded.

"Are you okay?" The concern in his eyes was almost overwhelming.

Salina forced a smile. "I'm fine. Just tired."

He raised an eyebrow as if unconvinced.

"Will?" Caroline called. "How many cucumbers should I get?"

"I'll be right back," Will said before joining his girlfriend.

Salina busied herself with arranging some herbs while the couple shopped. She tried to focus on her task, but her gaze kept wandering to Will, her jaw clenching every time Caroline touched his bicep or brushed her fingers over his hand.

She was definitely losing her mind!

She had completely reorganized her herb display by the time the two carts were full of produce.

"I think we're done." Caroline laughed a little as she pushed one of the carts to the counter with the cash register. "We left you a few things to sell."

Will feigned a weary expression as he pulled his wallet from his back pocket. "What's the damage?"

Salina added up the prices and then gave him the total. He fished out a stack of bills and began to count them.

"Will told me you have cousins who own booths here," Caroline said.

"*Ya*, I do. My cousin Christiana owns the Bake Shop across the way. Bethany has the Coffee Corner, and Leanna has the Jam and Jelly Nook."

Caroline touched Will's arm again. "I'd love to see what baked goods Christiana has in her Bake Shop. I'll take one of the carts with me."

"I'll be right there," Will told her.

"It was nice meeting you, Salina. I hope to see you soon." Caroline gave her a little wave and then pushed her cart into the aisle.

"Here you go." Will gave Salina her money.

"*Danki*." She counted the bills and then put them in the cash register drawer before handing him his change. "And here you go."

Will stuck the cash in his wallet. "Caroline wanted to come with me today."

"She's lovely." Salina fingered the edge of the counter.

He nodded. "She says she wants to get more involved in the restaurant."

"Oh." Questions swirled through her mind. She wanted to know everything. How did Will and Caroline meet? How long had they been together? Was he going to marry her? But her lips couldn't form the words. She just stared at him.

"I hope you have a *gut* day, Salina."

"*Ya*, you too." She leaned forward on the counter as he pushed the other cart out of the booth toward the Bake Shop.

Maybe someday she'd learn more about Will and Caroline.

But right now she couldn't stop thinking about how beautiful Caroline was and how happy she must make Will.

Why did that bother her so much? After all, didn't she make Josiah happy?

CHAPTER 9

Worry plagued Will as he pushed his cart into the Bake Shop. He couldn't stop thinking about the strange expression on Salina's face when she saw them come into her booth. She seemed different—somehow on edge and rattled. Had she and Josiah argued? Had something happened at home? He longed to know what was wrong, but he didn't know if he'd earned the right to ask. Their friendship was too new.

Still, he'd talk to her the next time they were alone—although that might be impossible if Caroline joined him for all his visits to the Farm Stand. Surely not, though. She still had to work in her family's bookstore.

He found Caroline talking to Christiana, who was standing behind the main counter in her booth.

"This is Will," Caroline announced as she gestured toward him. "Will, this is Christiana."

"Hi, Will." Christiana shook his hand. "I've seen you filling your carts at Salina's booth. You're her best customer."

Will pointed to the purchases in his cart. "That's because she has the best produce in town."

"I agree."

"You have to come by the restaurant," Caroline gushed. "Will is a *wunderbaar* chef. You'll love the food."

"I'd love to sometime."

"Did I hear someone mention that a cat lives in the market?" Caroline asked.

"*Ya.* She's a gray tabby named Daisy, but we haven't seen her in a while. We need to look for her. I hope she didn't run away or get hit by a car."

"I hope she's okay too." Caroline paid for a pack of chocolate chip cookies, and then they said good-bye to Christiana and headed into the aisle.

Will looked toward the Farm Stand and spotted Salina talking to a customer. He took in her pretty face but then felt a tinge of guilt.

Caroline took his arm and nudged him. "Let's go to the Coffee Corner. I want to meet Bethany."

"I really need to get back to the restaurant."

"Please?" She gave him her best puppy-dog look.

He sighed. "Fine, but let's make it quick. You know I have a lot to do before we open for lunch."

"Danki!" She took off ahead of him, hurrying past other customers.

Will followed her around the corner as the aroma of hazelnut coffee filled his nostrils. When they entered the Coffee Corner, he saw a half-dozen high-top tables where customers sat drinking coffee and eating donuts. A young Amish woman with blond hair and blue eyes stood behind the counter and smiled as an Amish man about her age spoke to her.

"That must be Bethany," Caroline said before pushing her cart to the counter.

When the young man left with a cup of coffee and a donut, the blonde turned to them. *"Gude mariye,"* she said.

"Hi. Are you Bethany?" Caroline asked.

"I am." Bethany looked at each of them. "How may I help you?"

"I'm Caroline, and this is Will. Will buys produce for his restaurant from your cousin."

"Oh, right." Bethany nodded at Will. "I've heard a lot about you."

"You have?" Will stood a little taller.

"*Ya*, I have. It's nice to meet you." Bethany's smile was bright and genuine. "Would you like a cup of hazelnut *kaffi*? I have regular too. And decaf. And I have plenty of fresh donuts—chocolate covered, plain, and sprinkled. What sounds *gut* to you?"

Will and Caroline left the booth each balancing a cup of coffee in one hand and pushing a cart with the other. Their chocolate-covered donuts sat on top of their carts. Then they stopped by the Jam and Jelly Nook and chatted briefly with Leanna, who was petite and looked to be in her midthirties. She, too, said she'd heard about Will, which he found surprising.

What had Salina told her cousins about him? The question sent heat swirling in his chest all the way back to the restaurant.

"That was fun," Caroline announced as they pushed the carts up the cement ramp at the back of the restaurant. "I'm so glad you let me go with you."

"I'm glad you went."

"The Farm Stand really is fabulous," Caroline continued as they pushed the carts into the kitchen. "I can see why you go there."

Will nodded as he flipped on the light switches, awakening the fluorescent lights and flooding the large kitchen with their warm glow. Roger was coming in a bit later today. He had an appointment to go to.

"I think you should set up a regular delivery from Salina."

Will turned to face her. "Really?"

"*Ya.* Your customers love her produce, and it's helping your business." Caroline placed her hand flat on his chest. "If this restaurant is our future, we should have only the best."

"Okay." He smiled. He'd love to ask Salina to set up regular deliveries for him. But then he nearly cringed as he realized the real reason for his enthusiasm. A business deal might mean he'd have the chance to get to know her better.

. . .

Salina put her rocking chair in motion as she sat on her grandparents' porch the following day. It was an off Sunday without a church service, and she was enjoying a visit with her mother's side of the family, including her favorite cousins.

She sipped from her glass of iced tea as she glanced out to the pasture, where her youngest cousins chased one another while their mothers chatted in the kitchen and their fathers gathered in the barn. The air was humid, but she could hear birds singing their summer songs, and her grandmother's colorful garden flowers swayed in the warm breeze.

"It's such a *schee* day," Christiana said as she sat beside Salina in another rocking chair.

"*Ya*, it's the perfect day for July." Bethany moved back and forth in the glider.

Leanna nodded as she sat down beside Bethany. "It is."

The back door opened, and *Mammi* appeared on the porch. She smiled at them. "I always know I'll find the four of you together."

"Sit with us, *Mammi.*" Bethany patted the empty rocker beside her.

"I'd love to." *Mammi* crossed the porch and sank into the rocker. "What's your latest news? I know you've heard some at the marketplace, so spill it!"

Salina laughed with her cousins as she looked at her precious grandmother. She loved *Mammi*'s sense of humor and zest for life. At eighty, she had gray hair and wrinkles, but those wrinkles outlined the same warm blue eyes she'd given Salina's mother. Although she was a few inches shorter than petite Christiana and walked with a slight limp because of pain in her knee, she still managed to keep up with her grandchildren and her great-grandchildren—even Leanna's thirteen-year-old son, Chester. She enjoyed hearing what was going on in their lives, and she was never short on good advice. Salina prayed she'd have many, many more years with her.

Mammi turned to Leanna. "Come on now, Leanna. I know you have something *gut* to share with me."

"Well . . ." Leanna turned toward Salina. "Salina has a new customer who's been buying up a lot of her stock."

"Really?" *Mammi*'s eyes lit up. "Who is she?"

"It's a man." Bethany elbowed Salina. "Go on. Tell her."

"Ow." Salina rubbed her arm and gave Bethany a look before turning back to *Mammi*. "His name is Will Zimmerman. He owns Zimmerman's Family Restaurant."

Mammi touched her chin. "Zimmerman? Is he Mennonite?"

"*Ya*, that's right."

Bethany's smile widened. "And he's very tall and *very* handsome."

"And he has a girlfriend," Salina added quickly.

Christiana nodded. "I met them both. They came by my booth yesterday."

"I met them too," Leanna said. "Caroline seems sweet."

"And she's beautiful." Salina got out the words and then stared down at her half-empty glass of tea. She couldn't seem to stop contemplating how Caroline had gazed at Will. It was as if the image was burned into her mind, taunting her. Why couldn't she stop thinking about them?

"How's Jeff?" *Mammi* asked Christiana.

"He's great. He's visiting relatives today."

"It sounds like things are going well for you two."

"They are. I'm hoping he asks *mei dat* for permission to marry me soon. I think I'm ready."

Salina heard Leanna gasp and Bethany squeal, and her head snapped up to stare at her cousin. Christiana was ready for marriage?

Mammi leaned over and touched Christiana's arm. "That's *wunderbaar*. I'm so *froh* to hear you say that."

Christiana beamed. "It just feels as if God has blessed our relationship, and I think marriage is the next step for us."

Bethany turned to Salina. "What about you?"

"What?" Salina blinked.

"Are you and Josiah ready to get married?" Bethany asked. Apparently her cousin wasn't going to let this go, but at least Jeff wasn't here this time.

"Uh, no. I don't think so." Salina rubbed at a knot that had suddenly formed in the back of her neck.

"Are you okay?" Leanna's eyes seemed to fill with concern.

"*Ya*. Sure." Salina nodded with such vigor that the ties on her prayer covering bounced off her shoulders. Then she shrugged. "I'm just not ready. I don't think it's our time."

"That's okay." Leanna smiled. "You'll know when you are."

Bethany stood. "Who wants more iced tea?"

Leanna stood as well. "I do. I'll walk inside with you." She and Bethany disappeared inside the house.

"I'm going to check on your *daadi*." *Mammi* limped down the porch steps and started toward the barn.

"What's going on with you?" Christiana asked Salina when they were alone. "You've been so quiet—as if you're lost in thought."

"How do you know you love Jeff?"

Christiana paused, and then her brow puckered. "I don't know, really. I just feel certain in my heart." She touched her chest. "An overwhelming feeling tells me he's the one God has chosen for me."

Salina stared at the horses in the pasture.

"Hey." Christiana touched Salina's arm. "I'm worried about you."

"I'm okay." Salina's eyes met hers. "I'm just struggling with how I feel about Josiah. Something just seems off between us."

"Give it time. Jeff and I went through a hard patch, too, and we came through it stronger."

"I guess I'll eventually figure it out." But as soon as she said the words, renewed doubt settled in her heart. What if she didn't figure it out? How long could she go on not knowing if Josiah was the man she was supposed to marry? How long would God let her go on?

Later that evening Salina stepped into her parents' kitchen, where she filled a glass with water. Then she walked through the family room where her parents were both reading. She was about to go up the stairs when *Dat,* sitting in his favorite wing chair, looked up from his devotional book. "Isn't Josiah coming to see you tonight?"

Salina stopped at the bottom step. "I don't think so, but I

haven't spoken to him since Tuesday, when we went out for supper."

Mamm put down her novel and looked at her over her reading glasses. "That's strange."

"Not really. We don't talk every day." Salina fingered her glass.

"Well, he's a busy man," her father said. "But I'm so glad you and Josiah are seeing each other. It's important for our community to stick together. Just like Neil married Ellen from his youth group, you'll marry Josiah. I'm the bishop, so you and Neil are examples for our community. You need to represent our family just as well as he has."

Salina's breath came in short bursts as her lungs felt squeezed so hard they might explode. She could never live up to her father's standards. She'd never be the daughter he wanted—probably needed and deserved.

"You and Josiah are just right for each other," he continued. "You've grown up together, and our families are close. Everything will be perfect when the two of you are married and have *kinner*. Then we'll share grandchildren with his parents."

"I'm going upstairs." Salina turned and started up the steps, hoping she'd find solace in her room, away from her father's suffocating expectations.

"I think I just heard someone knock on the back door," *Mamm* said. "Would you check, Salina?"

"Of course, *Mamm*." Salina walked back into the kitchen and set her glass on the table before walking through the mudroom and opening the back door. Josiah was standing there. "Hi."

"Hi." He pointed to the porch floor. "Do you have time to visit with me out here?"

"Sure." She pushed open the screen door and then joined him on the glider.

"We haven't talked in a few days," he said.

She pushed the glider into motion. "Are you okay?"

He sighed. "*Ya*. But I wanted to come to your *mammi*'s today. Then *mei mamm* insisted we all go to church in her cousin's district."

"Oh." Salina looked out at the pasture as the sunset pressed back the day, lighting the sky with vivid yellow and orange, the cicadas singing their nightly chorus as lightning bugs floated past the house.

Her mind swirled with confusion as her conversation with Christiana came to mind. Did she love Josiah? Did he love her?

But if she didn't marry Josiah, her parents would be so disappointed in her!

Her chest constricted with renewed pressure and anxiety. Would she ever discover the path God had planned for her?

"How's your work at the marketplace going?" Josiah asked. "Still good?"

"It's fine." She sank back against the glider. "Busy."

"*Gut.*"

Like a great canyon, silence stretched between them once again, and Salina wondered if Josiah had come to visit tonight only out of duty since that's what boyfriends are expected to do. Or did he truly *want* to visit her? But if he wanted to be there, why didn't he have anything to say to her?

After a few more beats of silence, Josiah finally spoke. "I was just thinking today about that day we spent at Cascade Lake when we were seventeen." He gave a little laugh. "That trip was a disaster."

Salina laughed as the details came to her. "*Ya*, it was. That was when I left the cooler of food at *mei haus*, right?"

"*Ya!* And none of us had any money to buy some because we had to pay our driver."

"That's right! We'd have perished in the sun if it hadn't been for the one pack of water Christiana brought."

"And I forgot my swimming trunks." He chuckled. "I planned to just watch everyone swim until Leroy Esh pushed me off the dock. My clothes were damp for the rest of the day."

They laughed together, and it felt good.

"That's one day we'll never forget," she said. "We have had some great adventures with our youth group."

"That's true."

As quiet fell between them again, Salina tried to imagine a life spent married to Josiah. Were all their best moments behind them? Would they sit at the supper table each night reminiscing because that's all they had to share?

Josiah's smile faded, and she wondered if he was just going through the motions in their relationship—not just with this visit tonight but every time they were together. And did the silence between them so often bother him as much as it bothered her?

She longed for the courage to ask him, but he stood. "I should go."

"Okay. *Danki* for coming by. I'll walk you to your buggy."

They strolled side by side, and then he turned and took her hand. But he only shook it.

"Have a *gut nacht*," he said as he climbed in.

"You too." As his taillights disappeared down the driveway, Salina shivered despite the humid air. She didn't know what God had planned for her and Josiah, but they needed to know before they made a big mistake.

CHAPTER 10

Will stepped into the Farm Stand Thursday morning and smiled as he watched Salina working on a bin of zucchini. Her brow pinched as she ensured the vegetables remained in a neat pile.

He stood silently for a moment and then crossed his arms over his chest. "You know, as soon as someone takes one of those, your perfect little stack is going to tumble."

She spun toward him and lifted her chin. "At least my booth isn't the mess your *bruder* said your office is."

"Ow." He winced and grabbed at his chest. "That felt like a barb."

"It was." She smiled, and her face lit up. "You thought you would sneak up on me, but I heard you coming as soon as you entered the building." She pointed at the bottom of one of his carts. "The wheels on that one squeak."

He nodded. "Well, that's *gut* to know. But I have a business proposition for you."

She tilted her head. "What do you mean?"

"How would you feel about setting up a midweek delivery to my restaurant? That would streamline our business arrangement." He gestured around the booth. "We can both save time if you delivered directly to my restaurant instead of dragging everything here and then my having to come get it. I also need to increase the amount I buy each week."

Her mouth dropped open a little, but no words came out. Then she said, "How would that work?"

"What if I paid you to deliver to me on Wednesdays? I could call you with my order on Tuesdays, and then I'll pay your driver to bring it all to me. Or I could come and get it from you."

She nodded slowly as if seeing the plan come together in her mind. "I'll just pay my driver and include the cost in my invoices. And I'll come with him to make sure you're satisfied. Will that work?"

"*Ya*. That would be great." He rubbed his hands together. "You can tell me what you want for a delivery fee."

"That sounds *gut.*"

Then her expression changed, but what flashed in her eyes was unreadable. "It was really nice meeting Caroline."

"She enjoyed meeting you too."

"How long have you been together?"

"Three years."

"Wow. That's a long time. Are you engaged?" Her eyes widened, and she cupped her hand to her mouth. "I'm so sorry. That was too bold and rude."

"It's okay." He held out his hand. "You can ask me anything."

Her expression relaxed.

"We're not engaged, but she'd like to be."

Her brow pinched again. "I don't understand what you mean."

He spotted two stools in the corner of the booth. "Can we sit and talk?"

"Of course." She led him to the stools, and they both sat down.

He folded his hands in his lap and looked at the floor as he tried to translate his feelings into words. "My family loves her, and her family loves me. I think everyone expects us to get married because we've been together so long, but I'm not sure if that's what I want."

Will looked up, and Salina opened her mouth but held back her words.

"What?" he asked.

"Will, I think—"

"Pardon me, Salina." A middle-aged Amish woman called out. "Where are your green peppers?"

"Hi, Ida. I'll be right there." Salina hopped down from the stool and turned to Will. "Excuse me."

"Of course." Will nodded, but disappointment zipped through him. He'd found someone who might understand how he felt about his dilemma, but their conversation had been cut short.

Will filled his carts with produce while Salina helped three more customers. Once they were gone, he pushed the carts to her counter, his mind whirling as he wondered what she'd been going to say before the woman interrupted them. Did she think he was wrong to doubt his feelings for Caroline? Or maybe she did understand what he was going through.

"I'm so sorry." She seemed scattered as she pulled out her calculator and began to use it.

He leaned forward on the counter. "Take your time." He ran his fingers over the wood while considering what else he could—or should—share about Caroline.

When voices sounded behind him, Will looked over his shoulder to see a group of *Englisher* women stepping into the booth. He gritted his teeth. So much for having more time.

Salina looked up at the crowd, and her shoulders sagged.
She seemed just as disappointed as he felt. She met his gaze and
gave him the total he owed. He paid her and then tapped the
counter. "May I get an order from you this Wednesday?"

"*Ya*, of course."

"Could I have your phone number?"

"Oh. Right." She pulled out a notepad and wrote on it. Then
she ripped off the piece of paper and handed it to him. "This is
the number to *mei dat*'s business, but you can leave a message
for me. I look forward to hearing from you."

He smiled as he folded the paper and slipped it into his
pocket. "I'll see you soon, Salina."

. . .

Salina stood at the counter in her basement kitchen and
scanned her list of items to pack for the next day. She tried to
concentrate, but her mind kept replaying her conversation with
Will that morning. She heard the sound of his voice as he'd
told her he wasn't sure about marrying Caroline.

Hearing Will's words had cracked open something inside
her. It was as if she had a kindred spirit in him—someone
who understood her and how she felt about Josiah. It was as
if Will had spoken *her* truth—said the words she'd longed to
say aloud.

She'd wanted to grab Will's arm and drag him out to the
back of the parking lot so they could talk alone. She'd wanted
to find out more about how he felt and then share her own feelings. She'd wanted to hear his opinion about her feelings for
Josiah.

For the first time in a long time, she'd felt as if someone

understood her. She and Will had a connection, a special friendship. If only they'd had more privacy and more time to talk!

Footsteps sounded on the stairs, and Salina looked up as her mother came down.

"What are you doing?" *Mamm* asked. "You've been down here a long time."

"I'm still packing for tomorrow." Salina held up the list she'd made before she'd left the marketplace.

"Do you need help?"

"Sure. *Danki*." Salina read off the items she needed, and *Mamm* took them from the pantry.

When they were finished, Salina leaned back against the counter and shared her news. "Will asked me to start making midweek deliveries to his restaurant beginning next week."

"How will that work?"

"He'll call me on Tuesdays with his order, and then I'll pay my driver to help me deliver the items on Wednesdays."

The basement door opened, and *Dat* came down the stairs. "What's going on down here?"

"Salina was just telling me she's going to start making weekly deliveries to Zimmerman's Family Restaurant." *Mamm* repeated what Salina had told her about how the deliveries would work.

"Tell me about Will Zimmerman," *Dat* said when he turned his attention to her.

"He's a *gut* man. He's an Old Order Mennonite, and he's impressed with my produce." Salina held her breath, praying her father wouldn't forbid her from supplying produce for Will. If he did, she'd never see him again. The idea sent near panic slithering through her body.

"And he's going to pay you a fair price?" *Dat* asked.

"*Ya.* He always has."

"It sounds *gut* to me." *Dat* turned to *Mamm.* "What's for supper tonight, Mary?"

Salina breathed a sigh of relief as her parents started up the stairs. She'd have a hard time waiting for Will's call. She just hoped they'd have a chance to talk when she delivered his first order.

· · ·

Salina walked out of Josiah's house with Bethany, Leanna, and Chester. Josiah's parents had hosted the church service this Sunday, and she and her cousins had just finished helping clean the kitchen after the noon meal.

"Did you happen to see Daisy at the market yesterday?" Bethany asked as they strode to their horses and buggies in the field out back.

Leanna walked beside her as Chester walked just ahead of them. "I was going to ask you the same thing."

"Daisy's missing?" Chester stopped and turned. When Leanna gave him a solemn nod, he asked, "Have you looked for her?"

"We did. Even Kent has looked, and I know as the market-place manager, he doesn't have time for that. But no one has found her." Bethany sighed. "I'm worried that something bad happened to her."

"We'll look again on Thursday," Salina said. "I'm worried about her too."

"I can help you look," Chester said. Salina was still getting used to how grown up Chester had become. This boy with his mother's light-brown hair and brown eyes was a teen now.

"That would be nice." Leanna patted his shoulder. Then she pointed to a group of teenagers standing by the pasture fence. "Why don't you go talk to your *freinden* until it's time for us to leave?"

"Okay." Chester headed off.

The three cousins walked in silence toward their family's buggies, and Salina's thoughts moved to Will. "I haven't had a chance to tell you Will Zimmerman asked me to start making midweek deliveries to his restaurant beginning this week." She explained their plan. "He wants to buy even more from me too."

"Wow," Bethany said with her usual enthusiasm. "His business will be that much more profitable for you, then."

Salina shrugged. "I suppose so."

"Will you have enough produce to supply both the restaurant and your booth?" Leanna sounded skeptical.

Salina hadn't thought about that. "I guess I'll see. I might have to cut back on what I sell at the market."

"Would that hurt your profit, though?" Leanna asked. "Would you make enough from supplying the restaurant to make up for what you would have made at the market?"

Bethany turned to Salina. "You'll just have to charge Will enough, right?"

"*Ya*, I suppose so."

Salina suddenly felt a headache forming behind her eyes. Had she made a mistake by agreeing to supply produce for Will's restaurant? She didn't want to lose her booth. She enjoyed spending time with her cousins and the customers who relied on her. Also, the booth was her special place, just like her garden and basement kitchen. She was in charge there, and she didn't have to make excuses for not being the perfect bishop's daughter or perfect deacon's sister. It was her business, and she couldn't allow anyone to take it away from her.

But wasn't that what *Dat* said marrying Josiah would do?

"It will work out," Bethany said as Salina shook away that thought. Then Bethany looped her arm around Salina's when they reached her father's buggy. "You'll make sure the prices are right. You've always been *gut* at that."

Josiah came up to them. "Prices for what? What are you all talking about?"

"Didn't Salina tell you the *gut* news yet?" Bethany said. "She's going to start making midweek deliveries to Will Zimmerman's restaurant."

"Really?" Josiah looked surprised. "That's fantastic."

"We were just discussing whether she'll have enough produce to sustain the booth and supply the restaurant," Leanna added. "Consensus is she'll be fine."

"Huh." Josiah gave Salina a long look. "I think so too."

Salina spotted Christiana and Jeff holding hands as they sauntered their way. Then she glanced at Josiah. He was standing at least two feet from her. Why did he maintain such a distance while Jeff always seemed to sit or stand close to his girlfriend? She supposed he could be honoring the sermon her father gave last month, reminding all the unmarried couples to maintain their purity. But Jeff was an honorable man, and no one—including her father—seemed to mind the affection he showed her cousin.

No, it couldn't be that. Josiah's kisses had always been few and far between. She could count on a peck on her cheek maybe once a month. And although she'd really begun to wonder about that only recently, it struck her that she wasn't disappointed. Was it time for her to face the truth? Was their relationship doomed to end because they were—and would always be—just friends?

She couldn't imagine her father ever accepting that idea when he was so determined she'd marry Josiah.

"Hey!" Jeff called from where he and Christiana now stood at his buggy. "Are you all coming to play volleyball at the Glicks' farm?"

Josiah turned to Salina. "Do you want to go?"

She shrugged. "I guess. Sure."

Josiah spun back to Jeff. "*Ya*, we're coming!"

"You all have fun." Leanna hugged Salina and then Bethany. "I'll see you at the market Thursday."

"Be safe going home," Salina told her.

"Do you want to ride with us?" Josiah asked Bethany.

"*Ya, danki*."

"I'll go get my horse." Josiah took off toward the pasture.

"Salina, I know I ask you this a lot, but are you okay?" Bethany said.

"*Ya*, I'm fine." Salina looked toward the pasture, willing her cousin to stop asking questions. But one of these days she'd have to have an honest conversation with Josiah about their relationship. Just not today.

CHAPTER 11

On Tuesday morning Will shifted a pile of papers aside as he searched for a notepad on his desk at the restaurant. He knew one was there somewhere. At least he thought it still was.

"Aha," he muttered when he found it. Then he carried it into the kitchen and began rooting through the refrigerator and pantry.

Roger rolled his neck as he came in. "Are you making a shopping list?"

"*Ya*, I have to call Salina today." Will smiled to himself as soon as he'd said her name. He couldn't wait to see her again tomorrow. Thoughts of her had haunted him throughout the weekend and all day yesterday. He longed to know if she'd thought about him too.

"You have to call Salina? Why?"

Will spun around. "Didn't I tell you? She's going to deliver produce here on Wednesdays from now on."

"No, you didn't tell me." Roger studied him. "How did this come about?"

"Caroline visited Salina's booth with me, and when she suggested I have Salina deliver to us midweek instead of my always going there, I made arrangements with Salina to deliver to us on Wednesdays." Will held up his notepad. "I'll call her with the list on Tuesdays. That's today."

"Oh." Then a smile turned up the corners of Roger's mouth. "Changing the subject . . . I've decided to ask Danielle if I can ride home with her today—so we can talk."

"Really? Are you going to ask her out?"

"I'm getting there. You can't rush these things." Roger crossed the kitchen floor and began pulling out pots and pans.

Will grinned and then continued working on his list. When he was finished, he returned to his office, once again scanning the mess. He needed to come in early one morning and organize this disaster. He'd begun to think of it as a real failing, and he didn't like that feeling.

He dug the phone out from under a stack of fresh invoices and then fished Salina's number out of his back pocket. He almost had her number memorized. She'd written her name, too, as if he'd ever confuse her with another Salina. She had such delicate, slanted handwriting.

He looked down at the floor and gritted his teeth. He had to stop thinking of Salina as more than a business associate, but he wanted her to at least be a friend—a good friend. Someone he could talk to and share his deepest fears with.

Shouldn't Caroline be that special friend?

Yes, she should be. So why wasn't she?

He punched in Salina's number. The phone rang several times, and then voice mail picked up, sending a man's voice through the line.

"You have reached Lancaster County Cabinets. We build and install custom cabinets. Please leave a message, and we will call you back. If you need to reach a member of the Petersheim family, please press two. Thank you."

Will pressed two, and at the beep he began to speak. "Hello, this is Will Zimmerman for Salina. I have my order for this week." He took a deep breath and then listed what he needed. When he finished, he said, "Thank you, Salina. I look forward to seeing you tomorrow."

He ended the call and leaned back in his chair. Yes, he did look forward to seeing her. But did she look forward to seeing him as well? Or had he scared her off when he'd confided in her about Caroline?

. . .

Salina sat on her rolling garden stool and pulled tomatoes off the vine before setting them in the large basket beside her. She hummed to herself as she soaked in the gorgeous, late-July weather. Her garden was the place where she breathed in God's beautiful creation and often prayed while she worked. Even more so than her basement kitchen, it was her solace at home.

She glanced around her and took in the half acre of colorful raised beds ripe with the fruits and vegetables she'd planted and cultivated with the help of God's glorious sun and rain throughout the year. Some plants were already past their season, but she had enjoyed tending everything in her garden this year.

When a screech sounded behind her, Salina turned to see her nieces running toward her with their mother in tow.

"Hi, *Aenti* Salina!" four-year-old Betsy Kay yelled. Her long, light-brown braids bounced off the shoulders of her green dress and black apron as she rushed toward her. Jayne, her two-year-old sister, looked like her miniature twin as she toddled forward with the same light-brown hair as their mother's and light-blue eyes as their father's.

"Hi, Betsy!" Salina pulled her in for a hug before hugging Jayne. "Hi there, Jayne. How are you today?"

The little girl pointed toward the tomatoes. "Red!"

"You're right. They are red." Salina laughed as she tented her hand over her eyes and looked up at Ellen. "Hi there. What a nice surprise."

"We were out getting groceries, and we decided to stop by and say hello." Ellen lifted Jayne just as her daughter reached into the basket of tomatoes. "Those are *Aenti* Salina's tomatoes. We shouldn't touch them."

"But do you girls want to help me pick some of the tomatoes?" Salina asked her nieces, and they clapped their hands in response. "Now, you lean over and gently pick the ones that are red, okay? Leave the green ones alone. They aren't ready yet."

Ellen sat Jayne back down on the ground.

"Okay." Betsy Kay turned to Jayne. "Let me see which ones you want to pick. Now pay attention."

Salina laughed as she stood and wiped her hands down her apron. "How is your week going, Ellen?"

"It's been fine. But Neil had to leave early this morning for a job he's finishing with your *dat* out in Reading."

"Oh. *Dat* didn't mention that."

"Ellen!" *Mamm* approached them. "I didn't know you were here."

"*Mammi!*" Betsy Kay wrapped her arms around her grandmother's waist as Jayne grabbed her leg.

"Hi, girls." *Mamm* sat down on the garden stool and pulled Jayne onto her lap. "It's so nice to see you."

"We were in the area shopping," Ellen said.

Mamm looked at Salina. "I came to tell you that you have a message on voice mail from Will Zimmerman."

"He must have left his order for the restaurant." Salina looked at Ellen. "Excuse me." Then she hurried to the building that housed her father's shop and office. She dialed voice mail and smiled as she grabbed a notepad and pen and started writing down his order.

Once the message ended, she listened to it a second time, enjoying the sound of Will's voice. He said he looked forward to seeing her tomorrow. She looked forward to seeing him too.

After she deleted the message, she stuck the list in her apron pocket before walking back to her garden, where her nieces were busy filling her bucket with tomatoes.

"Did he place a big order?" *Mamm* asked her.

"He did." She held up the list. "I need to start pulling it together."

"You get started on your order, and we'll finish harvesting your tomatoes," *Mamm* said.

"Just be cleaned up by five," Ellen said. "You and your parents are coming to our *haus* for supper."

"*Danki.* I'll be ready." Salina hurried inside. She would have Will's order together by then. Then all she had to do was wait for tomorrow to come.

. . .

As Salina sat between her nieces at the kitchen table in Neil and Ellen's large kitchen, she glanced at the custom cabinets and recalled how they were her brother's first solo installation. They were a special wedding gift for Ellen. At least they were part of her gift, along with the large, two-story brick home he'd saved up enough money to build for her on the other side of *Dat*'s pasture.

When Jayne squealed, Salina handed her a buttered roll and then turned back to her plate filled with generous portions of Neil's favorite meal—steak, mashed potatoes, green beans, and buttered noodles. Ellen always seemed to make this meal when she invited Salina and her parents to supper.

"One of the problems with this community is that the women are too concerned with making extra money," *Dat* was saying as he cut into his large steak. "They need to focus on the home and teaching their *kinner* to behave and follow the rules of the *Ordnung*. Their husbands can support them just fine."

Salina looked down at her plate as she forked some mashed potatoes. How she longed for her father's meal conversations to be light and easy. Instead, he turned them into lectures.

"I was just saying the same thing to Ellen the other day," Neil chimed in. "She knows her job is to worry about the *haus*, not running a side business like hosting meals or quilting. I'll worry about paying the bills, and she'll worry about our *kinner*."

Neil reminded Salina of their father in nearly every way. They had the same long nose, the same dark hair, the same light-blue eyes, the same bushy eyebrows, the same long beard, and the same focus on the good of the community. And all they wanted to talk about was how the community was failing to follow the strict rules of the *Ordnung*.

"That's right." Ellen smiled at Neil with love in her hazel eyes.

"This is why I have to visit homes and talk to parents about their teenage *sohns*." Neil continued swirling his fork through the air for emphasis. "Just the other day I had to have a tough conversation with Henry Blank about his eldest *bu*. He was seen driving a car again. And I heard he was drinking liquor with a group of *Englishers*. If Henry's *fraa* had been more focused on raising their *kinner* than on running her quilt business, I wouldn't have to go over there to talk to them. We wouldn't have these problems if the women were focused on teaching their *kinner* their proper roles in the Plain community."

Salina held back an eye roll as she placed some green beans in her mouth. Another meal, another lecture.

"I'll have to work this into one of my upcoming sermons," *Dat* said.

Salina buttered another roll and handed it to Betsy Kay. Then she lost herself in thoughts about Will and his order. She hoped her driver, Brian, remembered to arrive at seven thirty tomorrow. They had quite a bit to load into his van. But if he was on time, she could be at Will's restaurant by eight. Hopefully he'd wait while she and Will finished their conversation. She'd been about to give him her initial reaction to what he was saying when they were interrupted, but now she realized she wanted to hear more about his relationship with Caroline before she weighed in.

"That's what I keep telling Salina."

Salina's head popped up when she heard her father say her name. "Huh?"

Dat picked up his glass of water. "I was just telling Neil about how I've reminded you that you won't have your booth at the marketplace once you marry Josiah. You'll have too much to do keeping *haus*, and when the *kinner* come along, you'll be responsible for their welfare. You wouldn't want your *bruder* to have to visit you because your *kinner* were running around committing sins, would you?"

"That's right," Neil said. "I would hate that. It's tough enough being the deacon, but to have to deal with my own niece or nephew's bad behavior would make it even more difficult." Her brother smiled as if he hadn't just dropped a bomb on Salina's world.

The piece of steak in Salina's mouth suddenly tasted like sawdust from her father's shop. Not only did her father and brother see her married to Josiah and chained to a house, but they'd also decided her children would be unruly and sinful. She chewed slowly and then forced the meat down her dry throat.

"Why do you look so surprised, Salina?" Neil's smile was almost a smirk. "Did you really think you'd keep your booth after you're married? Leanna has hers only because her husband passed away. She's earning income so her parents won't have to be the sole support for her and Chester."

Salina felt a muscle jump in her jaw. If only her mother would say something, but she never did when Neil or *Dat* was lecturing her. As far as Salina knew, *Mamm* was in complete agreement with everything they said. And she knew Ellen was.

She turned to Neil and narrowed her own eyes. "I don't think I need to worry about that for quite a while," she said, nearly growling.

Neil set his fork on his plate. "What do you mean by quite a while?"

"I mean Josiah and I haven't even talked about marriage."

"You haven't talked about it?" Ellen leaned toward her as if trying to understand the words. "Why not? You've been together for a year now."

Salina stilled as all the adults stared at her. Had they all expected her to be engaged any day now?

"Marriage has never come up in conversation?" Ellen said, still pressing.

Salina cleared her throat. "No, it hasn't."

Ellen and Neil shared a look, and Salina scowled. She knew her brother was judging her, assessing her worthiness to even be in this family.

"Ellen," *Mamm* began, her voice a little too loud, "your mashed potatoes are just perfect tonight. I always seem to add too much milk."

Salina looked at her mother, who gave her a sad smile. At least *Mamm* had just saved her from more humiliation.

"*Danki*, Mary," Ellen said. "I'll have to show you my recipe. It belonged to *mei mammi*."

Neil turned his attention to *Dat*. "I need to discuss something with you. I received a letter from a church district in Kentucky asking for help. A member there gave birth to premature *zwillingbopplin*. The *bopplin* have been in the hospital for months now, and they need help with bills. I'd like to bring it up to the congregation in a member meeting after the next service."

Dat nodded. "We can discuss it after supper."

"*Danki.*"

Salina finished her supper and dessert in silence, grateful everyone else talked about people they knew in the community instead of focusing on her and her relationship with Josiah.

Salina and *Mamm* cleaned the kitchen while Ellen gave the girls a bath. *Dat* and Neil disappeared into the shop behind Neil's barn.

Confusion and irritation plagued Salina as she wiped down the counters. She kept replaying the conversation at the table. Maybe she and Josiah didn't belong together, but how could she break up with him when her parents and brother expected her to marry him?

What if Salina just expected too much from Josiah? Perhaps

God had chosen him for her, but she was too prideful and self-ish to appreciate him. He was everything a woman could want in a mate.

Mamm turned from washing the dishes at the sink and faced her. "Salina, you seem so lost in thought. Is something bothering you?"

Salina set the washcloth aside and rubbed at her temple where a headache brewed.

"*Mamm*, how soon did you and *Dat* discuss marriage?"

"I don't remember for sure. Maybe six months after we started dating." She paused. "I know you probably feel some pressure from your *dat*—from Neil and Ellen too. But we all feel sure God intends for you to marry Josiah. You know, just because he hasn't mentioned it yet doesn't mean he isn't thinking about it. Give him time."

"What if he doesn't want to marry me?"

"Don't be *gegisch*, Salina." *Mamm* smiled. "Of course he wants to marry you. Why would he have asked you to be his girlfriend if he wasn't already thinking about a future with you? Again, just give him time. You're both young."

Mamm paused again, and her smile faded. "Is this about your Farm Stand? I know you don't want to give it up, but it's part of being a *fraa*. You'll have to concentrate on your *kinner*. Maybe you can have a stand at your *haus* when the *kinner* are older. You and Josiah will figure it out. Don't let it upset you. We just want what's best for you and our community. I'm sure you understand that."

But a question still filtered through Salina's mind. What if what was best for the community wasn't best for her?

CHAPTER 12

Brian Clancy backed up his van to the loading dock behind Zimmerman's Family Restaurant at exactly eight o'clock the following morning. Then he turned to Salina in the passenger seat and smiled. "We're here."

"Thank you." Salina pushed the passenger door open and slipped out.

As she climbed up the steps, the back door of the building opened, and Will appeared pushing a cart. He looked so handsome dressed in a gray-and-blue plaid shirt, jeans, and suspenders. She also took in his strong jaw, wide shoulders, and muscular arms, then looked away as Roger came out behind him.

"Good morning." A smile broke out on Will's face, and her pulse skittered. His presence felt like a balm to her soul after her family's criticism last night. Her father's and brother's words about being a dutiful wife and Ellen's confusion over her lack of a marriage proposal still haunted her. Even her mother didn't seem willing to hear her heart. Seeing Will was just what she needed today.

"Hi." She gave him a little wave. "Will, this is Brian."

Will shook his hand. "Good morning." He turned to Roger. "This is my brother Roger."

"Nice to meet you." Brian shook Roger's hand.

Roger pointed to the van. "Are you ready?"

"Yup." Brian opened the back doors. "Let's get started."

Soon they were transporting Will's order into the kitchen, where he told them the places he wanted them to unload.

"Are you actually going to help or just supervise?" Roger joked as he set a crate of carrots on a counter.

Will rolled his eyes and pushed an empty cart toward the back door.

Salina silently marveled at the easy teasing between the brothers. If only she had that kind of relationship with Neil. But Neil had always found fault in her, even when she was a child. She vividly remembered him criticizing her for missing some crumbs when she'd swept the kitchen floor as a six-year-old.

After nearly twenty minutes, the van had been emptied, and the kitchen was full of fresh produce. Salina grabbed the invoice from the van and walked back inside. When she didn't see Will there, she peeked into the office, where she found him sitting amid the worst clutter she'd ever seen. Boxes, books, and papers were piled up not just on his desk but on the floor and surrounding bookshelves.

Will looked up and gave her a shy smile. "*Ya*, I know. It's a disaster. I need to organize it. Maybe Roger is right. Maybe you can help me someday."

She shook her head and gave a little laugh. "I'm not sure even I could help."

"I'm a lost cause, then." He chuckled and then nodded at the piece of paper in her hand. "Is that for me?"

"*Ya*." She handed him the invoice, and he pulled his checkbook from a drawer.

While he wrote out the check, she scanned the office. How long had it taken him to create this mess? How long would it take to organize it? That is, if organizing it was even possible. It might need a real overhaul first.

"What's on your mind?"

She turned toward Will and found him staring at her, his blue eyes intense and his expression full of empathy.

"Nothing." She shifted her weight on her feet and smoothed her hands down her apron.

He stood and handed her the check.

"Danki." She folded it and slipped it into the pocket of her apron.

"And *danki* for bringing my order." He leaned against the desk, his body still towering over her. "You're not yourself today. I could tell something was on your mind when you got out of the van." He pointed to her forehead. "You get this little dimple right there when something is bothering you. Do you want to talk about it? I'll listen without judgment."

Salina glanced behind her and found the doorway empty. Then she turned back to his concerned expression, and without warning, the frustration and irritation she'd been carrying for weeks broke free. "Do you remember how you talked about family pressure?"

He rubbed his chin. *"Ya*, I do. I'm so embarrassed for unloading on you. I hope you can forgive me."

"Don't be embarrassed. I can relate. *Mei dat* and *bruder* keep lecturing me about how I have to give up my booth at the marketplace if—when—I marry Josiah." She balled her hands into fists at her side. "Last night it became apparent just how completely they expect me to marry him. So do *mei mamm* and my sister-in-law. But what if I don't want to get married? What if I just want to work in my garden and sell my produce?"

Will nodded slowly as his eyes seemed to assess her.

"And what if Josiah doesn't even want to marry me? Sometimes he doesn't even act like my boyfriend. He just acts like a *freind*."

He stopped nodding, and she longed to know what he was thinking. But she went on, pointing at him. "You're a man. Maybe you can answer this for me. My family thinks it's strange that Josiah and I have been together for a year, but he hasn't even mentioned marriage. Does that mean he doesn't want to marry me? Lately, he doesn't even hold my hand or stand close to me. And he rarely even kisses my cheek. But Christiana and Jeff are always holding hands and standing close together. Does Josiah even love me? I don't know. He's never said so."

Will seemed to freeze, and his eyes widened in shock.

Uh-oh. She'd said too much. Heat blasted her cheeks, and Salina took a step back, ready to run away from Will and her humiliation. Why had she opened her heart to him like that? She didn't even really know him.

"I'm sorry." She took another step back. "I should go."

"No, wait." Will reached for her.

"I'll see you next Wednesday. Leave me a message with your order." Salina rushed from the office, bumping into Roger. "Excuse me," she muttered as she hurried out to the van and climbed into the passenger seat.

As Brian's van bumped across the parking lot, Salina stared down at her lap. She'd shared too much personal information with Will, and she could never take it back. She should have kept her relationship with him strictly professional, but now she'd crossed a line.

· · ·

Will stared at the empty doorway after Salina vanished, his mind spinning with disbelief. He ran his hand down his face as he recalled the hurt and sadness in her eyes as she shared her feelings. He'd been so stunned by her words that he hadn't been able to speak for a moment.

Josiah didn't tell her he loved her. Was he blind or just stupid? He would lose her if he didn't wake up soon. How could he risk a woman as smart, hardworking, beautiful, and sweet as Salina slipping through his fingers?

Will had longed to run after her, stop her, and tell her he thought Josiah was a moron and that she deserved better. He wanted to console her and tell her he believed she was wonderful and deserved a man who appreciated her. But it wasn't his business or his place to speak ill of Josiah.

Roger stuck his head in the doorway. "Why was Salina in such a hurry? Did you say something to offend her?"

"No, I didn't." Will stood straight. "She was upset about something her family said to her last night. I'd rather not say what since it was personal." He couldn't betray Salina's confidence and share her private feelings. He started toward the doorway. "Let's get all this put away. We have a lot to prepare before we open for lunch."

As Will set to work stowing the produce, thoughts of Salina continued rolling through his mind. He couldn't wait another week to see her. He would have to come up with some reason to visit the market so he could make sure she was all right.

She was his friend. She was important to him. And he was worried about her. As he moved some produce to the large refrigerator, an idea sparked in his mind. He would go to her booth tomorrow morning to buy what he needed to make his favorite stuffed peppers. Then he would invite her to come to the restaurant for lunch.

A smile overtook his lips as the plan came to life. Somehow he'd find a way to talk to her alone. That was the only way to be certain she was okay.

. . .

Salina straightened a stack of grocery bags under the counter and then looked up just in time to see Will stepping into her booth. He looked good in his green plaid shirt, and his inviting smile sent warmth radiating through her chest.

She touched her prayer covering and tried to smile, but humiliation pressed her lips together. How could she face him after what she'd revealed yesterday? "Will. Hi. Did I forget something on your list?"

"No, you didn't. But I'm in the mood to make stuffed peppers, and I don't have any peppers." He jammed his thumb toward her display of the vegetable. "May I buy all of them?"

"Sure."

He leaned against the counter, and his nearness made her feel dizzy for a moment. She held her breath, waiting for him to mention yesterday and everything she'd told him about her family and relationship with Josiah.

"How are you?" he asked.

"I'm fine." She lifted her chin as if trying to prove she was. "*Gut.*"

"And you?"

"Great." He tapped his fingers on the counter. "See, I have this local supplier, and she's selling me great produce. That makes my customers *froh*, which makes me *froh*."

She laughed as his comment made her relax a little. "I'm so glad to hear that."

"And it's so *gut* to see you smile and hear you laugh. I was worried about you after yesterday." His expression seemed full of genuine concern.

She blinked and tried to mask her surprise. He was worried? About her?

"Hi, Will!"

Salina looked past him as all three of her cousins walked into the booth.

Will spun and waved to them. *"Gude mariye."*

Bethany held up a cup, and the aroma of caramel coffee filled the booth. "Salina, since you didn't join us this morning, we brought you a cup." She handed it over, and Salina thanked her. Then Bethany looked at Will. "I'm sorry I didn't bring you some, but I didn't know you'd be here."

"It's no problem."

"What brings you here this morning?" Leanna asked.

"I came for peppers. I'm making stuffed peppers." He turned back to Salina. "You should come for lunch so you can eat some." Then he turned back to her cousins. "Actually, you should all come for lunch."

"Danki, but I can't," Christiana said. "Jeff and I have plans."

"I have plans with *mei sohn*, Chester," Leanna said. "He's coming so we can look for Daisy."

"Daisy is missing?" Will turned to look at Salina, and she nodded.

To Salina's surprise, he looked worried.

"She's been gone for more than a week now," Salina said.

"I'm sorry to hear that. I hope she isn't hurt somewhere," Will said.

"That's our fear too," Leanna told him.

Will turned to Salina again. "Will you come by for my stuffed peppers, then?"

"Oh, I don't know." Salina shook her head. "It's probably going to be busy today."

Bethany came around the counter and looped her arm around Salina's shoulders. "Let's close our booths for an hour so we can both go."

Salina stared at Bethany, who gave her a wide smile. How could she say no? She turned back to Will. "I guess we'll be there, then."

Will kept his eyes locked on hers. *"Gut."*

"We'd better get to our booths," Bethany announced. "The doors will be opening any minute. I'll come and get you at lunchtime, Salina."

As her cousins left, Will picked up his crate of peppers. "What do I owe you?"

Salina told him, and he paid her. Then he trained his intense gaze on her as she handed him his receipt. "I look forward to seeing you at lunch."

"I look forward to seeing you too." As he walked out of her booth, Salina wondered if he'd made an excuse to come see her today.

Surely not. He has a girlfriend, and my imagination is running wild.

CHAPTER 13

It's lunchtime," Bethany sang out as she walked into Salina's booth a few hours later. "I want to close for only an hour, so we need to get going."

Salina closed her register and locked the drawer with the key. "Why were you so determined to get me to do this?"

"I don't know." Bethany shrugged. "Will just seemed so eager for us to try his stuffed peppers. I didn't want to hurt his feelings."

Salina smiled at her cousin. "You're always so sweet and thoughtful."

Bethany snorted. "*Ya.* That's why the men are knocking down my door."

"You'll find someone soon. God has the perfect man in mind for you." Salina touched her shoulder. *And for me?*

"I just hope I find someone as nice as Jeff and Josiah."

"You will."

They exited the marketplace, bustling through the front entrance's double glass doors. When the traffic halted at the crosswalk on Old Philadelphia Pike, they stepped across the street.

"Have you seen Daisy today?" Salina asked as they walked the length of the parking lot to the restaurant's entrance.

"No." Bethany sighed. "I'm hoping Chester and Leanna find

her today. If not, I'm going to look for her after the market closes."

"I will too."

They entered the restaurant and were greeted by its tantalizing smells. Salina smiled when she spotted stuffed peppers listed on the chalkboard as the special of the day, along with the note about locally grown produce. She loved the idea of the people in town enjoying the food she'd grown.

They walked toward the podium, where someone already familiar to Salina stood.

"Salina. Hi!" Danielle waved to them.

"Hi, Danielle. This is my cousin Bethany."

"Nice to meet you." Their hostess picked up two menus. "Are you here for lunch?"

"We are." Bethany nodded toward the buffet. "Will told us to come for stuffed peppers."

"Gut." Danielle dropped the menus back into a basket and beckoned them to follow her. She led them to a table in one of the far corners. "How's this?"

"Perfect," Bethany said.

"What would you like to drink?"

"Water will be fine," Salina said.

"Ya, for me too," Bethany said.

"Okay." Danielle pulled a notepad and pen from her apron pocket and wrote on it. "I'll be right back. Please help yourself to the buffet. I'll let Will know you're here."

"Oh no." Salina held up her hands. "I don't want to bother him."

"It's no bother. Like I told you last time you were here, he'll want to know. I'll be right back." Danielle headed toward the kitchen.

"Let's get some of this delicious food." Bethany took Salina's arm and pulled her toward the buffet line. They each filled their plates with stuffed peppers, noodles, and green beans before making salads. Then they walked back to their table, where their glasses of water were already waiting for them.

Bethany ate a forkful of stuffed pepper and then moaned. "This is amazing."

"It is," Salina agreed after swallowing a bite. "Will is a talented chef."

Salina ate in silence as she contemplated her confusing relationship with Will. On one hand, she trusted him completely, and she wanted to be a close and dear friend. On the other hand, it scared her how easily she could open her heart to him. She couldn't find the courage to ask Josiah how he felt about her, but her feelings just flowed when she spoke to Will. Why was it easier to talk to him than to her boyfriend?

"So how are they?"

Salina looked up as Will slipped into the seat beside her, his expression eager as he pointed at her plate.

"The stuffed peppers? They're fantastic," Bethany said.

Salina nodded. "They are."

"Really?" His golden eyebrows careened toward his hairline.

"Truly," Salina said.

"*Gut.*" He rested his arms on the table. "I have a recipe, but I like to put my own spin on it."

"Will, where are the restrooms?" Bethany asked.

He pointed across the dining room. "Go toward the double doors and then make a right."

"*Danki.*" Bethany stood. "I'll be right back." Then she weaved through the knot of people and tables.

Salina suddenly felt self-conscious as she sipped her water.

Her mind whirled, trying to find something to say to Will after her embarrassing display the day before. He must have thought she was an emotional mess.

"I'm glad you came," he said. "I didn't think you were going to."

Salina swallowed and then fiddled with a napkin to avoid his gaze. She had to apologize to him, but she struggled to find the words. "I'm sorry for what I said yesterday. I shouldn't have shared so much with you. I know I made you uncomfortable. I promise it won't happen again."

"Are you kidding?"

She looked up and met his kind and genuine smile. "No, I'm not kidding. It won't happen again. I'm so embarrassed, and I'm sorry that I made our friendship so awkward."

"I'm not upset, and you could never make me uncomfortable. I'm honored you trusted me with something so personal. After all, I shared something similar with you."

"But we have a business relationship, and I crossed a line. I'm sorry for that. I hope you can forgive me."

He rubbed his chin as he looked at her, and she longed to crawl under the table.

"I understand this is a business relationship, but I don't see why we can't be *freinden* too. Right?"

She looked down at the table, afraid to let him see just how much she wanted his friendship. "I suppose so."

"*Gut.* I would like that." When she raised her head, he looked past her and smiled.

"I'm back," Bethany said as she sat down. "Will, this stuffed pepper is so flavorful. It might be the best I've ever had." She looked at Salina. "Don't you dare tell *Mammi* I said that."

"I won't." Salina smiled. She was grateful Bethany was there to take the pressure off. She looked at Will, and he grinned, seemingly amused with Bethany.

Danielle appeared again. "Is everything okay?"

"Perfect," Bethany said. "We're almost finished. Could we get the check?"

"No." Will shook his head. "It's on the *haus*."

"You can't keep giving me free meals." Salina pulled her wallet from her apron pocket and turned to Danielle. "How much do we owe you?"

"Uh . . . Well . . ." Danielle nodded at Will. "He's my boss, and I don't want to lose my job."

Salina turned to Will. "You have to let me pay you."

"Nope. Your money is no *gut* here." He pushed her wallet back. "It's the least I can do for you after you've helped me so much."

"*Danki*, Will," Bethany said.

Salina hesitated but then thanked him as well.

Bethany looked toward the clock on the wall. "We need to get going soon. I usually have another rush in the early afternoon."

Will stood and smiled at Salina. "*Danki* for coming. It truly means a lot to me."

The sudden intensity in his eyes sent yet another jolt through her. It was as if something had shifted between them. She felt an odd stirring in her chest—something new, something she'd never felt before. It was as if her heart had suddenly come alive. The sensation was exciting and terrifying all at once, and panic scratched over her skin.

This could not be happening. She couldn't allow herself to be attracted to Will. Not only were they both dating other people, but he was a Mennonite, not part of her community.

Her father would never approve. Nor would her mother or brother, and certainly not her sister-in-law.

"*Danki* again, Will," Bethany said.

"*Gern gschehne.*" Then he looked at Salina. "I'll see you soon."

"Okay," Salina managed to say.

Danielle said good-bye, and then she and Will left.

Salina and Bethany finished their meals and then headed back to the marketplace.

"That was just *appeditlich*," Bethany said as they walked toward the market.

"*Ya*, it was."

"Will is so nice."

"He is," Salina said, agreeing again.

Yet she felt as if she were drowning in confusion. She was falling for Will, but they could never be together. Then frustration set in. Why couldn't she feel these same emotions for Josiah? He'd been her friend since she was a child, and he was the man her parents wanted her to marry. The man God wanted her to marry, as far as she knew. Josiah was the one she belonged with, not Will.

But how could she ever talk sense into her heart?

CHAPTER 14

Will finished counting out the money in the register and then zipped the bank deposit bag. He glanced behind him to where Minerva was wiping tables and Danielle was vacuuming, and then he walked back through the kitchen to the office. After a minute or so of searching, he found his deposit slips.

"Danielle told me Salina came for lunch today." Roger had come to the doorway.

"*Ya*, she did. I invited her for stuffed peppers."

"Why?"

Will sighed. "What are you getting at, Rog? Why don't you just say what you're thinking?"

Roger stepped inside and closed the door. The frown on his face sent a wave of anxiety through Will, and it intensified when Roger spoke up. "You seem to have a crush on Salina."

"Whoa." Will held up his hands. "You're completely misinterpreting the meaning of a lunch invitation. Salina is my business associate and *mei freind*. That's it."

"I think it's more than that." Roger stood over Will. "I think you have feelings for her, but you can't admit it."

"Roger, I'm dating Caroline, and Salina is dating her boyfriend, Josiah. I care about her only as a *freind*. Okay?"

Roger shook his head. "I could tell something was going on yesterday when she almost knocked me over on her way out the door. What happened? Did you kiss her?"

"No!" Will jumped up from his chair. "I didn't kiss her, and I wouldn't. We were just talking. I already told you. She shared something that had upset her. And then she had to go. That was it."

Roger paused for a moment. "I think it's time for you to be honest with Caroline. Tell her you're never going to marry her instead of leading her on. She deserves to know the truth so she can find someone who truly wants her as his *fraa*."

"You're out of line. And I'm not leading Caroline on. I care about her. I'm just not ready to get married." Will nearly hissed the words. "I think you should worry about yourself and work up the courage to ask Danielle out."

"It's not the same thing at all, and you know that." Roger shook his head again as he moved toward the door, and when he reached it, he looked back. "Salina is Amish, and you're Mennonite. You really need to think about what will happen when her family finds out about you."

Will cupped his hand to his forehead. "There's nothing for her family to find out. Besides, Old Order Mennonite and Amish marry all the time. One of them just has to convert. It's not a big deal."

"Maybe not, but it's a big deal when you're interested in a *maedel* but dating someone else. You need to be careful. You're playing with fire."

Will leaned back in his chair as Roger disappeared. He tossed his pen onto the desk and buried his face in his hands.

Roger was right. Will *did* have feelings for Salina. He knew it for sure to the depth of his soul when Salina smiled and laughed today when he was in her booth. Seeing her happy had his heart soaring. But this *was* a dangerous situation.

Will couldn't act on those feelings. If he did, it could ruin too many lives, including Caroline's, Josiah's, and even Salina's. One more time, he thought about how he didn't want to hurt Caroline. She was precious to him, and she didn't deserve to be hurt.

He just had to remind himself constantly that he and Salina were only business associates and friends. Nothing more. Eventually these feelings would pass.

In the meantime, though, how could he pretend Salina hadn't already stolen a piece of his heart?

. . .

Will laughed as Irvin told another joke Sunday evening. Their parents, Roger, and Irvin's family were all gathered around the large table in his mother's kitchen.

Will glanced at Caroline beside him. She looked so pretty in a blue-and-white dress with a blue apron.

Karen, Irvin's wife, looked at Will. "How are things at the restaurant?"

Will nodded as he sliced his country fried steak. "They're *gut. Danki* for asking. It's been busy." He took a bite.

"And Will has added local produce to his menu." Caroline beamed at him. "His supplier is an Amish *maedel* who runs a booth at the Bird-in-Hand marketplace."

"Isn't the marketplace right across the street from your restaurant?" *Dat* asked.

Will swallowed. "That's right."

"How *wunderbaar*," *Mamm* chimed in. "I assume it's *gut* produce."

"The best." Caroline turned toward him, and her smile told him they were in this together.

Guilt coiled through him as he took a sip from his glass of iced tea. If only she knew what was going on in his mind. Why couldn't he erase these feelings for Salina? Caroline was right next to him, supporting him every step of the way. She should fill his daydreams, not Salina.

When Will thought he felt someone watching him, he looked across the table to find Roger staring, his eyes narrowed. It was as if his brother could read his thoughts, and the shame he felt made it hard to breathe.

Mamm turned to Heather, Irvin's five-year-old daughter. "Have you been helping your *mamm* at home?"

"Uh-huh." Heather nodded. "I'm learning how to use the washing machine."

"She's a great helper, Shirley." Karen touched Heather's nose, and Will couldn't help but notice once again how much the little girl looked just like her mother with the same blond hair, sparkling blue eyes, and small nose.

Karen touched her abdomen, and Will looked away. Irvin had recently told him he'd soon have two children, but Will didn't even know when he'd be ready to get married. How could he sort through all these confusing feelings?

"How's the construction business?" *Dat* asked Irvin.

"It's *gut*. We're working on several buildings right now."

"He's been working long hours, Gary," Karen told *Dat*.

Will relaxed as his family talked about Irvin's work for the remainder of supper. When they'd finished dessert, Caroline helped clean the kitchen while Will followed his father and brothers out to the porch.

"When are you going to ask Caroline to marry you, Will?" Irvin asked as soon as they all sat down on rocking chairs.

Will turned to his older brother. "Don't you get right to the point."

"Haven't you two been together three years now?" Irvin wasn't finished. "Neither of you is getting any younger. I already had a child when I was your age."

Will looked to Roger for help, but he kept his eyes focused on the porch floor as if it were the most interesting thing he'd ever seen. When Will met his father's gaze, though, he received a knowing look.

"What do you have to say, William?" *Dat* asked. "Irvin has a point. You're not getting any younger, and it's obvious that Caroline thinks the world of you."

"It's not that simple. You know it took every penny I had, plus a loan, to open the restaurant. Now I have to save up to buy a *haus*. I can't bring a bride home to an apartment."

"Why not?" *Dat* asked. "I was a poor farmer when your *mamm* married me." He gestured to the house behind him. "We didn't move into this place until after you were born."

"You need to stop being such a coward and just do it," Irvin said.

Will's gaze snapped to his. "Why are you picking on me tonight? What do you care if I get married or not?"

"You're thirty, Will. It's time for you to settle down."

Will looked at Roger again, but his younger brother only shrugged as if to say, *I told you so.* Then he looked away.

"Irvin is right," *Dat* added. "You and Caroline are meant to be together. It's time for you to propose. I'm sure she doesn't care where you live. She just wants to be with you. Don't wait too long. If you do, you'll risk losing her."

"And you'd regret that, Will," Irvin said. "Don't make that mistake."

Will looked out toward his father's rolling fields, and his heart sank. He was letting his family down. But how could he ask Caroline to marry him when it just didn't feel right?

. . .

"I had a great time tonight." Caroline reached over and took Will's hand in hers as he guided his horse. "I just love your family. They make me feel so welcome. I had fun talking to your *mamm*, Karen, and Heather while we all cleaned the kitchen. Heather is so funny. She was telling me all about how she loves to fold laundry." She balanced the chocolate pie on her lap he'd made for her family.

"Is that right?" Will gave her a sideways glance before returning his gaze to the road ahead.

"*Ya.*" Caroline squeezed his hand. "And Karen is due with their second *kind* soon. I wonder if it will be a *bu*. I imagine he'll be a junior. I can see your *bruder* wanting his *sohn* named after him." She turned toward him. "Would you want your *sohn* named after you?"

Will's stomach twisted. Now she wanted him to think about being a father? "I've never considered it."

"Oh, I have." She pulled her hand back to her lap. "I want us to have four *kinner*. It would be perfect if God blessed us with two *maed* and two *buwe*. I've even thought about names. For a girl, I like Diane and Arlene. Or Loretta after *mei mamm*. And for a *buwe*, I would want to name one Junior after you and the other Robert after *mei dat*." She turned toward him. "Do you like those names?"

"Sure." Will kept his eyes focused straight ahead as his horse moved through an intersection. But his body vibrated, and his nerves felt frayed. He was trapped like a caged animal at the zoo. Caroline loved him and his family. His family loved Caroline. They all expected them to marry. But how could he marry her if their relationship felt more like friendship to him?

He had been content when he first started dating Caroline—even up to recently. They had always had fun together, talking and laughing on dates or as they spent a quiet evening sitting on her parents' porch. But somehow the relationship had never grown beyond that stage. His feelings for Caroline had stopped evolving at some point. And now he didn't feel a spark for her like he felt for Salina, someone he'd known for only a short amount of time.

His relationship with Caroline felt stagnant, stuck somewhere between friendship and true, sustaining love. Would it be fair to marry a woman who didn't fill his dreams both day and night?

As Caroline kept talking about baby names and then how she wanted to decorate a nursery, he wondered if Salina felt the same suffocating despondency when her family discussed Josiah. Did she also believe she was held hostage to a similar circumstance?

"Did you hear a word I just said?"

Caroline's question broke through his thoughts as they arrived at her house, where he halted the horse and then turned toward her. "I'm sorry. What did you say?"

She pressed her lips together and shifted on the buggy seat. "You seem to be lost in thought. Is there something you want to talk about?"

He swallowed a sigh. He had plenty to talk about, but how could he even put his confusing thoughts into words. "I'm just thinking about everything I have to do at the restaurant tomorrow."

He nearly closed his eyes against the guilt he deserved for lying as she took his hand in hers.

"Sunday is a day of rest. Thinking about your chores can wait."

"Right." He took back his hand and pushed his door open. "It's getting late. Let's go."

They walked up the brick path to the back door, where the outdoor light sent a warm yellow beam onto the back porch.

"*Danki* again for the pie for my family. They'll love it." Caroline smiled up at him.

"*Gern gschehne.*"

"And *danki* again for inviting me for supper."

"I'm so glad you came."

She looked up at him expectantly, and he leaned down and kissed her cheek.

"*Gut nacht,*" he said before starting down the steps.

"Will," she called after him.

"*Ya?*" He turned to face her.

"I'll wait for you as long as you need me to. Even if it takes you another year to ask me to marry you, I'll be here. I love you."

He blinked as another wave of guilt crested inside of him. "I don't deserve you."

Something flashed in her eyes as she descended the steps and rushed to him. "Don't say that." She cupped her hand to his cheek. "I feel like I don't deserve you. You're so kind, hard-working, and handsome. I thank God every day that I have you in my life."

He swallowed a groan as he looked down at her beautiful

face. She deserved to know he was struggling with his feelings for her, but the thought of hurting her was still almost more than he could bear. She was a wonderful person with a gentle spirit. Maybe she was the one God wanted for him, and he just needed more time.

"*Danki* for being patient with me," he whispered as remorse choked back his voice.

"*Gern gschehne.*" She stood up on her tiptoes and kissed his cheek. "Be safe going home." She smiled at him and then headed back up the porch steps.

As Will watched her disappear into the house, he removed his hat and pushed his hands through his hair. Then he closed his eyes, lifted his face toward the dark sky, and opened his heart to God.

Lord, I'm so confused. My family wants me to marry Caroline, but I don't love her. I feel guilty, but the more I try to convince myself to marry her, the more confused I become. If I ask her to be mei fraa, *I'll wind up resenting her. I don't want to punish her by trapping her in an unhappy marriage. I can't bring myself to hurt her that way, but no matter what I do, I'll hurt her.*

What is the right answer? Should I marry her even though I'm afraid I'll eventually break her heart? Or should I break her heart now by telling her the truth? Lead me to the path you've chosen for me. Show me who you want me to marry—if anyone. Show me my future.

With a heavy heart, he climbed into his buggy and headed home.

CHAPTER 15

The following Wednesday morning, Salina glanced at her clipboard while standing in the kitchen at Will's restaurant. "So that's everything." She pulled the invoice off the clipboard and handed it to him.

"Great." He read the invoice and then smiled at her. He looked so attractive today in a red plaid shirt and dark-colored jeans. "I just need to get my checkbook." He motioned for her to follow him to his office.

"Okay." She lingered in the doorway as he wrote on the only uncluttered spot on the desk. "I see you've cleaned up," she said, teasing as she took in the chaos all around him.

He glanced up and raised an eyebrow. "I think you might need glasses."

"I was kidding."

He shook his head and snorted.

"The clutter would drive me crazy. How do you find anything in here?"

"I have a method." He ripped the check out of the book and brought it to her. When she took it, their fingers brushed, and a shudder ran up her arm.

"*Danki*," she managed to say as she slipped the check into her apron pocket.

"Do you like butterscotch pudding?"

"Who doesn't?"

He pointed toward the kitchen. "If you have a minute . . . I saved you some from yesterday."

"*Ya*, I think I can spare a minute. Brian doesn't mind waiting for me." Her heart seemed to turn over in her chest as she followed him to the large refrigerator. He'd saved her some pudding! That meant he'd thought about her. She tried to ignore the happiness she felt, but she failed.

The warm, sweet scent of freshly baked bread washed over her as she walked past a basket of rolls. She also noted how clean the kitchen was, especially compared to Will's office.

"I hope you like it." He pulled a small dish out of the refrigerator and fished a spoon out of a drawer. Then he handed both to her, and something that resembled pride filled his face.

"*Danki.*" She put a spoonful of the pudding into her mouth, and when the sweetness hit her taste buds, she closed her eyes and smiled. "This is fantastic."

He crossed his arms over his wide chest and tilted his head. "You don't think it's too sweet? Roger said it was. He always tells me I should follow recipes, but I like giving what I make my own flair."

She shook her head. "Roger is *narrisch*. It's perfect."

"Ah. Those are the best words to hear." His smile was back. "*Danki.*" He lifted a nearby stool and set it beside her. "Have a seat."

As she ate, she considered Will's story about living with his uncle and learning the restaurant business. She wanted to know more.

Will sank down onto a stool beside her. "You look like you're dying to ask me something. What is it?"

Could he read her thoughts? "I was wondering about how

you became a chef. You told me about your *onkel*, but you also said it was a long story. Would you share it with me?"

"Huh." He crossed his arms over his chest again and glanced at the clock on the wall. "How much time do you have?"

"I have until Brian tells me it's time to go."

He rubbed his chin. "Well, I was nineteen, and I was a little lost. My parents didn't know what to do with me, so they suggested I go see *mei onkel* Eddie. I went there not knowing what path God had chosen for me, and I left there with a purpose and a path."

"Why did you feel lost?" Finished, she placed the bowl and spoon on the counter next to them.

Will rubbed his left bicep as he looked down at his lap, and she wondered if she was being too nosy.

"You don't have to tell me."

"No, it's okay." He met her gaze, his expression warm. "I trust you. I just don't know how to put it into words. I guess I always felt as if my parents were comparing me to *mei* older *bruder*. They expected me to be baptized when I was seventeen, just like he was. Then they grew frustrated because it was taking me longer to figure out if I wanted to join the church. They didn't understand why I wasn't more like Irvin."

Salina's eyes rounded as his words sunk in.

Will reached over and covered her hands with his. "Are you okay?"

His palms were rough yet warm, and as her hands grew warmer under his, her pulse took on wings.

"*Ya.*" She looked up at him and experienced a startling burst of what felt like true companionship. "You said your parents always compare you to your older *bruder*. That's something else we have in common."

"You said something like that before." He released her hands. "It seems like we have a lot in common."

"*Ya*, it does."

A silence stretched between them, but unlike when she was with Josiah, the silence felt . . . comfortable. Yet Salina felt almost dizzy from this man's nearness.

Will leaned back. "Cooking is where I figured out who I was and where I belonged. It was as if God was guiding me to see that I could have a future as a chef and also in the church. I came back home, was baptized, and started working in a local restaurant to learn more and save for my own restaurant. Then I opened this place last year."

"Did your parents approve?"

"*Ya*." He nodded. "They were just *froh* I was finally baptized. Now . . . Well, they're pressuring me to marry Caroline and start a family."

She nodded slowly. "Just like my family is pressuring me to marry Josiah."

He blew out a breath. "Our lives are so similar it's almost scary."

"I know." When the look in his eyes grew intense, she glanced at the legal notepad on the counter. "Is that your menu list for the week?"

"It is." He picked it up and then gave it to her. "Today the special is meat loaf. My own recipe, of course. Tomorrow it's steak. Friday it's fish."

She reveled in his closeness once again. Her mind wandered toward a vision of riding in a buggy beside him. Walking in a park with him. Holding his hand.

Stop it! she chided herself. Her mind needed to stay far away from that place.

"Do you have a favorite cookbook?" she asked, trying to keep her mind from wandering again. She had to concentrate on being his friend and only his friend.

"I've collected a few. Well, more than a few." He turned and pulled four cookbooks out of a nearby cabinet before setting them on the counter beside her. "These are the ones I use the most, but I have a lot in the office here and at home too."

She ran her fingers over the worn bindings and smiled up at him. "I can see they're loved."

"What's your favorite kind of *kuche*?"

"Carrot, of course."

"I'll have to make you one."

"You don't have to do that."

"Salina."

Salina turned and found Roger standing in the back doorway. "Hi."

"I'm sorry to interrupt, but Brian said he's ready to go." Roger turned his gaze to Will, and the brothers seemed to share an unspoken conversation before Roger looked back at Salina. "He's waiting in the van for you."

"Oh." Salina looked at Will and was almost certain she saw disappointment in his eyes. "I'll see you next week."

Will smiled. "Take care."

"You too." Salina nodded at Roger and then hurried outside. She couldn't wipe the smile off her face as she climbed into the van.

. . .

"What are you doing?" Roger asked Will as soon as the back door clicked shut.

"Don't start." Will walked to the sink and began rinsing Salina's bowl and spoon.

Roger followed him. "She has a boyfriend, and you're practically engaged."

"Salina and I are just *freinden*, and I'm not engaged." Will placed the bowl and spoon in the dishwasher.

"How can you do this to Caroline? She's been loyal to you for three years now. She stood by you while you struggled to open this place. She always supports you, no matter what."

Will spun to face his brother as fury roiled under his skin. "What exactly have I done to Caroline?" He gestured around the kitchen. "I spoke to Salina. I *talked* to her. That's it."

"I'm not blind, Will. I see how you look at her. You light up when she's in the room. You were in a hurry to leave the *haus* this morning, and you've been grinning like crazy. I know that's because Salina was coming in today." Roger shook his head. "It's written all over your face. You care about her. What do you think will come of this?"

Will ran one hand across the back of his neck as Roger's words punched him in his gut.

"I'll tell you what's going to happen." Roger jammed a finger in Will's chest. "You're going to break Caroline's heart, and then you're going to wind up alone. And if you're not careful, you could get Salina in trouble with her family and her boyfriend."

"I know that. I just want to be her *freind*."

"Then you need to back off." Roger's voice lost a fraction of its edge. "She's your business associate. You should be depending on her for just that. And I know you don't want to hurt Caroline."

"That's the last thing I want to do. I care for her. She's a *wunderbaar maedel.*" Will nodded as anguish tightened around his chest.

"If you were *schmaert*, you'd ask Caroline to marry you before she gets tired of waiting. She loves you. Don't mess that up."

Will sank onto one of the stools as his shoulders slumped with a mixture of frustration and humiliation.

"We need to get to work," Roger muttered before walking to the freezer. "And I don't want to have this conversation again."

Will stared at the empty stool where Salina had sat and talked with him. He marveled at how easily he'd shared his past with her. She seemed to understand his confusion when he was younger, and her understanding intrigued him. He wanted to know more about her. Why did her parents compare her to her brother? Why were they pressuring her to marry Josiah? What did she want out of life?

But he didn't have a right to know more about her because Roger was right. He was dating Caroline, and Salina was dating Josiah. She was Amish, and he was Mennonite. But why couldn't he turn off his feelings for Salina? Why did his feelings for her grow each time they spoke? Caroline deserved so much more.

Guilt threatened defeat. Will couldn't continue this way. He had to stop this now before he hurt Caroline. He would build a wall around his heart and set boundaries. He'd commit himself to Caroline. She always made him a priority, and she gave him her heart. He would do the same for her. And he would keep his relationship with Salina professional. No more heart-to-heart talks.

From now on, with God's help, Will would be the boyfriend Caroline deserved.

Please, Lord. Lead me.

. . .

"Salina!" With his mother in tow, Chester rushed into her booth as Salina counted her money at the end of the following day. "We still can't find Daisy. I looked around again this afternoon, but there's no sign of her. I'm really worried."

"Oh no. I hope she's okay." Salina closed her bank bag and shook her head.

"*Ya*, I told Chester we'd look for her again tomorrow." Leanna touched her son's arm. "We need to get going. Are you heading out, Salina?"

"Not yet." She gestured toward her displays. "I asked my driver to give me an extra forty-five minutes to do some inventory tonight."

"Don't stay too late." Leanna gave her a little wave as she and Chester said good-bye.

"See you tomorrow," Salina called after them, also waving at a few of the other vendors as they left. Then she turned her attention to her booth, and holding a clipboard in one hand, she began tallying fruits and vegetables.

When she heard footsteps behind her, she spun around. Will was there, smiling at her. "Hi. What are you doing here?"

"I was hoping to catch you, and I just made it inside before they locked the doors. I ran out of butterhead lettuce today. I guess I didn't calculate correctly when I gave you my order."

"Oh." Salina gestured toward her display of lettuce. "How much do you need?"

"Quite a—" His brow furrowed. "Did you hear that?"

"Hear what?" Salina looked behind him.

"I thought I heard crying. It almost sounded like a baby." He turned and peered into the aisle.

"I think everyone has gone for the day." Salina stepped into the aisle and then heard a sound that resembled both a yowl and a cry. She froze in place. "Is that Daisy?" She turned to Will and grabbed his arm, then quickly released it. "She's been missing! Help me find her."

"Okay."

"Daisy! Daisy!" she called as they followed the sound of the cries to the far corner of the market, near the restrooms. The mewing grew louder, and she quickened her steps as her heart began to pound.

"Daisy? Where are you? Are you hurt?"

The sound grew even louder when she came to a corner clogged with empty boxes and pallets.

"Daisy?" Will called. "Is that you?"

They began to root through the boxes, and when Salina came to a large one, she saw something move. She peered into the box as Will sidled up beside her.

"I think she might be in here." Salina tried to ignore Will's familiar scent, but it wasn't easy.

"Let me see." He lifted the box, and his handsome face broke into a smile. "Salina. Wait until you see this." He pulled the box closer to her, revealing Daisy with three kittens. "She's a mommy now."

Salina clutched her hand to her chest as she blew out a happy gasp. One of the tiny kittens was black and white, a second was almost pure black, and a third was a brown-and-orange tabby. Will set the box down on the floor.

Salina fell to her knees. "Daisy! You had kittens." She looked up at Will, who grinned at her. "I can't believe it."

"I know." He smiled down at the little family, and his warm expression sent more happiness twirling through her.

"We've been so worried about her. I'm so glad she's okay." Salina touched Daisy's soft head as the kittens nursed.

Will knelt beside the box and touched Salina's arm. "I'm glad I heard her crying."

"I am too."

They sat in silence for several moments as they watched the kittens, both leaning in close and studying the little balls of fur.

"They're so tiny," Will whispered.

"I know." Salina clicked her tongue. "Look how they nurse. Daisy is such a *gut mamm*."

"She is." Will shook his head. "It's the miracle of life right here before our eyes. I know we've both grown up with animals, but it never ceases to amaze me when little ones are born. The way God creates new life is incredible."

She nodded and took in the brightness in his expression. He looked just as overwhelmed by the sight as she was.

Then she suddenly felt the intimacy of this moment. This was a bad idea. She had to sell him the lettuce, finish her inventory, and get home. It was inappropriate for them to be alone together.

Salina stood. "Kent, the market manager, is probably still here. We should tell him we found Daisy and see if he'll allow her to stay in his office."

"That's a *gut* idea. Let's go." Will carried the box as Salina walked beside him toward the other end of the market.

They found Kent sitting at his desk, and he looked up at them. "Salina, I didn't realize anyone was still here." He nodded at Will. "Hello."

"We found Daisy," Salina said. "Actually, my friend Will did."

"She had kittens." Will held out the box, and Kent peered in.

"Wow." He shook his head. "I was so worried she'd been hit by a tourist zooming by somewhere on Old Philadelphia Pike."

"Would you consider keeping her and the babies here in the office so they'll be safe?" Salina asked. "I'm afraid another animal might hurt them."

"Of course." Kent moved a couple of plastic containers from the corner and then motioned for Will to set down the box. "They can stay here. I'll put out food and fresh water for Daisy too."

"Thank you." Salina smiled as she looked down at the kittens.

"And I'll take her to the vet to get her and the kittens checked out," Kent said. "We all care about Daisy."

"That's perfect," Salina said. Then she turned to Will. "We'd better get your lettuce so you can get back to the restaurant. I'm sure Roger needs you."

"I can't believe we found her with kittens," Will said as they walked back to her booth, his smile still bright. "What a blessing that we were here to help her."

"I agree." When they reached her booth, Salina began packing up the lettuce for him. Then she gave him a price, and he paid her.

"*Danki* for coming by," she said.

"Of course." He nodded. "See you soon."

As he walked away, Salina felt her smile fade. She had to do her best to never be alone with Will again. Her attraction to him had already grown too strong, and she couldn't risk losing her heart to someone she could never have.

• • •

"How is your arrangement with Will going?" Bethany asked Salina. They were sitting with Leanna in the Coffee Corner two weeks later.

"It's going well." Salina picked up her cup of that Friday's flavored coffee special—butter pecan—determined to convey that her relationship with Will was nothing more than friendship, which it was. It had to be.

"I can't believe it's been four weeks since I started delivering to his restaurant," she said. "Like you, Leanna, I was a little worried I might not have enough produce for his weekly delivery and the booth, but it's been fine."

Salina continued after taking a sip. "He's so nice. Every time I make a delivery, he lets me sample one of the desserts he's serving on the buffet that day. One Wednesday it was butterscotch pudding. The next Wednesday it was carrot *kuche*, my favorite. Last week we had *kaffi kuche*, and then this past Wednesday it was Boston cream pie. I can't wait to see what he'll have next Wednesday. He said he might try to make—" She realized her cousins were staring at her, wide-eyed, and she divided a look among them. She'd said too much, but she pretended she didn't know why they were reacting that way. "What?"

"Salina," Leanna said, "do you have feelings for Will?"

Genuinely embarrassed, Salina felt her cheeks burst into flames. "No, of course not! We're just business associates."

Leanna and Bethany shared a look, and a flicker of irritation hit.

"Just say what you're thinking," Salina said.

"I think you might be too close to him," Leanna said. "You seem really excited whenever you mention him."

"*Ya*, I agree," Bethany chimed in. "You do seem to like talking about him."

"Trust me. Nothing is going on between us. We get along well, and we work together. That's it." Salina looked up at the clock. "I need to get going."

"*Ya*, it's about that time." Leanna sighed as she stood up. "I'll see you both later."

"Are you joining us for lunch?" Salina asked.

"No, I have to close up early today, so I'm going to work through lunch. You two enjoy your break, though." Leanna waved as she left.

"Do you want to eat outside today?" Bethany asked.

"Actually, I was hoping to run to the bookstore up the street."

"I'll come with you if you want company."

"Oh. Okay. I'll see you around one." Salina tried to hide her disappointment. She wanted to buy Will a gift to thank him for letting her sample his desserts every week, and she had hoped to run to the store alone. Now she'd have to tell Bethany why she was going, and she would have to convince her the gift wasn't more than a thank-you token for a friend.

No matter how hard it still was to suppress her true feelings for Will, he remained her friend.

CHAPTER 16

W hat exactly are you looking for?" Bethany asked Salina as they walked down the aisle at the Sunshine New & Used Bookstore a few blocks away from the marketplace.

Salina walked past displays of greeting cards and Amish Country knickknacks as she breathed in the smell of musty old books mixed with the aroma of an apple pie–scented candle burning nearby. She stopped in the used cookbook section and began perusing the selections. "I'm looking for a cookbook."

"Why do you need it?"

"It's a gift."

Salina felt Bethany's stare burning into her back, but she kept looking at the books.

Bethany stepped closer to her. "Is this about Will again?"

"It's just a thank-you because he's a *gut* customer, and—"

"Salina, listen to me." Bethany clamped her hand around Salina's forearm as her signature smile dissolved. "What would Josiah think if he found out you're buying gifts for Will?"

"It's just one cookbook. And it's used. Not even new!" Salina yanked her arm out of her cousin's grasp. "It doesn't mean anything."

"I think Josiah would disagree." Bethany pointed a finger at her. "How would you feel if he bought a gift for another *maedel*? Wouldn't that hurt your feelings and make you wonder about his loyalty to you?"

"I'm not cheating on him." Salina lowered her voice as she heard other people in an adjacent aisle. "I would never do that."

Bethany didn't look convinced.

"Do you really think I would?"

"No." Bethany's frown softened as she shook her head. "But I think you're putting your relationship in jeopardy. I agree with what Leanna said. You're getting too close to him."

Salina turned back to the shelf and picked up an old Betty Crocker cookbook she recalled her grandmother using. "Look at this one. I think he might get a kick out of it."

When Bethany didn't respond, Salina moved to the front counter, where a young Old Order Mennonite woman with blond hair and brown eyes stood ready to assist them.

"May I help you?" she asked.

"I'd like to buy this book, please." Salina pulled her wallet out of her apron pocket.

"Of course." The young lady flipped it over to look at the price. Then she rang it up on the cash register and gave Salina the amount. Salina paid her and then was given her change.

"Salina? Bethany?"

Salina turned to see Caroline Horst coming toward them. Her eyes widened as she forced a smile. "Hi."

Bethany gave Salina a sideways glance, then said, "How are you, Caroline?"

"*Gut.* What brings you here today?"

"I wanted to pick up a cookbook." Salina pointed to her purchase, still in the young lady's hand.

"How nice. That's a classic." Caroline pointed to the other woman. "This is *mei schweschder*, Irene."

Now Salina saw the family resemblance in their hair, eyes, and pretty faces. "Oh, hi, Irene." Then she looked back at Caroline. "Is this your family's store?"

"*Ya*, it is." Caroline walked behind the counter and took the cookbook from her sister. Then she slipped a bookmark with the store's name and hours on it into the cookbook and put it into a bag.

"That's *wunderbaar*." Salina took the bag from her. "We have to get going." She smiled at Irene. "It was so nice meeting you." Then she turned back to Caroline. "I hope to see you again soon."

Caroline smiled. "I'd love to see you too. I'm sure I'll visit your booth again with Will, and I'm so glad you stopped by."

"Have a *gut* day," Bethany said. Then she and Salina headed out the door.

Salina took long strides down the street, making Bethany work to keep up.

"I can't believe that's Caroline's family's store," Salina said.

"I can't believe you just bought a book for Caroline's boyfriend at her family's store."

"It's just a little something. It's not a big deal." Salina crossed the street, Bethany right behind her. "Let's stop by the restaurant on the way back to the marketplace," Salina threw over her shoulder.

Bethany grabbed Salina's arm and pulled her into a halt as soon as they reached the other side. "Why now?"

"Why not?"

"Don't you think you should wait until Wednesday to give it to him?"

Salina shook her head. "No, I don't. I want to give it to him now." She started toward Will's restaurant.

"Salina, I really think you should reconsider what you're doing."

"It's just a cookbook, and I'm grateful for his business."

"I think it's more than that, and you know it. What would your *dat* say if he knew you were taking a gift to a Mennonite man?"

"I'm not dating him."

"But what would he say?"

"Other women have left the Amish to marry an Old Order Mennonite, and they weren't shunned."

Bethany gaped. "You want to *date* him?"

"That's not what I said. I'm just saying it's not forbidden for Old Order Amish to be with Old Order Mennonite."

"That may be true, but have you forgotten your *dat* is the bishop? How would it look if his *dochder* left the Amish church for a Mennonite?"

Salina clamped her lips shut so tight that she felt a muscle flex in her jaw.

Bethany gestured widely. "Aside from your *dat*'s embarrassment, how would Josiah feel about this so-called friendship with Will?"

Salina harrumphed. "Giving him a thank-you gift is not a crime!"

"Are you sure that's all this is? Because it still seems like it's more than that."

Salina gritted her teeth and tried to ignore Bethany's comments as they walked one more block and then to Will's restaurant. As usual, the parking lot was full of cars, and a line of horses and buggies waited at the hitching posts.

They walked inside, and Salina made her way up to the hostess station. Danielle was there.

"Salina. Bethany. Hi," she said. "Would you like a table?"

"Actually, I'm wondering if I can see Will." Salina held up the bag. "I have something for him."

"Sure. You can come into the kitchen." Danielle beckoned them to follow her.

"Danielle!" Another waitress called to her. "I need your help."

Danielle hesitated, but then a waitress named Minerva walked over. "Go help Valerie. I'll take them back. I need to get more fried chicken for the buffet." She turned to Salina and Bethany. "Follow me."

Bethany sat down on one of the benches by the door. "I'll wait here."

Salina hurried to catch up with Minerva. As they weaved in and out of the tables, she noticed plates piled high with fried chicken, roast beef, mashed potatoes, peas, and corn. Some of the children, though, were eating burgers or another one of the sandwiches offered.

As they neared the kitchen, her hands shook. She hoped Will would like her gift but not think she was silly for bringing it to him now instead of waiting for her next delivery. She also hoped the book was a worthy gift after all the joy he'd brought into her life.

. . .

Will pulled a large pan of fried chicken out of the oven and set it on a counter before placing another pan inside. Then he started placing the ready chicken on a large tray with a pair of tongs.

"Will."

He turned toward Minerva as she walked into the kitchen. "*Ya?*"

"You have a visitor." She stepped aside, letting Salina in.

As usual, he had a ready smile for her. He just had to keep it friendly. Only friendly.

"What a nice surprise." Then worry hit him, and he dropped the tongs into the pan. "Is everything all right?" He wiped his hands on a cloth as he walked toward her.

"*Ya.* Everything is fine." Her smile seemed unsure, yet she looked beautiful in a pale-blue dress that complemented her eyes. She held up a white plastic bag. "I bought you something, and I wanted to drop it off. I hope it's okay."

"Of course it's okay." He tossed the cloth onto a nearby counter and then adjusted the chef's hat on his head.

Minerva walked over to Roger. Will had forgotten he was even there. "Could I take another tray of fried chicken out?" she asked. "The buffet is getting low."

"I'll carry it for you, Minerva. Would you please get the door for me?" Roger gave Will a pointed look as he walked by him with the tray of chicken.

Will ignored him. "What have you got there?"

"It's just a little gift to thank you for being such a *gut* customer." She held out the bag but then pulled it back. "It's kind of *gegisch*."

"I'm sure it's not silly."

"Here." She handed him the bag and then folded her arms over her black apron.

Will pulled out a cookbook and grinned. "Betty Crocker. I love it."

"Do you already have it?" Her expression seemed hopeful.

"No, I don't, but *mei mammi* did."

"Mine too!"

They laughed, and an overwhelming warmth flowed through him. He felt a deep connection pulling him to Salina—like always. But he shoved it away as he had again and again in the last month. Those feelings were dangerous, and to indulge them would be wrong.

"*Danki*. I'll enjoy it." He flipped the book open, and when he spotted a bookmark from Caroline's store, he almost gasped. Had she been there when Salina bought the cookbook? He seldom mentioned Salina in Caroline's presence. It would crush her if she knew Will harbored feelings for another woman.

He looked up at her. "I'll find a new dessert to make and share it with you next Wednesday."

"I look forward to it." She took a step back. "I should let you get back to work."

The kitchen door swung open, and Minerva came back in. "Roger asked me to tell you to get more fried chicken ready for the oven. Also, the salad bar is running low."

Will smiled. "*Danki*, Minerva. I have more salad bar fixings ready to go. We'll take them out together." He turned his gaze on Salina. "I do have to get back to work. Have a *gut* afternoon."

"You too." Salina gave him a little wave and then disappeared through the swinging doors.

Will set the cookbook on the counter and then crossed to the large refrigerator, where he pulled out containers filled with salad bar ingredients. He could tell Minerva was watching him as he carried what he'd prepared earlier to the counter, where a couple of trays sat waiting. Although she didn't speak, he could feel her judgment.

Will plastered a smile on his face as he and Minerva carried what he'd gathered out to the buffet. He felt his heart reaching for Salina, but he would do everything in his power to push those feelings away and keep her at arm's length—for Caroline.

CHAPTER 17

Rain drummed on the restaurant roof as Salina handed Will his invoice Wednesday morning. "It's really coming down out there now."

"It sure is." He pulled his checkbook from his pocket and leaned on the counter as he wrote.

Salina placed her hands on her waist and glanced out the back window. The sudden shower began to beat harder, and a rumble of thunder sounded in the distance.

Will handed her the check, and she slipped it into her apron pocket. "*Danki*," she said.

"As usual, I have something for you to taste. I think I've started to trust your opinion more than anyone else's!" He opened the refrigerator. "You have to close your eyes, though."

"Okay." Her heart seemed to trip over itself as she closed her eyes and licked her lips.

"Open your mouth." His voice sounded close to her ear, sending shivers dancing up her spine. She did what he asked, then felt something touch her tongue before a sweet, smooth, chocolaty taste tantalized her taste buds. She sighed as she closed her lips and swallowed.

"What do you think?"

"It's incredible." She opened her eyes. "Chocolate mousse. Wow. The best ever."

"It's from the cookbook you gave me."

"Really?"

"Uh-huh. I made a few modifications, of course." He held out the spoon.

Without a second thought, Salina licked it, and the intensity in Will's eyes sent a shock wave through her. The moment felt intimate. Sacred. Both the hair on her arms and the blood in her veins electrified.

Someone behind her let out a gasp, then almost an angry hiss. "Will! What's . . ."

When Salina turned, she found Caroline watching them, her eyes wide. Every muscle in Salina's body clenched before panic jolted her away from Will.

Caroline held a box in one hand, and her other hand was clamped over her mouth. She looked back and forth between Will and Salina and then took a shaky step backward, stumbling before righting herself.

For some reason, Salina noted the continued beat of the rain on the roof above them, a steady cadence counting the seconds as she stared at Caroline, unsure what to do as humiliation dug its claws into her shoulders. She wanted to run. She wanted to hide. But most of all, she wanted to apologize to Caroline. How could she share such an intimate moment with another woman's boyfriend?

She was a sinner. What would her father and brother say if they saw her now?

"Caroline." Will tossed the spoon into the sink and then walked over to her. "I didn't expect to see you this morning."

Caroline shook her head, and her brown eyes sparkled with unshed tears. "I-I thought I'd surprise you with donuts." She opened the box lid. "I didn't think you'd have company, though." She turned her eyes on Salina.

"How thoughtful." Will's voice sounded almost shrill. "They smell great."

"Would you like one, Salina?" Caroline's tone seemed to warn her to turn down the offer.

"No, *danki.*" Salina forced a smile. "I need to go. It was nice seeing you again, Caroline." She glanced at Will. "See you next Wednesday."

Will nodded, and she thought she saw an apology in his eyes.

Salina hurried toward the back door but stopped when she spotted three buckets in the corner. Water was dripping into them from the ceiling. She spun to face Will. "Your roof leaks?"

"*Ya,* it has for a while."

"You should call Josiah's roofing company. They can fix it." She walked to the counter that held a pen and notepad. She wrote down the name of Josiah's company and the number. "Call them."

"I will." Will gave her a weak smile. *"Danki."*

Salina glanced at Caroline's frown and then hurried outside, guilt drenching her more than the rain ever could.

. . .

The back door clicked shut, and Will turned to Caroline. Sick shame poured through him like the rain dripping through the ceiling. He opened his mouth to apologize, but she held up her hand, silencing him.

"How long has this been going on?" Her voice was shaky.

"Nothing is going on." He worked to keep his tone even. He didn't want to alarm her.

"I'm not blind, Will." She crossed to the counter and set the box of donuts on it. Something seemed to catch her eye, and she lifted the Betty Crocker cookbook and opened the cover. When she turned to face Will, her eyes were swimming with tears. "She bought this for you."

"*Ya*. To thank me for being a *gut* customer."

"She came to my family's bookstore"—she pointed to her chest—"And bought a gift for you. You're *my* boyfriend, but she bought this for *you!*" Her voice broke as the tears spilled onto her cheeks. Then she dropped the book on the counter with a loud thud that echoed around the kitchen.

"Caroline, please don't be upset. Salina and I are just *freinden* who work together. I would never hurt you like that." He reached for her, but she pushed him away. His guilt dug deeper. This was exactly what he'd wanted to avoid.

"Don't!" She held up her hand again. "Just don't." She wiped her cheeks, and then her eyes flared. "You care about her, don't you? Don't lie to me."

"We're business associates, and that's it."

"I don't believe that for a second! I had a feeling you two liked each other. I could detect the attraction. I tried to convince myself I was just being paranoid and insecure. You said you cared about me, and I believed you even loved me—even though you've never said the words. But today I saw the truth with my own eyes. She's the *maedel* you want. Not me!"

Caroline sucked in a breath and then covered her face, tears seeping through her fingers.

"*Ach*. Caroline." Will pulled her into his arms, feeling the crush of disgrace. She didn't deserve to be hurt like this. He was sure she would push him away, but to his surprise, she rested her cheek against his chest as she cried.

"I'm so sorry," he whispered into her prayer covering, his

voice sounding weak to his own ears. "I never wanted to hurt you. Salina is only *mei freind*. I would never be unfaithful to you. *You* are my girlfriend."

Then Caroline did pull away from him, but gently. She sniffed as she took a tissue from the pocket of her gray apron and wiped her eyes and nose. "I feel like we're falling apart, Will. When you're with me, you act like you'd rather be somewhere else."

He rubbed at a knot in his shoulder. "I'm sorry I haven't been a better boyfriend to you. I know I work long hours, and I'm always exhausted when we're together. I'll make more of an effort to be present when I'm with you."

She looked down at the floor and then back up at him, only the patter of raindrops filling the silence between them.

"Do you still . . . care for me?" Her eyes seemed to plead with him to not just say he cared for her but to say that he loved her. But he couldn't lie.

"*Ya*, I do." And he did care for her. He also wanted to love her. He wanted this relationship to work. They made sense together. They *should* work as a couple.

"But do you still want to be with me?"

"Of course I do." He rested his hands on her shoulders. "I'll do my best to make this up to you." Then he let his hands fall to his side, exhausted by the intensity of their discussion.

"Okay." She took in a shuddering breath. "I was going to tell you I can stay and help you for the rest of the day. But I'll just go to my parents' store. I'll see you soon." She turned and started to walk away.

"No." He took her arm and gently pulled her back. "Stay. I want you to." He pointed to the refrigerator. "I made you a coconut cream pie last night. I was going to surprise you with it later."

She hesitated. "Are you sure you want me to stay?"

"*Ya.*" He leaned down and kissed her cheek. "I want you here."

"*Danki.*" She gave him a watery smile. "You're the only one for me, Will."

As he pulled her close for a hug, he closed his eyes and sent a prayer to God. *Lord, please help me grow closer to Caroline. She's the one you've chosen for me. She must be.*

Then he moved to the refrigerator, and when he opened it, he ignored the chocolate mousse inside. "Why don't you try a piece of this pie right now? Of course, I changed up the recipe. And we can have one of those donuts later!"

. . .

Salina washed bundles of fresh celery in the downstairs kitchen sink as rain pounded against the basement windows. All morning her mind had replayed her encounter with Will and how her body had reacted when he fed her the sweet chocolate mousse. Worse, she'd licked the spoon he held as if it were the most natural thing in the world.

She'd never before felt such an attraction to a man. Her heart had never sped up for Josiah—not once—and the realization confounded her. What could she do to stop these feelings for Will?

Remorse wrapped around her throat as she visualized the pain in Caroline's eyes when she found her and Will together. How could she hurt another woman that way? She was so embarrassed and humiliated. Her family would berate her if they knew about her actions. She had to stop sinning and start behaving like a dutiful Amish daughter and sister.

She also had to put her inappropriate feelings for Will aside and concentrate on being a virtuous girlfriend to Josiah. After all, Josiah could be the man God had chosen for her. She just needed more time to develop her feelings for him.

The basement door opened, and heavy footsteps sounded on the stairs. She looked up as Josiah appeared with a large paper bag.

She turned to greet him. "Hi. What are you doing here?"

"I brought lunch." He set the bag on the small table in the center of the basement. "I'm off work today because of the rain, and since we haven't talked in a while, I thought I'd surprise you."

"*Danki.*" She smiled. Josiah was a thoughtful boyfriend. She swallowed back more guilt as the truth hit her—she'd known him for so long that she hadn't appreciated what a good man he was and how worthy he was of her affection and loyalty.

They sat down at the table, and he pulled two turkey subs, two bags of chips, and two brownies out of the bag. After a silent prayer, they began to eat.

Salina took a bite of the sub. When she'd swallowed, she smiled and said, "This is *appeditlich.*"

They ate in silence for a few moments, but the sound of the rain filled the basement.

"Have you been working down here all morning?" Josiah finally asked.

"No. I delivered to Will's restaurant earlier. When I got home, I started washing and sorting the produce I harvested on Monday and Tuesday." Her thoughts turned to Will's ceiling. "I gave him your company's name and phone number. The roof of his restaurant has a few leaks."

"*Danki.*"

"How has work been for you?"

"Still busy."

Josiah told her about his projects as they finished eating, and Salina was happy to listen.

"Would you like help with your produce?" Josiah asked as she gathered the wrappers from their food and tossed them into the trash can.

She hesitated. "Are you sure you have time?"

"*Ya.*" He gave a little laugh. "I told you. I can't work today. That's why I'm here. And I wanted to spend some time with you."

"That's so kind of you." She walked to the sink. "You can wrap the celery in plastic bags after I wash it."

"I think I can handle that."

As Salina washed more celery, Josiah placed it in plastic bags and then tied the ends with rubber bands. They worked in silence for several minutes. How could she regularly remind herself to appreciate how wonderful Josiah had always been?

A thought occurred to her. Maybe he was here because he didn't feel appreciated.

"Are we okay?" Her question seemed too loud in the quiet basement.

Josiah stopped working and turned toward her, his forehead wrinkled. "What do you mean?"

She gestured between them. "I mean us. Our relationship. Is it okay?"

"I'm *froh*. Are you?" She heard no trace of hurt in his voice.

She smiled as relief hit her. "*Ya*, I am."

"*Gut*. I don't want anything to change."

She nodded. "Okay."

As they returned to work, her shoulders relaxed for the first time in weeks. Maybe she'd just forgotten how much sense her relationship with Josiah made. Everyone must be right. She belonged with him, and she had to try harder to make things work with such a *gut* man.

CHAPTER 18

Will swiped his hand across his forehead as he walked through the restaurant's back parking lot the following Wednesday morning.

"It's September, but it still feels like August," Roger commented.

"*Ya*, it's definitely hot and humid," Will said, agreeing with that assessment.

When an engine sounded behind them, Will turned to see two work trucks pull in.

"The roofers are here," he said.

Roger continued toward the restaurant. "You can talk to them, and I'll get to work inside."

"All right."

The passenger door opened on the first truck, and Josiah hopped out.

Will waved and then walked over to shake his hand. "*Danki* for coming today. The leaks have been getting worse the past few weeks."

"It's no problem." Josiah pointed behind him toward his crew. "We can fix it today. I'll give you an estimate first."

Will waved off the offer. "Salina recommended you, so I trust you to give me an honest price."

"I'll still work it up. I want to be sure you're satisfied before we get to work."

"Sounds *gut*."

Josiah shook his hand again. "I'll be in as soon as I have the quote ready."

Will walked into the kitchen, where Roger was already pulling out the cookware they'd need. They worked in silence as they made preparations for the day's cooking and baking.

Will smiled as he pulled out the cookbook Salina had given him the week before. He planned to use it today for his baked ham. Then his smile faded as he recalled how upset Caroline was when she walked in on him and Salina. Will had felt terrible for hurting her, and he'd tried to make it up to her all weekend.

He'd visited her Friday night and then again on Sunday, taking her gifts each time. On Friday he'd surprised her with a bouquet of flowers and a book by her favorite author. On Sunday he took her a quesadilla casserole and a Boston cream pie. Caroline seemed pleased with the surprises, and he prayed that they helped make up for his past mistakes. He was determined to make things right between them.

Although thoughts of Salina still invaded his mind, he'd vowed to be a better boyfriend to Caroline. And he'd resolved to rid his heart and mind of feelings for Salina. He prayed for strength every night, and he was relying on God to guide his heart down the appropriate path.

Will found the recipe for baked ham and began gathering the supplies he'd need. He was already at work when the back door opened, and Salina walked in with a cart full of her produce.

"*Gude mariye*," she sang. "I see Josiah and his crew are

here." Her smile was brighter today, and she seemed different, although he couldn't put his finger on how. Maybe it had something to do with her boyfriend. Maybe Josiah had finally wised up and told her he loved her.

"Hi. *Wie geht's?*" Will said.

"I'm great. How about you?"

"Fine." Will turned to Roger. "Can you help us get the rest of the delivery inside?"

"I can." Roger smiled at Salina. "*Gut* to see you."

They brought in the supplies, and then Will paid Salina before walking her out to where Roger stood talking with Brian.

"I hope you have a *gut* day," Salina told him as she approached the passenger side of the van.

"Are you going to work in your garden today?" Will asked.

She nodded. "*Ya*. That's what I normally do on the days I'm not at the marketplace, after I help *mei mamm* with chores. I'm also canning, so I'll have something to sell all winter."

"Tell me about your garden." He leaned against the van beside her, eager to satisfy the curiosity he'd had about it from the first day he entered her booth. "How big is it?"

"It's a half acre."

"Wow." Now he could imagine it with more detail. "Does anyone help you work in it?"

"Sometimes." She looked past him toward the business next door. "My small nieces like to help, but they really just play in the dirt. *Mei mamm* helps some, but I don't really expect anyone to help me. It's my garden, but it's also my special place. I love working in the soil. It gives me a chance to pray and reflect on God's glory and all my blessings."

She seemed embarrassed, but he marveled at her skill and the joy she found in her work. "Do you live far from here?"

"No." She pointed down the road. "Do you know where Beechdale Road is?"

"*Ya.*"

"If you turned onto Beechdale and drove about a half mile down, you'd see our *haus* on the right. There's a sign for Lancaster County Cabinets, *mei dat*'s business. You can't miss it. His showroom and workshops are behind our *haus*. My garden is back there too."

"Okay." He nodded, making a mental note.

"You should stop by if you're in the area," she said. "I'd love to show you my garden."

Salina looked as though she might have regretted the invitation as soon as she'd given it, but he responded without hesitation. "I'd love to see it. You have such a great variety of produce. I can't even imagine how *schee* it is in full bloom."

"Well, it's a sight to see, but I don't mean to sound prideful." She smiled at something beyond his shoulders. "Hi."

"Hi." A smiling Josiah came up beside Will and nodded at Salina. "How are you?"

"Fine. You?"

"Hot and sweaty. It's already humid out here."

Will's gaze slid to Salina. Despite the smiles, he must have been wrong to think this relationship had improved. Their conversation was so clinical and cold. It was as if they were only friends—or even just acquaintances—instead of a couple who'd been dating for more than a year.

Even so, a twinge of jealousy surprised Will. He didn't have the right to be jealous of Josiah, but the feeling was there, taunting him.

Josiah handed him a piece of paper. "Here's the estimate. You need quite a bit done." He pointed to the roof. "I recommend replacing most of the shingles on this side."

Will rubbed his chin as he examined the estimate. "Looks fair to me."

"All right, then. We'll get started." Josiah looked at Salina. "I'll see you soon."

"Be safe up there." Salina turned her attention to Will as Josiah and another worker took a ladder from one of the trucks. "I need to get home. Have a *gut* day."

"You too." Will said good-bye to Brian and then stood on the loading dock ramp as he and Salina climbed into the van and drove away. He stared at his feet then. What was he thinking? Visiting Salina's home to see her garden was a bad idea. What if Caroline found out?

When he thought he felt someone watching him, he glanced up at the roof. Josiah was staring down at him. Will nodded without a smile, and Josiah responded in kind, his face set like stone.

. . .

Salina placed a platter of pork chops and a bowl of buttered noodles in the center of the kitchen table that evening, next to the green beans and carrots. When a knock sounded on the back door, she turned to *Mamm*. "Are you expecting company?"

"No." *Mamm* shook her head. "Go see who it is."

Salina stepped through the mudroom and opened the door. She was surprised to find Josiah, holding his straw hat in his hands. "I didn't know you were planning to stop by."

"I just finished work, and I wanted to see you."

"Oh." Salina glanced behind her as *Mamm* stepped into the mudroom.

"Who is it?" *Mamm* asked.

"Josiah."

Mamm's expression brightened. "Invite him for supper. We have plenty."

"Would you like to join us for supper?" Salina opened the storm door wider. "We're having pork chops."

"That would be nice. *Danki.*" Josiah stepped into the mudroom and hung his hat on an empty hook.

The three of them entered the kitchen and found her father already sitting at the table.

"Josiah." *Dat* stood and shook his hand. "I'm so glad you could join us tonight."

Salina took her usual spot at the table while Josiah washed his hands. Then he sat down across from her, and after prayer, they all filled their plates.

"I imagine you and your *dat* are staying busy," *Dat* said.

Josiah nodded as he swallowed. "We are. And I'm running my own crew now. We repaired the roof at Zimmerman's Family Restaurant today." He glanced at Salina and looked almost as if he disapproved of something. Was it Will? But why would he?

"That's *wunderbaar,*" *Dat* said. "You must be making a *gut* wage now."

Salina swallowed three times in rapid succession as she stared at her father. Was he truly going to ask questions about Josiah's salary? How rude!

Josiah hesitated but then nodded. "I'm doing okay."

"Do you have enough money saved to build a *haus* yet?" *Dat* asked.

"*Dat!*" Salina exclaimed, mortified.

Dat glared at her, and she looked down at her plate.

"I think I'll have enough saved up soon," Josiah said. "*Mei dat* has offered to help me as well."

Salina kept her eyes focused on her plate as she took a bite of her green beans. Could this meal get any more embarrassing? She prayed her father wouldn't ask Josiah when he was going to propose!

"That's great news. You can start planning your future, then." *Dat* sounded pleased. "I think you have a *gut*, solid future with your *dat*'s company. I'm so *froh* to hear it."

"*Danki.* We've had a few bumps in the road, but I'm still learning."

"And you'll continue to learn. You're on the right track. It's so important that our young people choose to work in our community. They need to stay close to home. Just like they should marry within our community."

Salina swallowed a sigh. Every supper discussion still turned into a sermon.

"How's your cabinet business going, Lamar?" Josiah asked.

"Oh, it's great. Neil is taking over more and more of the operations, and he's doing a fantastic job."

Salina snuck a peek at her father's proud smile. Did he ever brag about her the way he bragged about Neil? She doubted it. As she'd realized before, Neil was the one who did everything right while Salina was the disappointment. She'd never live up to her father's high standards—especially if he knew she and Will had become not just business associates but good friends.

Another thought hit her. Did Josiah suspect she had feelings for Will?

Josiah and her father continued talking about business as they all finished supper, sampling one of Salina's apple pies for dessert. Then the men stepped outside, and Salina and her mother started cleaning the kitchen.

They worked in silence, but then *Mamm* turned to Salina as she dried a dinner plate. "It was nice of Josiah to surprise you tonight. He's so thoughtful."

"*Ya.*" Salina washed another plate and glanced out the window. She could see *Dat* and Josiah coming out of her father's workshop.

"Are you upset about something?"

Salina turned to her mother. "I am. *Dat* embarrassed me at supper. Why did he have to go on about Josiah's success and then ask if he had enough money to build a *haus*? It was impolite to bring that up."

"Your *dat* is just worried about your future, Salina. He's looking out for you, and I'm sure Josiah understands that."

"But I'm not sure of my future." Salina turned her attention back to the soapy water, afraid she might be sharing too much with her mother. What if she told *Dat*?

"What do you mean?"

Salina glanced out the window again. Now her father and Josiah were standing by the barn. They didn't look like they'd be back anytime soon. Maybe her mother would understand.

"*Mamm*, I'm not sure what I want or what God has planned for me. What if my future isn't with Josiah?"

"Not with Josiah? Are you two having problems?"

"No. I just don't know if we're meant for each other."

"But you've been together more than a year now. The last time we talked about him, you said he hadn't discussed marriage. He still hasn't brought it up?"

"No, he hasn't." Salina kept her eyes focused on a bowl as she rinsed it. "I'm not sure he wants to marry me, and I don't know if I want to marry him."

Her mother took a deep breath, and Salina didn't dare look at her.

"*Dochder*, have you been honest with him about your doubts?"

Salina shook her head and handed her mother the bowl.

"Do you think you might break up with him?"

"I don't know." Salina began to wash another bowl as confusion continued to roll over her. Her thoughts turned to Will and his handsome face, electric smile, and kind eyes, but she quickly dismissed them.

Mamm touched her shoulder. "You should be careful. Think this through before you break off your relationship with Josiah. He's a *gut*, hardworking, Christian man. Your *dat* and I have known his parents since we were all *kinner* in school. We grew up together, attended the same youth group, and stayed close after we were married. They're like our family. It would mean so much to us to see you and Josiah marry and start a family. Your *dat* is supportive of your relationship with him, and that's important. If you tell Josiah you don't want to be with him, you might wind up regretting it, and then he might not take you back."

"I know," Salina whispered as she began washing utensils.

Her mind knew her mother was right, and she'd vowed to work on her relationship with Josiah. But her heart still believed he might not be the man God had for her. And that had nothing to do with Will.

. . .

Later that evening Salina sat on a bench beside Josiah, sipping from a glass of iced tea as she gazed out over her garden, taking in the rows and rows of late-season vegetables God had given her. Above them the sunset lit up the sky with vibrant shades of yellow and orange as the frogs sang their colorful chorus all around them.

Salina breathed in the familiar scent of moist earth as her body relaxed. But when she glanced at Josiah, she found him sitting ramrod straight, staring ahead. She sensed irritation coming off him in waves.

She angled her body toward him. *"Was iss letz?"*

He looked down at his full glass of tea and then up at her, his lips twisted into a frown. "Do you like Will?"

She held back a gasp. Josiah did have suspicions, then. But she'd vowed to make her relationship with him work, and she couldn't hurt him with the truth.

"What do you mean?"

"Do you care about him?"

She searched his eyes, determined that her response would alleviate his concern. "I like him as a *freind*."

He looked toward her brother's house in the distance as he settled against the back of the bench. "I think he likes you as more than a *freind*."

She tried to ignore the tingling that traveled all the way down to her toes. "But there's nothing more to our relationship than business and friendship."

Josiah gave a little snort as he ran his fingers through the condensation on his glass.

"What does that snort mean?"

He looked up at her. "I noticed today that he seemed really *froh* to talk to you. And I saw the way he looked at you." He sipped his tea, and she tried to hold back the shock his words caused.

She never thought Will's feelings for her were . . . more. But could Josiah be right? No. It wasn't possible.

"He's just friendly, that's all. Toward everyone."

She searched her mind for a change of subject. "By the way, remember I'm hosting the youth gathering on Sunday. It's going to be fun, but I have a lot of preparation to do. *Mei mamm* and I have a long list of chores."

Josiah had just stared toward her garden as she talked. But now he looked at her, and she was sure he had more to say about Will. Then he straightened his shoulders as though he'd decided to let the subject drop. How she wished he would.

"I can help you set up the Ping-Pong table and the volleyball nets," he said. "But I better go now."

They walked to the driveway together and then stood by his horse and buggy.

"*Danki* for supper. It was *appeditlich*." He leaned down and, surprisingly, kissed her cheek. Yet her heartbeat didn't speed up, and she felt no emotion at all. If God wanted her to marry Josiah, why didn't this man warm her heart the way a future husband should?

"*Gut nacht*," he whispered in her ear.

"*Gut nacht*," she said as he climbed into the buggy. "Be safe."

As his horse and buggy moved toward the road, Salina looked up at the clear night sky and prayed.

Please, Lord, guide my heart. Help me love Josiah if he's my future and remove my feelings for Will.

CHAPTER 19

I think we have everything set for tomorrow," Roger said as he wiped down the largest counter in the restaurant's kitchen Friday night.

Will peered inside the refrigerator and shook his head. "No, we don't. We have a problem." He picked up a container of tomatoes. "We won't make it through tomorrow with just these." He set the container back into the refrigerator and then turned to his brother. "Can you get Danielle's driver to take you home?"

"I was going to ride home with Danielle anyway. But what are you planning?"

"I'll see if I can get Austin to take me by Salina's *haus*, and I'll buy enough tomatoes from her to last until Wednesday."

Roger narrowed his eyes and tilted his head. "Do we really need tomatoes? Or is this just a reason to see Salina?"

Will opened the refrigerator and pointed to the small package. "Do you think this is enough to make it until Wednesday?"

"No, but I don't think we need more tonight."

"I do, and I'm the chef around here. We have enough to do in the morning."

"Whatever you say, boss." Roger threw his hands into the air and then pulled off his apron. "See you later."

"Rog," Will called after him. "Wait."

Roger turned and looked at him. "What?"

"How are things going with Danielle?"

Roger's expression softened. "We're getting to know each other. She's really sweet, and we get along well."

"When are you going to ask her out?"

"Soon." Roger rubbed the back of his neck, a gesture Will had always seen him do when he was nervous.

"What are you afraid of?"

Roger pursed his lips. "What if she says no?"

Will grinned. "Trust me. She won't say no."

"Don't worry about me." Roger pointed at him. "You need to worry about what you're doing to Caroline by spending so much energy on Salina. Trust me when I tell you you'll regret it." He turned and started toward the exit. "I'm leaving."

After Will locked up, he climbed into Austin's van. Austin had no problem taking the short ride to Salina's house. But when he steered into the driveway just past the Lancaster County Cabinets sign, Will's heart pounded with doubt. Maybe this was a bad idea. Hadn't he concluded he shouldn't visit Salina's house when they'd talked about her garden?

But this was different. He needed those tomatoes.

"I won't be long," he told Austin before walking up the driveway to the two-story, white house with the wraparound porch. He scanned the property, taking in the large, red barn and four matching workshops that sat in front of a pasture fence.

Beyond the pasture, he spotted Salina's vast garden, and he smiled. It was more glorious than he imagined. The garden was large, and the raised beds, surrounded by fencing, seemed to reach the sky. The rows were uniform, and the plants were green and beautifully tended.

"May I help you?"

Will spun to find an Amish man, who looked to be about

his age, staring at him with a stern expression. He was just about Will's height, and he had the same light-brown hair and bright-blue eyes Salina had. His beard matched his hair. Could this be Salina's brother?

"I'm looking for Salina," Will said.

The man's eyes narrowed with what looked like suspicion. "And who are you?"

"I'm Will Zimmerman." Will held out his hand, and the man hesitated before shaking it. "Salina supplies produce for my restaurant, and I need to get some tomatoes."

"Oh. Come with me." The man started up the path toward the back porch.

Will followed him up the steps and then stood on the porch as he disappeared into the house. A few moments later the man reappeared with Salina in tow.

"Will. Hi." Her smile was bright as her gaze roamed his face. "What are you doing here?"

"I ran out of tomatoes, and there's no way I'll make it until Wednesday. Could I buy some from you now?"

"Of course." She looked at the man and then back at Will. "Have you met *mei bruder*, Neil?"

"*Ya*. We're *gut freinden*. Right?" Will grinned at Neil, who frowned and then walked past him down the steps. Will held back a chuckle. Did Neil ever smile?

"Tell *Dat* I went home," Neil called over his shoulder as he continued down a path toward the pasture.

"He's a real jokester," Will muttered.

Salina laughed. "Give me a minute, and I'll get your tomatoes. What kind do you need?"

"I'll take what I can get. But do you have cherry for the salad bar?"

"I do. Wait here." She slipped back into the house, and the storm door clicked shut behind her.

He walked to the end of the porch and leaned over the railing as he watched Neil stalk down a path to a large brick house on the other side of the pasture. Then he scanned the whole property, marveling at the beautiful pasture and buildings. Her family was truly blessed.

A few minutes later Salina returned with a large bucket. "I don't have as many as I thought, but we can go pick some." She pointed toward her garden. "It shouldn't take us long."

"Oh. That would be nice." He walked beside her and gave a low whistle as they approached the garden. He took in the rows and rows of raised beds full of colorful crops. "This is more amazing than I imagined."

She turned toward him. "You imagined my garden?"

"I did." He walked over to the tomato plants and touched one. "These are magnificent."

"*Danki.* But it's the end of their growing season, so they're starting to peter out." She set the bucket on the ground. "Go ahead. Pick some."

He pulled several red tomatoes off the vine and set them in the bucket. Salina worked beside him. Then he moved to the cherry tomatoes and pulled off a handful.

He turned to Salina. "May I try one?"

She laughed. "Of course. Go ahead."

He popped one into his mouth and smiled at the sweet taste. "Delicious."

"I'm glad you like it."

They worked side by side until the bucket was full, and then they walked back to the house.

"I just need to wash them and put them in a crate for you."

"*Danki.*"

"*Mei dat* was in Lancaster today for work, so we're just about to sit down to a late supper. Would you like to stay? Even if you already ate, we can offer you dessert. I bake, too, you know."

He hesitated. Had he heard her correctly? Was he just invited to her family's table for a meal?

A look of alarm flickered over her face. "You don't have to stay. Don't feel obligated."

"I'd love to stay, and I am hungry. But I need to let my driver know."

"Tell him you'll call him when you're ready."

"Okay."

Excitement sizzled through Will's veins as he made his way to the van, ignoring the misgivings that told him he should just go home. He had the chance to spend time with Salina, and he didn't want to pass that up. But then he went a little cold. After meeting Neil, he had to wonder what it would be like to meet her parents—especially her father.

. . .

Salina looked across the table at her guest, and her heart fluttered. Will sharing a meal with her family was a dream come true.

For a moment she tried to imagine what it would be like to have him by her side for the rest of her life—sharing meals with him daily, seeing him sitting across from her in the married men's section at church, riding with him in their buggy to town, raising a family together.

She bit her lower lip and looked down at her chicken noodle

casserole. She was torturing herself with these fantasies, and she needed to stop before she went crazy. Will would never be a member of the Amish church, and he would never be her husband. She had to stop allowing her brain to manufacture these silly thoughts!

"Where are you from, Will?" *Dat* asked.

Will wiped his mouth with a napkin. "I'm from Lititz."

"What does your *dat* do?"

"He's a dairy farmer. *Mei* older *bruder* is in construction, and *mei* younger *bruder* runs the restaurant with me."

"Are they all baptized in the Old Order Mennonite church?"

Will nodded. "*Ya*. They are."

"*Gut*." *Dat*'s expression was bishop stern. "What made you want to open a restaurant?"

"I was inspired after spending a summer with *mei onkel* in New York State. I worked in his restaurant, and I realized that was what God had called me to do with my life."

Salina watched Will as he continued talking about his restaurant and love of cooking. He never lost his easy expression despite her father's somber tone. He seemed perfectly at ease, and her admiration for him swelled.

"Your restaurant sounds *wunderbaar*," *Mamm* said. "Salina has told us the food is delicious."

Will smiled at Salina. "I have to credit her for helping with that. My meals wouldn't be so great without her produce."

Salina felt her cheeks flush, and she looked down at her plate. When she glanced up, she found *Dat* frowning at her, and she averted her eyes.

Mamm turned to *Dat*. "We'll have to go there, Lamar."

"I'd love for you to come. Please do." Will turned to *Dat*. "Your meal will be on me."

Dat watched him for a moment and then looked at *Mamm*. "We'll see."

Salina's stomach twisted with foreboding. *Dat* didn't approve of Will. She was certain he'd tell her why later.

"Salina tells me you make cabinets," Will said. "What are your biggest sellers?"

Dat seemed surprised by the question, but he began talking about his business. When they were ready for dessert, Salina served her cherry pie with coffee.

After dessert, *Dat* and Will stepped out to the porch, and Salina and her mother started cleaning.

"What's your rush?" *Mamm* asked as Salina quickly carried the dishes to the counter.

"I don't want to leave Will alone with *Dat* too long."

"Why not?"

"Because *Dat* was grilling him. I don't want him to feel uncomfortable."

Mamm faced her. "Why is it so important for you to make him feel comfortable?"

"He's *mei freind*."

Mamm's expression hardened. "Salina, he's not a member of our community."

"I know, but he is a *gut* customer, and I want to stay on *gut* terms with him."

Mamm paused and then waved her off. "Go outside. I'll finish in here."

"Are you sure?"

Mamm spun around and waved again over her shoulder. "Go before I change my mind."

Salina kissed her mother's cheek. "*Danki.*"

She hurried out to the porch, where *Dat* was talking about

the importance of community. No surprise there. Will blessed her with a wink and a grin, and she bit the inside of her cheek to stop the laugh that threatened to bubble up from her throat.

"Will," she said, "you only got to see my tomatoes. Would you like to see the rest of my garden?"

Dat spun to face her, and she held her breath, waiting for his censure.

Instead, he said, "It's getting late. I'm sure Will has to get home."

"I'll just give him a quick tour." Salina smiled at Will and then started down the porch steps. Excusing himself, he joined her, and they walked side by side to the garden.

"I'm sorry about *Dat*." She was careful to keep her voice low. "He gets a little worked up when we have company. I used a tour of my garden as an excuse to get you away from him."

"It's fine. I enjoyed meeting your parents." He walked toward the fig trees that stood at the edge of the garden, then turned toward the lettuce beds. "I envision you weeding the garden with the sun on your back as you pray."

She took in his handsome profile, and her eyes moved to his lips. She looked away before her thoughts got the better of her. "Do you pray while you cook?"

"*Ya*, I do."

"You said you weren't certain you wanted to be baptized before you went to visit your *onkel*. And you find your connection to God through cooking?"

"*Ya*. When I started cooking with *mei onkel*, a lot of things started making sense. I realized I did belong in the church and that I was supposed to be a chef, not a farmer like *mei dat*. I found a connection with God I never felt when I was working on the farm." He turned toward her. "Did you ever doubt your place in the church? I mean, before you were baptized?"

Salina looked out toward the pasture as she gathered her thoughts. "I was ready to join the church with *mei freinden* when I was a teenager, but I was also expected to join the church since *mei dat* is the bishop and *mei bruder* is the deacon."

Will's mouth dropped open. "Your *dat* is the bishop? I had no idea." He cupped his hand to his forehead. "As a Mennonite, I never should have come here. No wonder he was talking so much about community. I'm so sorry." He began backing away from her.

"No. No." She grabbed his arm and then released it, realizing how improper it was to touch him. "You're welcome here. We're *freinden*."

He seemed unconvinced.

"I mean it, Will. Please don't leave yet."

His expression wavered. "Okay."

They stood in silence for a moment, and her thoughts spun. She wanted him to stay all evening. She wanted to talk until they ran out of words. But she knew their time was running short.

"You said your *bruder* is the deacon?" Will asked. "Is that why you feel like you're always compared to him?"

Salina sighed as she shrugged her shoulders. "*Ya.* Plus, *mei bruder* can do no wrong in *mei dat*'s eyes. He's the perfect *kind*. He's learning *mei dat*'s business, he married a *maedel* from the community, and he has *kinner*. He's the perfect bishop's offspring, unlike me." She couldn't quell the resentment that always lingered just below the surface.

Will looked confused. "What could you have possibly done wrong?"

"I never seem to do anything right. I'm not married. I'm not even engaged. I'm supposed to get married, give up my booth at the marketplace, and live the godly life of a *fraa*."

"Do you want to get married?"

"I think so. If I fall in love and feel God leading me to the right man."

"You don't love Josiah?"

She looked at him, and her brain froze for a moment. "I-I mean, I've known him since we were kids. Like I mentioned to you before, our parents all grew up together, and they stayed close after they were married. Josiah was my first *freind*—other than my cousins, of course. We always got along and had a *gut* time together."

She laughed a little as a memory came to mind. "When we were about seven, he told me he would marry me. I was so thrilled back then."

She shook her head, and Will smiled.

"But then things got complicated after we started dating. I do care about him, but . . . I don't love him like a *fraa* should love her husband." *I don't feel the spark I feel for you.* She looked away and shut her eyes for a moment, stunned at her own honesty.

Then she turned back toward him and took a deep breath. "Do you love Caroline?" Her heart seemed to stop as she awaited his response.

Will looked out over her garden. "I care about her, but my feelings are complicated. I know she loves me, though. Maybe too much."

Once again Salina felt as if an invisible force was at play between them. She felt closer to Will than she'd ever felt to Josiah, and it scared her. And then her thoughts turned to Caroline. She had to think of her, not herself.

"I'm hosting a youth gathering here on Sunday. We're going to play volleyball and Ping-Pong. You and Caroline should come."

Will hesitated, but only for a moment. "I'll ask her if she wants to come."

"Gut." She smiled.

Will looked over his shoulder. "I should get going. It's getting late, and your *dat* looks . . . antsy."

She glanced behind her and found her father sitting on the porch, watching them. Her mother had joined him. "You're right."

They entered her father's workshop, and Will called his driver. Then they returned to the porch and collected his tomatoes, which she'd washed and put into a crate before they sat down to supper.

Will said good night to her parents and thanked them for the meal, and then Salina walked him to the driveway to wait for his driver.

"I'm so glad you came by tonight," she told him. "I had a nice time."

"I did too." He shook her hand, and once again, she felt a spark skip up her arm. "I hope we'll see each other on Sunday."

"I do too."

"Salina!"

She spun and saw her brother running toward them. "Haven't you listened to your voice mail messages? Josiah's father just called me. Josiah has been in an accident."

"What?" Salina's stomach dropped.

"Is he okay?" Will asked.

Neil glared at him and then focused on Salina. "He fell off a ladder, and they've taken him to the hospital."

Salina gasped and cupped her hand to her mouth. "*Ach* no." She looked at Will. Here she was, spending time with him while her boyfriend was at the hospital—injured! What was she doing?

Her eyes stung with tears. "I need to go to him. I need to call my driver." She looked at Will. "I have to go."

Will's expression filled with concern. "Do you want me to go with you?"

"She doesn't need you," Neil snapped. "She has family."

Will blanched. "I understand."

Salina turned toward the workshop they'd just left.

"What's going on?" *Dat* called from the porch.

"Josiah got hurt on a job. He's in the hospital," Neil called to him.

Salina felt as if she were in a fog as she rushed to the phone. Nightmare scenarios swirled in her mind. How badly was Josiah injured?

As she dialed Brian's number, she prayed. *God, please let Josiah be all right. Please heal him. And forgive me for spending time with another man.*

When Brian answered, she asked him to come right away and take her to the hospital. Then she hurried out to the driveway to wait. Josiah had to be okay. He just had to.

CHAPTER 20

Salina hurried through the emergency room doors with her parents close behind. She spotted Josiah's younger sister, Lizzie, sitting in the corner with her boyfriend, Joe, and ran over to her.

"Lizzie!" Salina called. "How is he?"

Lizzie stood and gave her a hug. "He's going to be okay, but he gave us quite a scare." She clicked her tongue. "I'm so grateful he only broke his left leg."

"His leg? I'm so sorry. Can I see him?" Salina asked as her parents joined them.

"*Mamm* and *Dat* are with him now. Maybe you can see him when they come out."

Salina nodded as she stared toward the double doors that led to the treatment area. She wrung her hands as guilt tangled up her insides. She should have been at the hospital sooner! If she hadn't asked Will to stay for supper, she would have checked her messages.

Mamm touched Salina's shoulder, and she jumped with a start.

"Sit, *mei liewe*." *Mamm* rubbed her back. "You're making me *naerfich*."

"I can't sit." Salina shook her head. "I'm too worried." She moved closer to the ceiling-to-floor windows. Then she stared at the cars coming and going in the parking lot for what seemed like hours, but she knew from the clock on the wall that it was only forty-five minutes. Her mind spun with not just worry but shame as she imagined Josiah suffering in pain without her.

When she saw his father walking toward her, she turned toward him. "Ira! How is he?"

Ira gave her a weak smile. In his midfifties, he shared his son's dark hair and eyes, along with a matching beard that held a hint of gray. "The Lord blessed Josiah today. He doesn't have a concussion, although he has a throbbing headache. But he'll go home with crutches and a cast. It will take time for his broken leg to heal. And his bruises." He shook his head. "The Lord truly looked after him when he fell from that height. His injuries could have been so much worse."

Salina clasped her hands together. "Praise God! May I see him?"

"*Ya*. Jean can take you back. She's over there giving our *dochder* an update." Ira pointed to where his wife stood.

"*Danki*." Salina joined Jean, who was sharing the same news with Lizzie, Joe, and her parents.

"Hi, Salina." Jean pulled her in for a quick hug. If it weren't for her graying brown hair, Jean and Lizzie could nearly pass for sisters. They not only had the same hair color but the same hazel eyes and facial features. "I'm so glad you could come."

"We came as soon as we heard," *Dat* told Jean.

Salina touched her arm. "Ira said you might take me to see Josiah."

"Of course." Jean motioned for Salina to follow her to the double doors.

They walked through them together and down the hallway

past several treatment rooms. The smell of bleach filled Salina's senses, and the hum of fluorescent lights buzzed in her ears as men and women dressed in scrubs hurried past. She fiddled with the hem of her apron as they approached the last room on the left.

Jean drew back a curtain and then gestured for Salina to walk in.

Salina sucked in a breath when she saw Josiah lying in a bed dressed in a blue hospital gown. His face was pale, and his body was covered in a white sheet. She spotted a bulge under the sheet, indicating he had either a splint or a cast on his left leg. An IV was attached to his arm.

He gave her a grin as she came closer. "You're a sight for sore eyes."

"I'll give you two some privacy," Jean said before dropping the curtain and slipping away.

"How are you?" Salina pulled the only chair to the side of his bed and took his hand in hers as she sat down.

"I've had better days." He gave her a goofy grin. "But the painkillers are helping."

"What happened?"

He sighed and looked down at his leg. "I was climbing the ladder and got distracted. One of the guys on my crew called me, and I turned to look at him. Next thing I knew, I was on the ground and in the most tremendous pain." He snorted. "I'm a klutz." He looked at her. "I'm glad you're here."

Tears filled her eyes. "I should have been here sooner. If I had known you were hurt, I would have come, but I—" The tears began to fall.

"Hey. Don't cry, Salina. I'm going to be fine." He rubbed her hand. "I'll be on crutches for a while, but I'll be okay."

She pulled out a handful of tissues from a box by his bed and wiped her eyes. She had to get control of her emotions as guilt pushed her too close to a sob.

"They said I might go home later tonight," Josiah told her.

"That's *gut*."

"And I can still come to your youth gathering. I just won't be much help with the setup."

"Don't worry about that. You just need to heal."

He squeezed her hand. "I will. *Dat* said I did this for some time off." He rolled his eyes. "He thinks he's so funny."

Salina smiled.

"There's your smile." He leaned back in the bed and sighed. "What a day."

"*Ya*, that is true," she whispered. *You have no idea.*

Salina sat with him until he fell asleep. Then she kissed his forehead and returned to the waiting room, where she gave both Lizzie and Jean a hug. "Please let me know when Josiah is home."

"We will," his mother said. "*Danki* for coming."

Salina and her parents were quiet during the ride home. Then as she stepped into the kitchen, she yawned and glanced at the clock on the wall. It was nearly nine thirty.

"*Gut nacht*," she told her parents before heading to the stairs.

"Salina, wait," *Dat* said. "We need to talk about that Mennonite."

She bit her lower lip as her heart sank.

"I don't know what you were thinking when you invited him to stay for supper, but I'm going to set you straight." His tone was gruff, but she wasn't surprised. "Will is not from our community, and it's inappropriate for you to have a relationship with him. Besides, you're dating Josiah, and it's a sin for you to be unfaithful to him."

"I'm not being unfaithful to Josiah, and I'm not in a relationship with Will. He's a business associate and a *freind*, and that's all."

"It was obvious to me that he'd like more from you, and I will not allow it. He's from Lititz, he's not part of our community, and you belong with Josiah. If Will continues to pursue you, I will forbid you from supplying his restaurant with produce." *Dat* wagged a finger at her. "You need to keep your relationship with him professional. I expected better from you."

"I'm not doing anything inappropriate," Salina said, insistent. "You always believe the worst in me, and you shouldn't." There was a tremor in her voice. "Just because I'm not Neil doesn't mean I'm a complete disappointment." She divided a look between her parents. "It's been a long night, and we're all exhausted. We just need to go to bed. *Gut nacht*."

Despondent, she made it to her bedroom before all the emotions from the evening poured out of her in tears. Then she dropped onto her bed and hugged her pillow before realizing what her father had said. He thought Will wanted "more" from her, and he'd accused him of pursuing her. *Did* Will think of her as more than a friend? Josiah suggested the same thing, yet he seemed to have forgotten all about it now.

"Please, God," she whispered. "I don't know what Will thinks, but my family is pressuring me to marry Josiah. I don't want to hurt him, and I know Will would never want to hurt Caroline. The guilt is overwhelming. And I feel terrible for not being with Josiah when he needed me. If I'm supposed to be at his side for the rest of our lives, please stop these feelings I have for

Will. And if he has feelings for me, stop those too. I'm waiting
for you, Lord. Only you can help me find my way."

. . .

Will heard a tap on his front door as he flipped on the light in
his living room. He opened the door and found Roger standing
on the porch.

"Let me guess," Will began. "You're here to lecture me about
seeing Salina tonight. To tell me what a bad idea that was."

Roger held up a finger. "How did you know?"

"Because you like to constantly remind me that I should
stay away from her." Will sighed as he opened the door wide.
"Come in."

Roger stepped inside and sat down on the sofa. "You were
there awfully late."

"I know." He shook his head. "They were having a late supper, and Salina invited me to stay. While I was there, her *bruder*
came over and told us Josiah was hurt in an accident at work.
He fell off a ladder."

Roger gasped. "What happened then?"

He described how Salina had reacted to the news and how
she'd called a driver to rush her and her family to the hospital.
But he kept to himself how hard it was to see Salina so upset
about another man.

"Well, I hope she's okay—and that Josiah is too." Roger
paused. "How was meeting the rest of her family?"

"Her father grilled me up one side and down the other." Will
dropped into the chair across from him. "I found out he's the
bishop in their district, and her *bruder* is the deacon."

"Yikes."

Will scrubbed his hand down his face. "I know what you're thinking. I need to stay away from her. The thing is, she's become important to me. She's a welcome *freind*."

"But she's also an Amish bishop's *dochder*. And she obviously cares about Josiah."

"I know."

Roger leaned forward and folded his hands as if saying a prayer. "Concentrate on being her *freind* and only her *freind* if you can't just stick to a professional relationship. Otherwise, this won't end well."

"I agree," Will said. But it seemed like an impossible feat.

. . .

Will sat in the passenger seat of Austin's van the following evening. "Could we make a stop on the way to my house?"

"Where?" Austin said.

"Caroline's."

"Sure. We can do that."

"Thanks." Will cupped his hand over his mouth to suppress a yawn as the van bumped down the road.

It had been a long and busy day, but it also didn't help that he hadn't slept much the night before. He'd tossed and turned with his thoughts stuck on Salina and how connected he'd felt to her in her garden. He'd longed to talk to her all evening long and learn more about why her father compared her to her brother and found her lacking. How could the man criticize Salina, a daughter who was not only smart, hardworking, and kind but perfect in every way?

Will inwardly cringed. *But she's the bishop's* dochder! *And the deacon's* schweschder! *And I'm committed to Caroline!*

Not only was he wrong entertaining feelings for a woman other than his girlfriend; he was risking getting Salina into trouble if her father realized Will cared for her. Plus, he had no right to interfere in her relationship with Josiah, whom he'd managed to learn had only a broken leg. Salina cared for the man, even if her feelings were muddled.

Oh, how he could relate to muddled feelings. But one thing was clear. Even though his heart got more and more attached to Salina each time he saw her, she was off-limits. Why couldn't he suppress these feelings? Wasn't he strong enough to control his emotions? After all, he was a grown man!

He should have declined her invitation for him and Caroline to attend her youth group event, too, but he didn't think he could force himself to completely avoid her. Yes, just last night he'd agreed with Roger that he had to keep their relationship professional. But then when she'd asked him to stay for supper . . .

He sighed. Having Caroline there would help.

"We're here." Austin turned and looked at him. "You don't seem like yourself. Are you all right?"

"Yeah." Will faked a smile. "It's just been a long day." He pushed his door open. "I won't be long."

"Take your time."

"Thanks." Will jogged up the driveway and then up Caroline's back steps to knock on the door. Soon he heard footfalls in the mudroom, and the back light flipped on before the door opened. Caroline stood in front of him, clad in a pink bathrobe covering a white nightgown.

"Will, hi." She pushed open the storm door and stepped onto the porch. "Is everything okay?"

"*Ya.*" He pushed his hands into the pockets of his jeans.

When another yawn hit him, he covered his mouth with his hand. "I just didn't get much sleep last night."

She cupped her hand to his cheek. "Why not? Are you *krank*?"

"No, I'm not. I just had a lot on my mind."

She looked worried. "Do you want to talk about it?"

"No, but *danki* for asking." He glanced toward the driveway, where the headlights from Austin's van bathed the gravel in a warm glow. Then he faced Caroline again. "Do you have plans for tomorrow?"

She searched his eyes. "No. I was going to just rest here. Why?"

"We've been invited to a youth gathering in Bird-in-Hand. Do you want to go?"

"Oh, how nice. Who invited us?"

"Salina."

Caroline's pleasant expression flashed away, but then a serene smile took over her lips. "Sure. I'll go if you want to."

"It will be nice to meet some new people and have some fun. I'll pick you up after lunch." He leaned down and kissed her cheek. "*Danki* for putting up with me. Sleep well, *mei liewe*." He turned to go.

"Will. Wait." She grabbed his hand and pulled him toward her. "What's going on?"

"What do you mean?"

"You're acting strange and distracted. Talk to me."

He blew out a deep sigh. "I'm just tired, and I wanted to see you. That's all."

She smiled, seeming satisfied with that. "I'll see you tomorrow, then. Get some rest."

"I will." He kissed her cheek again and then hurried off to the van.

Will waved at Caroline as the van backed down the drive-way. Then as Austin headed toward his home, Will realized he had to extinguish his feelings for Salina for good, and that meant they couldn't even be friends. It was the best solution for everyone concerned. If his heart could make it through the youth gathering in one piece, then he would find a way to keep his relationship with her strictly professional.

. . .

Salina lifted a platter of peanut butter spread and started for the Esh family's back door. As usual, she and the other women serving lunch after the service were preparing lunch in the kitchen before heading to the barn.

"Hey." Bethany caught up with her, a stack of plates in her hands. "How's Josiah?"

"He was in pain when I visited him after I left the market yesterday, refusing to take any more medication. I took him a chocolate cake from Christiana's Bake Stand, his favorite, but he didn't have much of an appetite. He said he'd stay home from church this morning, but he still wanted to come to the youth gathering this afternoon to see everyone."

"I feel so bad for him."

"I know."

"I want to ask you something." Bethany leaned in closer. "Have you noticed that Christiana has been acting weird all morning?"

Salina glanced at her as they approached the barn. "I did notice she's been really quiet. I don't think she's said much more than *gude mariye* to me. Well, other than giving me one-word answers to my questions."

"What do you think is up with her?"

Bethany halted as they reached the barn doors. So did Salina. "I don't know. We'll have to ask her."

Bethany's face filled with concern. "Do you think she and Jeff broke up?"

"No, I doubt that." Salina stepped inside and looked across the barn. Then she nodded toward where Christiana and Jeff stood talking, both grinning from ear to ear. "Check that out over there. I think they're fine."

Bethany stared at their cousin. "Huh. Interesting." Then she turned to Salina. "Are you ready for this afternoon?"

Salina shrugged. "I guess so. *Mamm* and I cleaned like crazy when I got home from visiting Josiah. Neil came over and put up the volleyball nets for me. I'm as ready as I'll ever be."

"It will be fine." Bethany's signature bright smile was back. "After lunch we'll head to your *haus* and have some fun."

Salina helped serve lunch to the men, moving from table to table and passing out the bowls of peanut butter spread while Bethany gave out plates. They made another trip to the kitchen and then moved through the barn filling coffee cups while the other women put out plates of lunch meat, bread, and pretzels. Dessert included a variety of pies the women had baked the day before.

After the men finished, Salina and her cousins ate at the long tables with the other women before helping clean up from the meal.

"Are you ready to go have fun?" Christiana asked her cousins as they all walked toward their buggies. "I am." She smiled at them, but Salina still wondered if something was going on.

As she climbed into her parents' buggy, she hoped Will was on his way to her house. Of course, he'd have Caroline with him, and knowing that made excitement and guilt war inside of her. But by inviting them, she'd wanted to prove she could accept their relationship and maintain her relationship with Josiah.

Yet as she glanced out the buggy window, she knew she had to prepare herself. Who knew what the afternoon had in store?

CHAPTER 21

"What can we do to help?" Bethany asked as Salina stood with her cousins and Jeff once they'd all arrived. Chester was there too.

Salina tapped her chin as she reviewed a mental list. "Well, I need someone to get the volleyballs out of the barn." Then she snapped her fingers. "And the Ping-Pong table is in that far workshop, just past the cabinet showroom. Jeff, can you get it and set it up? Then would you please pull out the folding tables and set them by the back porch? We can put the snacks there."

"Consider it done," Jeff said.

"*Danki.*" Christiana gave him a sweet smile before he turned and walked away.

"I'll help you!" Chester rushed after Jeff.

"He's such a *gut* helper," Salina told Leanna.

"He is. I hope he stays that way." Leanna rubbed her hands together. "Should we start making lemonade and iced tea?"

"*Ya.*" Salina waved for them to follow her into the house. "We need to bring all the snacks out too."

They headed into the kitchen, where they pulled out the food she and her mother had prepared the day before. They had chips, homemade peach salsa, cookies, brownies, crackers, pretzels, and popcorn.

Before long the Ping-Pong table was ready to go by the driveway, and the four cousins had placed the snacks on the folding table. Salina stood on the porch as her church friends began to arrive. Soon their buggies were lined up in the far field, and their horses stood in the pasture and grazed.

"Salina!" Bethany called. "Josiah is here!"

Salina spun to see Jeff helping Josiah out of his father's buggy. Josiah balanced himself on his crutches and laughed at something Jeff said before he hobbled toward her.

"Josiah!" Salina met him halfway. "How are you doing?"

"I'm exhausted, but I really wanted to come. *Mei schweschder* and her boyfriend brought me." He pointed a crutch toward a picnic table over by the volleyball nets. "Could you help me get situated there? I can rest my leg on the bench and watch the games."

"Wouldn't you be more comfortable in the recliner in the *schtupp?*" Jeff asked.

"We have a chaise lounge in the barn," Salina said.

"I'll get it!" Chester ran toward the barn and came back a few moments later dragging the chair.

Soon Josiah was resting while enjoying popcorn and a glass of iced tea, watching the volleyball game Jeff, Christiana, and a group of friends had started. Nearby, another group cheered for friends playing Ping-Pong.

"Do you need anything else?" Salina asked him.

"I'm all set." He winked at her. "Go take care of your guests. I'll call you if I need anything."

Salina walked to the porch, and from there she took in the knot of friends gathered around the folding table, sampling the snacks. But her heart sank as she scanned the familiar faces for the one she longed to see. Will was nowhere to be found.

Later Bethany sidled up and draped her arm across Salina's shoulders. "You seemed *froh* to see Josiah, but you've been moping for the past hour. I've kept my mouth shut, but you know me. I can't keep it shut for long. Now, I want you to tell me what's wrong."

"Nothing." Salina feigned a smile. "I'm just tired. I forgot how much work it takes to organize a youth gathering."

"Nice try, but I don't believe it. Talk to me. Is it Josiah?"

"Why would it be?" she asked—a little too quickly.

Bethany stared. "I'm worried about you. What is it?"

"I'm fine. Really." Salina turned toward the house.

"Does it have to do with Will?"

Salina froze, and trepidation trickled down her back.

"It does, doesn't it?"

Salina scanned the area, making sure no one had heard what Bethany said. Then she faced her. "Why do you think it's Will?"

"Please, Salina." Bethany snorted. "I'm not stupid. You've always been excited to see him, and you even bought him a gift. Maybe you thought you convinced me otherwise, but I know I'm right. Does Josiah suspect? He doesn't seem—"

"No." Salina shook her head. "He did wonder, but I assured him Will and I are just *freinden*. I told *Dat* the same thing when—" She clicked her tongue. "Wait. Do Leanna or Christiana know?"

"Oh, so now you're admitting it. Progress. Maybe they do, although I haven't discussed this with them. But I don't see how long you can keep this a secret. You know they've been suspicious before."

Salina looked toward the driveway again, her disappointment increasing by the minute. "I was hoping he and Caroline would come today."

"You invited them?" Bethany looked aghast as Salina nodded. "When?"

Salina shared how Will had stopped by Friday night and stayed—until she got the word about Josiah's accident.

Bethany's eyes narrowed. "Don't you think it's strange that you're both dating other people yet obviously have feelings for each other?"

"I don't think Will feels that way about me, but I do think we both feel trapped."

"Trapped?"

"I'm expected to marry Josiah, and he's supposed to marry Caroline. But he's told me his feelings about her are . . . confusing."

Bethany shook her head. "Are you sure he's not just playing both sides? And anyway, you're not trapped. You can marry whichever Amish man you want to marry."

Salina gave a sarcastic laugh. "Tell that to *mei dat*. According to him, I can marry only Josiah. I was 'encouraged'"—she made quotation marks with her fingers—"To date him, and now I'm 'encouraged' to marry him."

"I think your *dat* would understand if you told him you didn't want to marry Josiah."

"You don't know *mei dat* as well as you think you do."

Bethany opened her mouth to say something, but she was cut off.

"Salina, could we get more lemonade?" Katie Esh called.

"*Ya*, of course." Salina walked down to the food table and retrieved the two empty pitchers. "I'll bring it right back."

Salina followed Bethany into the kitchen and reached for a wooden spoon.

"Salina, I truly believe you need to think long and hard

about this," she said as Salina mixed up the lemonade. "And you should be honest with Josiah."

"Shhh." Salina craned her neck to make sure no one could hear them. "We can't talk about this here. My parents, Neil, Ellen, and the *maed* are all in the *schtupp*."

Bethany opened her mouth, and Salina shot her a warning look.

"Let me help you." Bethany grabbed the second pitcher and began to fill it with water.

Once the lemonade was made, they carried it out to the table, where Salina gathered two empty bowls to refill them. She turned to walk back to the house and almost slammed right into Caroline.

"Hi!" Caroline grinned. "May I help you with those?" She reached for one of the empty bowls.

"Caroline. Hi." Salina breathed the words as relief rolled through her. She looked past Caroline to where Will stood talking to Josiah and Jeff, near the two volleyball nets. *He made it!*

Will met her gaze and waved. She replied with a smile, and then she turned to Bethany, who gave her a disapproving look.

Ignoring her cousin, Salina turned back to Caroline. "How are you?"

"I'm great. *Danki* for having us today." Caroline motioned toward Will. "Will stopped by last night and told me you'd invited us to come. I was so surprised, but it's always nice to make new *freinden*." She turned to Bethany. "How are you?"

"*Gut. Danki.* I'm glad you and Will could join us." Bethany picked up a half-empty bowl. "I think I'll get more popcorn." Then she gave Salina another look and headed to the back porch.

Caroline gestured in that direction. "Let me help you get more snacks."

"Great." Salina walked with Caroline into the house and then into the kitchen.

"You have a lovely home," Caroline said.

"*Danki.*"

"Will told me your *dat* is a cabinetmaker."

"*Ya*, he is." As she replenished the snack supply, Salina thought she could feel Bethany's stare on her back. She longed for her cousin to just go back outside. Why did she have to make this situation even more uncomfortable?

"And he's the bishop too?"

"That's right." Salina picked up one of the bowls, and Caroline and Bethany took the others.

Caroline wasn't done asking questions. "Is it tough being the bishop's *dochder*?"

Salina paused, unsure of how to respond. "*Ya*, I suppose it is."

"I imagine you feel the pressure to act a certain way." The concern in Caroline's eyes felt almost too much to bear. Assuming it was genuine, how could the woman hold any sympathy for Salina at all? Then again, Will had probably convinced her that his relationship with Salina amounted to no more than friendship based on business. She was sure that's how he really felt.

Salina decided to change the subject. "Let's get these snacks outside before the group holds a protest," she said, starting for the door.

The three women set the snacks on the table, and as Caroline and Bethany filled plates with snacks for themselves, Salina walked toward the makeshift volleyball courts. She stopped in her tracks when she spotted Will playing on a team with Jeff. He served the ball with grace and strength.

Will turned toward her and grinned as he pushed his hand through his glistening hair. She returned the smile, and as their gazes locked, she couldn't help feeling happy.

Then she looked to Will's right and found Josiah staring at her from the sidelines, his dark eyes narrowed. Was that a mix of hurt and disappointment in his expression? Maybe anger too?

She dreaded facing what she knew to be true. He'd seen something loving in her gaze trained on another man. She smiled weakly in his direction, but it was no use. Her cheeks flared hot, and she turned on her heel and almost ran toward the house.

CHAPTER 22

Salina held her breath until she reached the porch, where Caroline now sat with Leanna, Bethany, and Christiana, lost in conversation as they ate and sipped their drinks. Salina finally took a breath of relief, grateful that Caroline didn't seem to have noticed her watching Will.

Salina climbed the steps and sat down on the glider beside Christiana. She listened to the women chatting for a moment or two before she was drawn to the makeshift volleyball court again. First noting that Josiah had disappeared somewhere, she watched Will again, but then she forced her eyes away.

"How long have your parents owned the bookstore?" Leanna was asking Caroline.

"They opened it before I was born. They started out with a small store by our *haus* in Lititz. Then they moved to Bird-in-Hand when the business grew big enough to sustain a storefront. They like the quaint small-town feel of Bird-in-Hand." Caroline pushed a piece of popcorn around on her plate.

"Do you sell only books?" Christiana asked.

"No. We also sell greeting cards, knickknacks, school supplies, and candles."

"We need to check it out," Leanna said. "What are your bestsellers?"

"Well, the tourists love Amish knickknacks and signs with Scripture verses. They also like the books, of course." Caroline went on as Leanna and Christiana listened with what seemed like rapt attention.

Salina looked at Bethany, who was staring at her with a serious expression. Great. Then she glanced at Caroline, and shame hit her anew. Suddenly the weight of Bethany's judgment and Josiah's disappointment pressed against her chest as well.

"Excuse me," Salina mumbled as she stood. Then she hurried into the house, the storm door clicking shut behind her. She leaned forward on the kitchen counter, sucking in a deep breath to stop threatening tears.

How could she allow her feelings for Will to drive a wedge in all her relationships? Between her and Josiah. Between her and Bethany. But she was in too deep, and she couldn't find a way out.

Oh God! Help me!

She covered her face with her hands as guilt tried to suffocate her.

"Talk to me." Bethany came up behind her and placed a hand on her shoulder.

"I'm losing my mind," Salina said, her voice muffled by her hands. "I know I'm wrong to have feelings for Will, but I can't deny it."

Bethany sighed. "I know, but you have to think this through, Salina. You can't let your heart rule your life."

"What?" Salina let her hands drop to her sides as she spun to face her cousin. She was careful to keep her voice low. "How can I *not* let my heart rule my life? Aren't we supposed to follow our hearts when we fall in love?"

"Do you think your *dat* and *bruder* would ever accept Will?"

"No," Salina whispered.

"Well, then you have to ask yourself if Will is worth losing your family." Bethany spoke with a soft voice, but her words couldn't have held more weight.

Salina glanced toward the doorway just as Will walked in. She did her best to hide her surprise as heat rose in her face, but she knew it was useless. "Hi."

"Hi." Will gave her a funny expression. "I was wondering where the restroom is."

She pointed to the doorway leading to the hall. "It's through there. On the left."

"Danki." He nodded at Bethany and then disappeared.

Salina covered her face with her hands again and groaned. "What if he heard us? I will just pass out from embarrassment. Why does this keep getting more and more complicated?"

"I'm sure he didn't hear us," Bethany said. "We were talking softly."

"I don't know."

"Come on." Bethany took her hand and tugged her toward the mudroom. "Let's go back outside and act like nothing is wrong, okay?"

"No." Salina shook her head.

Bethany tugged at her again. *"Kumm."*

"I need a minute." Salina pulled her arm back. "Go. I'll be out after I get myself together."

Bethany hesitated but then nodded. "Fine, but don't stay in here all day. Josiah will wonder what's wrong." Then she turned and left.

Salina leaned back on the sink and rubbed her temples

against the headache now throbbing behind her eyes. She had to get her emotions in check. But how could she when her feelings for Will nearly consumed her?

. . .

Will washed his hands and then stepped out of the bathroom into the hallway. He hoped Salina was still in the kitchen—alone. Then he'd have a chance to talk to her even though he regretted even coming today.

What had he been thinking? All he wanted was to take Salina's hand and lead her out to her garden, where they could sit on the bench and talk for the rest of the afternoon. But he couldn't enjoy that luxury when his girlfriend, her boyfriend, and the rest of her community were all here. He felt like a heel thinking about Salina while Caroline sat on the porch talking to her cousins.

He stepped into the kitchen and found Salina leaning back on the sink, rubbing her forehead. Worry took hold, and he was glad Bethany had gone.

"Salina?"

"Huh?" She jumped. "I'm sorry. You scared me." She pressed her hand to her chest.

"Are you okay?" He walked over to her.

"*Ya.*" She gave a little laugh.

"You sure? You look like you have a headache." He took another step toward her, almost close enough to touch her.

"I'm fine." She smiled up at him. "I'm so glad you're here. I was afraid . . ."

"Afraid?" That he wouldn't come? Did that mean she cared for him as much as he cared for her?

She looked away as if embarrassed. "*Ya*. I was afraid something might have happened to you and Caroline." Then she met his gaze again and pointed in the direction of the porch. "Caroline is so sweet. She seems to fit in well with my cousins. She was telling us all about her parents' bookstore. Christiana and Leanna want to visit there soon."

He leaned back on the counter beside her. He didn't want to talk about Caroline or Josiah. He longed to tell her that he cared about her. But he knew he was playing with fire just standing here with her alone. And after today their relationship would be strictly professional. It had to be.

She turned toward him. "What's on your mind?"

"I ran out of cucumbers yesterday. I suppose you can't sell me more, huh?"

She grinned as she wagged a finger at him. "You know I can't sell anything today. It's against our rules to work on Sundays. However, I could give you some cucumbers as a gift."

"If you give them to me, I'll pay you on Wednesday."

"Okay." She glanced down at her apron and then back up at him. "You looked like you were having fun playing volleyball."

"I was."

"You're a *gut* player."

Will studied her eyes, and the reality that they would never be together threatened to crush his heart. Salina belonged to Josiah.

"I'm sure Josiah is a *gut* player too—when he's not in a cast," he told her.

Her smile faded as if she understood the underlying meaning of his words. "*Ya*, he is."

"I imagine he's a much better player than I could ever be."

"That's not true," she whispered.

Voices sounded from the family room, and Salina's mother entered the kitchen followed by a woman who looked to be about his age. Salina shifted away from him and smoothed her hands down her apron.

"*Mamm*. Ellen." Salina turned to Will, and he could see the alarm in her eyes. "Will, you've already met *mei mamm*, Mary. This is my sister-in-law, Ellen. Neil's *fraa*." Then she looked at Ellen. "This is Will Zimmerman. I supply produce for his restaurant."

"Hi, Will." Mary's posture seemed stiff as she nodded.

"Hello." Ellen's expression was almost grim as she held out her hand.

"It's nice to meet you, Ellen." Will kept a smile on his face as he shook her hand. It was limp. "Salina invited my girlfriend and me to join her *freinden* today."

"How nice." Ellen's cold expression didn't match the sentiment in her words.

The back door burst open, and Caroline appeared in the doorway. She looked around the kitchen before her eyes landed on Will.

"This is Caroline, my girlfriend," Will said. "Caroline, this is Salina's *mamm*, Mary, and her sister-in-law, Ellen."

"So nice to meet you," Caroline said. Then she turned to Will. "Are you going to play volleyball? We're looking to start another team." She paused. "We're still a team, right, Will?" Her words seemed to hold a deeper meaning as she held his gaze.

"*Ya*. Of course we are." Will nodded at all three Petersheim women. "Excuse us."

Then he followed Caroline out the door and down the porch steps. But he felt as if he'd left his heart in the kitchen with Salina.

. . .

"Ellen and I were tired of sitting in the *schtupp* with your *dat* and *bruder*, and the *kinner* are napping in my bedroom," *Mamm* said. "Do you need help with anything, Salina?"

"I was just going to check the snack table." Salina opened the pantry and pulled out a bag of pretzels.

Mamm took the bag from her and then retrieved a bag of chips. "I'll do that and see what else you need." She headed outside.

Salina was aware of Ellen's gaze on her as she took a jar of peach salsa from the pantry. When she turned, Ellen was standing beside her, eyeing her with what could only be called suspicion. Anxiety pricked at her as she worked to keep her expression pleasant. "Do you need something, Ellen?"

"I'm worried about you." Ellen glanced toward the doorway and then back at Salina. "But I don't want Neil or your *dat* to hear me. Neil told me he met Will Friday night and could tell you two have feelings for each other. I thought that couldn't be true since you and Josiah have been together so long, and we've all believed you would get married sometime soon. I was certain he'd misinterpreted your friendship with the Mennonite."

Ellen looked at the doorway again and lowered her voice even more. "But I saw it for myself just now. You and Will *are* attracted to each other. Do you realize how dangerous that is?"

"Listen, Ellen. You've got this all wrong."

"Do I?" Ellen lifted her chin. "Neil is concerned, and if you're not careful, he'll tell your *dat*."

Salina shook her head. "No need. *Dat* made his position

clear after he met Will. But it doesn't matter. There's nothing to tell him or anyone else."

"I don't believe you. And if word gets around that you and Will are having a secret relationship, it will ruin your reputation and embarrass your parents and Neil. Is that what you want?"

"No." Salina's body vibrated with trepidation.

"Then I suggest you stop whatever is going on between Will and you. Josiah is a *gut* man, and he will be a *gut* provider for you and your future family. Caroline seems like a lovely *maedel*. I know you, Salina. I know your heart. I don't believe you want to hurt Will's girlfriend, but you could."

Salina nodded as the truth of Ellen's words stabbed at her, stealing the breath from her lungs.

"Your *dat* is fair, and so is Neil, but Neil will talk to you if he has to. You know he's the one the congregation calls when a member isn't following the rules. Don't make him have to do that. It will be such an embarrassment for our entire family."

Ellen's expression warmed. "Please, Salina. Use your head. Right now you're caught up in the excitement of meeting someone new, but it's not true love. It's not a love that will sustain you for a lifetime. Only a man like Josiah can provide that. He's a member of our community—a true, solid Amish man."

Renewed confusion twisted Salina's insides. Was Ellen right about Will? Was he just a fleeting fantasy while Josiah was the true future she needed? Maybe her sister-in-law's counsel was the sign she'd asked God to send, but she wasn't sure.

The back door opened, and *Mamm* walked back into the kitchen. She reached for the jar of salsa in Salina's hands. "We need to replenish the salsa bowl. It's popular today. Nothing beats your peach salsa." She walked to the pantry. "We also need more crackers and *kichlin*."

"I'll get the *kichlin*." As Salina moved to the counter, she tried to digest everything Ellen had said. She had to stay away from Will—before the situation grew any worse. That might be the only way she could get over him.

CHAPTER 23

Will laughed when the ball hit the net after he smacked it toward the opposing team.

"As tall as you are, I thought you could do better than that," Caroline said, teasing him.

"I think I'm off my game." He shook his head and then glanced toward the porch where Salina sat talking with her cousins. He and Caroline had been playing volleyball for what seemed like an hour now, but Salina had never left his mind.

He also couldn't help but notice the shift in her mood ever since her mother and sister-in-law had come into the kitchen. He'd also heard her friends ask her to play volleyball, but she declined.

"Let's go," Josiah barked from the sidelines, his frustration seeming to be aimed at Will. "Why don't you play instead of talking about it?"

After retrieving the ball, Will tossed it to the opposing team.

"This is fun, isn't it?" Caroline touched his arm.

Will smiled at her. "*Ya*, it is."

"I'm glad you're playing." Then her expression grew serious. "I like to win, though. Let's do it."

"I'll do my best." Will turned his attention back to the game, but he kept an eye on the porch.

. . .

Salina sipped lemonade as she sat on a rocker beside Bethany. Next to her, Jeff and Christiana shared the glider, their legs brushing together as they moved it back and forth. Josiah had gone home with Lizzie and Joe an hour ago, telling her he was tired. But she knew he must be hurt. She just didn't know what to do about it.

Leanna sat on the other side of Bethany, looking out toward the volleyball games. "I appreciate how everyone is so nice to Chester and allows him to participate."

"He's a great kid," Jeff said. "He's always so polite to everyone."

Leanna sighed. "Marlin would be so proud of him."

Salina's chest constricted. She couldn't imagine the depth of Leanna's grief after losing her husband.

"I'm sorry, Leanna." Bethany's voice was soft.

"*Danki*." Leanna gave her a sad smile and then squeezed her hand. "I appreciate that."

"I think it's been a *gut* day," Christiana commented. "I've had fun." She looked at Jeff. "Have you?"

"Of course I have." Jeff took her hand in his.

Salina moved her gaze to the volleyball games and watched as Will served the ball and the opposing team missed it. Caroline cheered and then hugged Will, and Salina's spirit sank as Ellen's warning echoed in her mind.

"It's almost time to go home. Do you want to play again?" Jeff asked Christiana.

She shrugged. "If you do."

Jeff stood and looked at all the other women. "Do any of you want to join us?"

Bethany pushed her rocker into motion. "I'm fine sitting here on the porch."

"I'll stay here too," Leanna said.

Jeff looked at Salina, and she shook her head.

"All right, then." Jeff again took Christiana's hand in his as she stood. "We'll play for all of you." Then he led Christiana down the steps.

"I still think there's something up with them," Bethany said as soon as Jeff and Christiana were out of earshot. "They've seemed glued to each other more than usual lately. Christiana doesn't have lunch with us at the marketplace anymore. She doesn't even come for *kaffi* in the morning. And she acted so strange at church today."

Leanna finished her iced tea and set her glass on the porch floor. "I think they're engaged. Or about to be."

Salina turned toward her. "You do?"

Leanna nodded.

"Did she tell you Jeff was going to propose?" Disappointment swirled through Salina. Why hadn't Christiana told her first? They used to be so close, like sisters. Yet Salina had been so caught up in Will lately that she hadn't made much effort to talk to Christiana. Maybe she didn't deserve to know first.

"No, she didn't tell me anything. I just have a feeling." Leanna picked up a pretzel from the plate on the small table next to her and ate it.

"I think you're right," Bethany said. "I get that feeling too. I guess we should be prepared for a wedding soon."

They all sat in silence as they watched Christiana and Jeff join Will's team.

"*Mamm!*" Chester called from the second game nearby. He was waving vigorously. "Come play with us."

"I think you need to go play volleyball," Bethany said with a laugh.

Leanna frowned. "I guess I have to, huh?"

"Have fun," Salina said. "Show those *buwe* how it's done."

"You must need glasses, because I'm the shortest one here." Leanna stood and then slowly headed down the steps. She turned back toward them and added, "Pray for me."

"You've got this," Bethany told her.

As Salina once again watched Will play and Caroline clap and look up at him adoringly every time his serve was good, shame pounced around her soul. The more she thought about it, the more she realized Caroline had to have been hurt when she found her with Will—again. She must have wondered why he hadn't come back to her. She'd seemed desperate for Will's attention when she asked him to play volleyball. And her comment about their being a team wasn't lost on Salina. She understood the double meaning, and it was true. Caroline and Will were a team. Salina was the outsider, Caroline's enemy.

She was a horrible person. And that included what she'd done to Josiah today.

"I hate to sound like a parrot, but are you all right?" Bethany asked.

"No. For one thing, Ellen cornered me in the kitchen and gave me some unsolicited advice." She'd decided to dismiss what Ellen told her as a sign from God. Why would he use Neil's wife—of all people?

Bethany angled her body toward Salina. "What did she say?"

Salina told her, and Bethany's eyes widened a little more with each point. "She made it clear that I had to watch my step before I embarrass my family and have a visit from *mei bruder*."

Bethany was silent as she looked down at her lap.

"Why don't you just say what's on your mind, Bethany? I can take it."

Bethany raised her head. "I think Ellen is right. I know you, Salina. You're a *gut* person, and you care about other people's feelings. I know you don't want to hurt or disappoint your family or Josiah. And like Ellen, I know you don't want to hurt Caroline. You should appreciate Josiah and concentrate on making your relationship with him work."

Salina closed her eyes for a moment and then nodded. She needed to settle her mind about this once and for all. "You're right."

"*Gut.* I'm glad you agree. Everything will work out for the best, then. I promise you. God is in control." Bethany reached over and patted her arm.

"I know he is."

Before long, the volleyball games came to a close. The men took down the nets and stored them and the Ping-Pong table while the women cleaned up. Once everything was stowed, Salina's friends began leaving, thanking her as they said good-bye.

Salina's heart lurched when Will and Caroline approached her, holding hands.

Caroline released Will's hand and then hugged Salina, pulling her close as Salina awkwardly patted her back. "*Danki* for such a fun time."

"*Gern gschehne.*" Salina looked up at Will. "I'm so glad you both could come."

"I am too. I just called for our ride." He lifted his eyebrows. "But could I still get those cucumbers? I'll pay you on Wednesday."

"Oh. I almost forgot." Salina rushed into the house and down to the basement kitchen, where she filled a plastic crate with cucumbers. When she walked back outside, Will and Caroline were talking with Jeff, Christiana, and Bethany. She took in Caroline's sweet smile, and once again, shame hit her hard. Caroline deserved Will. She had held his heart for the longest time, and Salina was only interfering in their relationship. It was time to let him go.

Will turned toward her and held out his hands. "Add these to my bill."

"Don't worry about it." She shook her head. "Consider them a gift."

"Don't be *gegisch*. I can't take these for free. You'd make money if you sold them at the market."

"It's fine." She took a step back as if putting distance between them would stop her heart from longing for him.

Will's smile faded, no doubt sensing her sadness. *"Was iss letz?"*

Caroline came up behind him and placed her hand on his bicep. "Austin is here. He was just around the corner when you called." She smiled at Salina. "See you soon."

Salina gave them a wave and then walked up the porch steps and disappeared into the house, her heart cracking open with each step.

. . .

"I had fun today," Caroline said as she and Will stood on her front porch.

"I did too."

And yet Will pondered Salina's sad expression before they

left. Had he said or done something to hurt her? And why would she give him the cucumbers for free? He had to add money to his check this week to make sure he covered the cost. She couldn't afford to give away produce, and he didn't want to cheat her out of a profit.

"Bethany, Christiana, and Leanna were so kind to me," Caroline continued. "But . . . Salina was awfully quiet. It seemed like she was distracted or upset about something."

"Really?" Will did his best to sound surprised by her observation.

"Will, do you care about Salina?"

He managed to stay calm and shake his head. "I've already told you I'm not interested in her as more than a *freind*. You can trust me, Caroline. I won't be unfaithful to you."

Caroline nodded, but her lips formed a frown. "She's in love with you, you know."

Will's heart seemed to somersault at her words. "No, she's not." His voice sounded rough, as if the words had scraped out of his throat.

"I think I'm right. It's pretty easy to tell when a *maedel* is in love. It's obvious by the way she stares at you and the way she smiles at you. She seems to seek you out, and she hangs on your every word. I can't blame her. I know how special you are."

Caroline touched his arm. "Tell me the truth this time, Will. Do you love her?"

"Caroline, you have nothing to worry about. Please, let's drop this." But he wasn't being completely truthful. His emotions were a jumbled mess. All he knew for sure was that he cared for Salina—and he'd just lied to his girlfriend.

Was it love?

Maybe.

Caroline said good night and then went into the house, but he just stood there. He felt stuck at a crossroads. No matter which direction he chose, someone would get hurt. If he pursued Salina, he would hurt Caroline. If he proposed to Caroline, he would lose Salina forever—and hurt himself.

If only he could make a decision that wouldn't hurt anyone at all.

CHAPTER 24

On Tuesday evening of the following week, Salina sat on her garden stool, leaning over her bed of zucchini as she pulled another ripe one from the vine and dropped it into a bucket. The humid mid-September air closed in around her, and she swiped her arm over her forehead. She was ready for cooler temperatures in Lancaster County.

She'd helped *Mamm* clean up from their evening meal before she headed outside to clear her head. It had been almost a week and a half since she'd hosted the youth group at her house, but her heart and mind still churned with Ellen and Bethany's warnings and her guilt over hurting Caroline.

When she'd delivered Will's produce last Wednesday, she'd kept her conversation with him short and professional. She hadn't allowed herself to chat or joke with him. He insisted on paying for the cucumbers she'd given him at the youth gathering, and she'd accepted the payment before hurrying out to the van and leaving. She had to keep distance between them even though it was breaking her heart.

She'd seen Josiah a few times since the youth gathering, stopping by his house to see how he was healing and taking a meal to his family. He'd also invited her to visit with them on Sunday. Their relationship seemed strained, though, and she had to force herself to be attentive toward him. She kept praying that her feelings for Josiah would transform into love, but that prayer had not yet been answered.

"Salina!"

She turned and spotted Christiana and Jeff waving from the driveway. She stood, then wiped her hands down her apron and carried the bucket of zucchini to where they stood. "Hi. What are you two doing here?"

Christiana looked at Jeff and then back at Salina. "We're looking for Neil. Ellen said he's here."

"Oh." Leanna's words echoed through Salina's mind. Christiana and Jeff had to be getting engaged if they were looking for Neil. Couples met with the deacon when they wanted to get married.

"I haven't seen him, but he might be in the workshop with *Dat*. I'll look for you."

"*Danki*," Jeff said before gazing down at Christiana with a big smile on his face.

Salina set the bucket of zucchini on the porch steps. "You can have a seat."

Once at the workshop, she tapped on the door and opened it, finding her father and brother standing at a workbench, discussing a project.

"Christiana and Jeff are here to talk to you, Neil," she said as they turned to face her.

"Oh?" Neil looked at *Dat* and then back at her. "Would you ask them to come back here?"

"Sure." Salina went back to the porch. "They are in the workshop," she told the couple. "You're welcome to go in there."

"*Danki*." Jeff took Christiana's hand as they walked down the porch steps, and her cousin gave Salina a nervous smile.

Salina watched them disappear into the workshop, her mind

spinning. Christiana, her best friend, was getting married. That meant a wedding would come soon, and then she'd move into Jeff's house at his father's farm.

Would Christiana give up her Bake Shop at the market? Would she become a mother in another year and be too busy to talk to Salina? Not that she'd been forthcoming with her cousin about her dilemma with Josiah.

"Did I hear someone out here?" *Mamm* asked as she stepped onto the porch from the house.

"Christiana and Jeff are here to meet with Neil."

"Really?" *Mamm* smiled. "Are we going to have a wedding this fall?"

"I guess so."

"That's so exciting." *Mamm* waved Salina toward the house. "Come inside. Let's get out a *kuche*. We'll celebrate with them."

Salina washed up and changed into a fresh dress and apron as *Mamm* put on a pot of coffee and took out a pound cake she'd baked the day before. The coffee was ready just as *Dat*, Neil, Christiana, and Jeff stepped into the house.

"We have some news," *Dat* announced.

Salina held her breath.

"We're getting married the second Thursday in November," Christiana said, and Salina and her mother clapped.

Salina pulled Christiana into a hug. "I'm so *froh* for you," she whispered in her ear.

"*Danki.*" Christiana squeezed Salina's hand. "I can't believe it. I'm so excited."

"I know you are." Salina shook Jeff's hand. "Congratulations."

"*Danki.*" Then he pushed his hand through his curly hair, and the curl that always hung over his forehead bounced back into place.

"Let's celebrate!" *Mamm* said. "We have *kaffi* and *kuche*."

They all sat down at the table, and after a prayer, *Mamm* cut the cake and distributed pieces while Salina poured the coffee.

"So. The second Thursday in November," *Mamm* said. "You have just two months to get ready. That's pretty quick."

"I know." Christiana glanced at Jeff. "But we don't want to wait any longer than that. Jeff already has a *haus*, and we're ready." She looked at *Mamm*. "I have to decide what color I want Phoebe and me to wear. Then I'll have to start making the dresses and plan the menu." She turned to Salina. "If it's all right, Jeff and I want to be the ones to tell everyone, so please don't tell Bethany and Leanna."

Salina crossed her heart. "I won't spoil your secret. It's your news to tell."

"*Danki.*" Christiana smiled. "I wanted you to know first, though."

Warmth filled Salina's chest. Maybe she wouldn't lose her best friend after Christiana was married.

"When did you talk with Freeman?" *Dat* asked Jeff. Freeman was Christiana's father.

"Last week." Jeff grimaced. "It wasn't easy, but he did say yes."

Everyone laughed.

"*Mei dat* isn't so easy to talk to," Christiana said.

"That's an understatement." Jeff groaned, and everyone laughed again.

Salina's mind swirled as she tried to imagine herself married to Josiah—sharing a home with him, making his breakfast, eating supper with him every night, spending the rest of her life with him at her side. She felt no excitement, no longing.

Yet the thought of having Will all to herself sent her senses spinning. She could imagine herself cooking by his side, laughing and teasing as they prepared a meal together. Fantasies of Will working beside her in the garden filled her mind—chasing each other through the rows of vegetables and weeding together in the sunshine. Then she imagined sharing a home with him, having a family with him, and growing old beside him, and her heart warmed.

Oh, that was the future her soul craved!

She squashed her fantasy as she sipped her coffee. It would never happen, because Will could never be her future.

Please, God. Help me know what to do. I can't go on this way.

When they finished their cake and coffee, Christiana and Salina helped her mother clean the kitchen and then joined the men, who were talking in the driveway.

Salina hugged Christiana as she and Jeff stood by his buggy. "You deserve all the happiness possible."

"Danki." Christiana smiled at her. "Don't worry. You and Josiah will get here."

Salina managed not to cringe, and yet something inside her seemed to shift. Maybe it was time to tell her family the truth.

Mamm hugged Christiana next. "We're going to have so much fun celebrating you and Jeff."

"Danki, Aenti Mary," Christiana said before climbing into the buggy.

Jeff said good-bye to everyone, and then he climbed into the driver's side of the buggy before guiding his horse down the driveway.

"I need to get home," Neil said. *"Gut nacht."*

"See you soon," *Mamm* told him.

"And I'll see you at work tomorrow," *Dat* said.

Salina waved at him before heading back into the house.

"Salina, I guess you and Josiah will be the next ones to ask permission to get married," *Dat* commented as he hung his straw hat on a peg by the back door and then led them into the kitchen. "Now that Jeff has asked Christiana to marry him, maybe Josiah will be inspired to ask you. Sometimes marriages happen in phases. Once one couple gets engaged, another does."

"That's true," *Mamm* said as she sat down at the table. "After your *dat* and I got engaged, our *freinden* Reuben and Lydia did too."

Salina's hands trembled as she looked at her parents. Here was her opportunity. *Thank you, God. Please give me the strength I need.*

"I don't think we'll be next."

"Oh, you just might be." *Mamm* gave her an encouraging smile. "You never know. Josiah could surprise your *dat* with the question any day now."

Hadn't her mother heard anything she'd said to her that night Will stayed for supper?

"*Mamm*, it's not going to happen. Please stop pushing the issue."

"Salina, why would you say that?" *Dat* asked as he remained standing.

"Because we still haven't discussed it. I don't think he wants to marry me, and I'm not so sure I want to marry him."

Dat's eyes narrowed. "Why would you date someone if you didn't think it would lead to marriage?"

"Maybe I did at first, but now I don't know." Salina wrung her hands as the truth bubbled out. "Maybe it's because you're *freinden* with his parents, but you've always pressured me to date Josiah. I don't think it's ever really been my choice."

Dat blinked and had the nerve to look offended. But he did sit down. "I never pressured you."

"You've always pressured me." Salina ticked off examples on her fingers. "You've pressured me to be perfect, like Neil. You've pressured me to represent our family like a dutiful Amish *dochder*. When I was old enough, you pressured me to be baptized. Then you pressured me to date Josiah. Now you're pressuring me to marry him, but you've never once asked me what I want."

"Salina." *Mamm*'s voice held the hint of a warning.

"How can you say that?" *Dat*'s voice rose as he nearly spat the words. "I've always made sure you had what you wanted." He pointed toward the back windows. "When you wanted a garden, I made sure you had room to grow what your heart desired. When you wanted a booth at the marketplace like Bethany and Leanna, I made that happen too. I even built you a second kitchen in the basement." His tone took an ugly turn. "You're just an ungrateful *kind*."

"That's not true." The words scraped from her throat. "I've always been thankful for what you've done for me, but I never asked to date Josiah. You chose him for me to date, and now you're choosing him to be my husband. I should be able to choose who I want to marry." She wiped away furious tears.

Dat's expression warmed. "But I only want what's best for *mei kinner*, and Josiah is the best choice for you, Salina. He cares about you. He'll always work hard to take care of you."

And then his expression hardened again as if he were ready to give a sermon to the congregation. "Maybe you don't feel the love you want to feel now, but you will. It's time for you to become a dutiful *fraa*. You're the bishop's *dochder*, and you need to set an example for the other *maed* in this community."

Salina shook her head. "I'm not going to be an example. You can't tell me when it's time for me to marry. I'll make the decision, because it's a decision I have to live with for the rest of my life."

Dat opened and closed his mouth, and for the first time in her life, Salina was certain her father was speechless.

"Salina." *Mamm* hissed another warning.

"It's my life, *Dat*." Salina's hand trembled as she pointed to her chest. "You need to let me live it the way I choose." She divided a look between her parents and then started toward the back door. "I'm going back outside."

She hurried to her father's office, where she knew she'd find a voice mail message from Will. It was Tuesday, and she needed to hear his voice. It was the only solace she craved. She punched in the number for voice mail and then pushed the buttons with the right code. After a beep, Will's voice rang through the line.

"Hi. This is Will Zimmerman. I'm calling for Salina. Hey, Salina. It's time for my weekly order."

As he recited his list, Salina balanced the receiver on her shoulder and wrote down the order. A tear trickled out of the corner of one eye, and her heart swelled at the sound of his deep, soothing voice. She longed to call Brian and ask him to take her to Lititz so she could visit with Will and pour out her sorrows to him. He was the only person who seemed to truly know her and understand her. If only she could tell him how she felt about him!

But she couldn't do that. She had to be strong and keep her relationship with him strictly professional. At least she could count on that level of relationship, and she couldn't run the risk of losing it. If she could see him only on Wednesdays, that had to be enough to sustain her bruised soul.

As his message ended, she finished writing the list. Then she erased his message and hurried back into the house and down to the basement kitchen to fill his order. Her parents knew the truth now, and she wouldn't think about Josiah just yet. Tomorrow morning she'd see Will, the only bright spot in her week.

. . .

Will took the invoice from Salina and glanced at the total, then back up at her. But then he looked away. Just like the week before, she hadn't smiled once, and the storm in her blue eyes was tearing a hole in his soul.

He looked at her again and found her staring at the floor. He had to find a way to make her smile.

"So," he said. "This is what you're charging me now, huh? How about I give you my arm and then a leg?"

"What?" Her eyes snapped to his, and for the first time since she arrived, she seemed to be truly looking at him.

"I'm kidding. I'm trying to make a joke so you'll smile."

"Oh." She stared at him, and her expression was just as despondent.

"Please tell me what's wrong."

"It's nothing." She cleared her throat and then pointed at the invoice. "I charged you what I always do."

"I know." He gestured toward his office. "I need to get my checkbook. If I can find it, that is," he said, joking again. But she didn't laugh.

He walked into the office and wrote out the check. Then he ripped it from the book and took it to her.

"Here you go." He held it out, but when she reached for it, he snapped it away, holding it up too high for her to reach. "I'll give this to you after you tell me what's bothering you."

She said nothing.

"Salina, you're breaking my heart. Please tell me."

Her lower lip trembled, and alarm gripped him. "What happened?"

"Christiana and Jeff got engaged. They met with *mei dat* and *bruder* yesterday, and the wedding is in November." She dabbed her eyes as tears welled.

Will grabbed her arm and pulled her into the office, closing the door behind them. "Talk to me." He held on to her arm, enjoying the feel of her warm, soft skin. "Do you not like Jeff?"

She shook her head. "No, it's not that. Jeff is great. He's perfect for Christiana."

"Okay." He searched her watery blue eyes. "Then what is it? Why are you so upset?" He took her hand and moved his thumb over its back.

"After Christiana and Jeff left *mei haus* last night, *mei dat* started pressuring me again to marry Josiah." She paused to wipe away tears with her free hand. "He said I need to set an example for the community and the other *maed*. That I need to be a dutiful *fraa* since I'm the bishop's *dochder*. He wouldn't listen to me when I told him I don't think I want to marry Josiah. He just kept telling me he wants what's best for me and that I need to realize how Josiah will be a *gut* husband and provider."

Images of Salina married to Josiah—living with him, having children with him, loving him—pummeled Will's mind, sending jealousy roaring through him.

"I tried to tell him I don't think I belong with Josiah. I feel so trapped, Will. It's like my life isn't my own. I keep praying, asking God to lead me down the right path. And he gave me the opportunity to at least tell my parents the truth last night.

But they still believe Josiah is my future, and I don't feel it in my heart."

She touched her chest. "Josiah still has never told me he loves me, and I don't love him—at least not like I should love someone I'm meant to marry."

She shuddered. "We're really just *freinden*. How can I be a loving and dutiful *fraa* to a man who's truly only a *freind*? I think he only asked me to be his girlfriend because his family pressured him as much as mine pressured me."

She looked up, and her expression seemed to plead with him. "If Josiah is God's plan for me, wouldn't it feel right? Wouldn't the idea of marrying him bring me joy? I see the joy in Christiana's eyes. She looked elated last night. I don't feel that when I imagine spending my life with Josiah. Doesn't that mean he's not the man I'm supposed to marry?"

"It sounds like he's not." Will released her hand, grabbed a handful of tissues from a box on the floor, and handed them to her. "I don't know the answer, but I believe God wants us to be *froh* with the spouse he's chosen for us."

Salina wiped her eyes and nose with a tissue and then tossed it into the trash can before turning toward the door. "I'm sorry. I shouldn't have come today. I should have just asked Brian to bring you your order. I've shared too much."

"Salina. Stop." He gently took hold of her arm and turned her toward him. "You haven't shared too much." He swiped the tip of his finger across her soft cheek to wipe away a stray tear. "I'm always *froh* to listen. That's what *freinden* are for, okay?"

She nodded, and her lips quivered.

"Have you told your *dat* everything about how you feel?"

"No. But I told you. He doesn't listen. He just gets angry. And this time he accused me of being an ungrateful *kind*."

Will gritted his teeth at the thought. "I'm sorry he does that to you."

"I don't think there's any solution to this." Her voice quavered. "I think I'm stuck with Josiah, and he's stuck with me. I don't know how to cope."

"What if you told Josiah how you really feel? And asked him how he really feels about you? From what you've told me, he might be feeling some of the same things you are—even though he does care about you. He might feel just as trapped as you do. If you're both honest, maybe you can convince all your parents that you don't belong together."

"You could be right."

He sighed as he touched her cheek again. "And remember, Salina, you can always talk to me. I will always listen without judgment. I'm here for you anytime."

"*Danki.*" She reached up and touched his cheek, too, and he shivered at the intimate contact. "I appreciate that more than you'll ever know."

He smiled, and then he felt an overwhelming urge to kiss her. He leaned down, but right before his lips brushed hers, he froze, stunned at his lack of self-control.

Suddenly, the door opened, and Roger stared at them, his eyes round and his mouth open.

Embarrassment overcame Salina's face as she jumped back. "I need to go. I'll see you next Wednesday." She muttered a good-bye and hurried out of the office.

Will sat down on the edge of his desk, hugging his arms to his chest as his own embarrassment set in.

"What are you doing?" Roger said, his tone a demand for honesty. "Why did you have her in here alone with the door closed? Have you completely lost your mind?"

"Roger, listen to me," Will began as his voice shook. "It's not what you think. She needed someone to talk to, and I—"

"What about Caroline?" Roger seemed to grind out the words.

Will nodded as a new level of guilt gnawed at him. When Salina changed toward him, he'd gone back on his promise to himself to keep his distance from her and keep their relationship professional. He couldn't stand to see her unhappy.

Why wasn't he stronger? He could do better than this! He hung his head in shame.

"How would Caroline feel if she found you in your office alone with Salina?"

"It's not like that." Will forced his words through barely moving teeth.

Roger tilted his head and gave him a pointed gaze. "Isn't it, though? Isn't Salina the *maedel* you think about all day long? Isn't she the one you dream about at night?"

Will swallowed against sudden dryness in his throat. "I'm trying my best to keep my feelings for Salina in check."

"It's not working, though, is it?" Roger stepped closer and jammed a finger in Will's chest. "I'm not blind, Will, but I think you are. You need to admit to yourself that Salina is the *maedel* you love."

"I have work to do." Will pushed past him and marched into the kitchen, but he heard Roger follow him. He busied himself with moving pans around to avoid his brother's accusing glare. "I don't have time for this."

"Well, you'd better make time before it all explodes in your face."

Will's shoulders sagged as Roger's words rolled over him. What was he going to do?

CHAPTER 25

The large, dark clouds clogging the blue sky seemed to reflect Salina's mood as she worked in her garden later that day. She bent over the winter squash bed and yanked out the weeds, hoping the work would help weed out her heartbreak and humiliation after the way she'd behaved with Will that morning.

She couldn't deny how good it had felt to share her deepest feelings with him. He had listened to her and respected what she'd had to say. And he'd offered advice. She could tell Will truly cared for her. But that didn't mean he cared more for her than he cared for Caroline.

Salina ripped out another weed and tossed it into a nearby bucket. She glanced up at the sky and sucked in a breath. Will had touched her cheek and pleaded with her to share her feelings. How comforting it was when he touched her. She felt safe and protected when she was with him, more than she'd ever felt with Josiah.

And she was certain he'd almost kissed her! They were both dating other people, but Will had almost kissed her! What if Caroline had walked in instead of Roger?

Why was being with Will so much easier than being with Josiah? Why did his touch feel so right and natural when Josiah's elicited no feelings at all? Why did a man who wasn't a part of her community feel like the right man for her? She'd asked God for help, and she believed he had, first with advice from Bethany—and even from Ellen—and then with a clear opportunity to tell her *dat* the truth about how she felt, at least in part. Yet it also felt like he was torturing her by keeping Will in her life but not allowing her to be with him.

But God didn't torture people. She knew that.

"I'm so confused, God," she whispered. "It's as though I'm full of weeds like my garden. I can't find a way to weed out my sin when my heart is being pulled again and again to Will, and I think I'm just torturing myself. Please help me clean out my soul. Help me be the *dochder* my parents need me to be."

She yanked another weed as tears began to flow.

. . .

"Have you seen the kittens?" Bethany asked as Salina sat with her cousins and Jeff at the Coffee Corner the next morning.

"I haven't, but I bet they're getting big," Leanna said. "Chester asked me about them, though, so I need to bring him here to see them."

"Oh, they are big," Bethany said. "I just love the black one Kent named Chubby."

"Aww, that's a cute name," Leanna said.

Salina lifted her cup and breathed in the scent of the pecan nut flavor. She longed to be happy and smiley like Bethany, but she didn't have the energy today to even pretend. Even though she was sure God was still at work to resolve her dilemma, she couldn't see it, and her mind was spinning with the same confusion that had kept her up most of the night. She wished she could have just stayed home.

But if she had stayed home, her parents would have grilled

her, asking what was wrong. Although her mother had brought up the subject once, she couldn't admit she really was considering breaking up with Josiah. They would never understand.

"Jeff and I have news," Christiana said. "We're getting married on the second Thursday in November."

Bethany clapped her hand over her mouth before she and Leanna squealed in unison. Then they jumped up to hug Christiana and shake Jeff's hand.

"That's *wunderbaar*!" Bethany sang. "Welcome to the family, Jeff."

"*Danki*." Jeff beamed as he took Christiana's hand in his.

"I had a feeling this was coming," Leanna told them. "I'm so *froh* for you."

Bethany turned to Salina. "Did you know?"

Salina nodded. "I did, but only because they came to talk to *mei bruder* on Tuesday, and he was at our *haus*." She nodded toward Christiana. "I was sworn to secrecy, though. The happy couple wanted to share the news themselves." She smiled at Christiana. "And I am very *froh* for them too."

"*Danki*." Christiana smiled at her. Then she looked at Bethany and Leanna. "I hope we can all go shopping for the wedding together. I've asked Phoebe to be my attendant, but I want you all involved, okay? You're like my other *schweschdere*. I want you all to know how special you are to me."

"Of course we know." Leanna rubbed Christiana's shoulder and then took her seat again.

"We're here whenever you want us to help," Bethany chimed in.

"*Danki*. I want to make green dresses for Phoebe and me. I think that color will look nice—depending on the shade, of course."

"Oh *ya*!" Bethany gushed. "Green will be perfect with your red hair."

"I told her that too," Jeff said.

"Then I was thinking about the table decorations . . ."

As Christiana talked about her ideas for the wedding, Salina's thoughts turned to Josiah. She'd spent most of last night considering Will's advice to have an honest conversation with him, to ask him how he really felt about her. But what would be the right words? She debated just cutting to the chase, asking him if he loved her and imagined a future with her.

But her true fear was that he would say yes. If he did envision a future with her, she would have to tell him she didn't feel the same way about him. How would he take that news? Would he be heartbroken?

"Well, it's time to head to our booths," Leanna said as she stood. "You all have a *gut* morning—and sell a lot!" She waved as she walked out of the booth into the aisle.

"You too." Christiana climbed down from the ladder-back chair. "I'll see you all later."

"Bye," Jeff said as he and Christiana trailed behind Leanna.

Salina lingered as Bethany walked to the counter and set out more empty cups.

"You knew, huh?" Bethany waved a cup at her. "Even though you were the first because they had to go to your *haus* to find Neil, I'm sure Christiana would have wanted to tell you first. You two have always been so close, being the same age."

"But I'm close to you and Leanna too." Salina leaned on the counter. "Could I ask you something?"

"Sure." Bethany's eyebrows rose. "What's up?"

Salina ran her finger over the wood grain. "Do you think Josiah loves me?"

Bethany gave a little laugh. "Why wouldn't he?" Then her smile dimmed. "You don't think he does?"

Salina shook her head. "No, I don't. At least he's never said he does."

"Maybe it's just hard for him to express his feelings." Bethany leaned her arms on the counter as a frown appeared on her face. "Is this about Will again?"

"No. It's more than that." Salina told her how her father had started pressuring her to marry Josiah again after Jeff and Christiana got engaged. "But I think I need to break up with him. I do care about Josiah, but as a *freind*."

"Are you sure that's the answer?" Bethany asked. "You two seem to get along so well. And friendship can be a *gut* foundation for marriage."

"I can't marry someone I don't love like a *fraa* should." Salina looked down as she absently drew circles. "And like I said before, I don't think Josiah loves me that way either. I need to talk to him about this, but I don't know what to say. We never have deep conversations. We just talk about old memories, work, and mundane things. I don't know how to open up to Josiah and be honest with him." *Like I do with Will.*

"I think you're right. It sounds like you two should have been honest with each other a long time ago."

"I know." Salina's eyes filled with tears. Why did she cry so easily these days?

"Hey." Bethany stepped from behind the counter and hugged her. "It will be okay. God is in control, and he'll give you strength as you figure this out."

"*Danki.*" Salina pulled a tissue from the pocket of her apron and blotted her tears. "I'm so grateful for you."

Bethany smiled. "I'll listen anytime."

"I'd better get going. I'll see you later, okay?"

"You be strong." Bethany held up an empty coffee cup. "Do you need another one for the road?"

"I'm fine. But *danki*." Salina waved and then walked out of the booth and down the aisle.

As she passed Jeff's booth, she spotted Christiana standing close to him, laughing. When he kissed her cheek, Salina bit back the bitter taste of envy. If only she could be that close to Will. If only he could kiss her cheek and make her feel better. How she craved his touch and comfort.

But you're both with other people.

Salina tried to ignore the voice in her head. She might not be with Josiah for long, but what did that matter if Will stayed with Caroline?

"Salina!" Sara Ann followed her into the Farm Stand. "How are you?"

Salina touched her forehead and forced a smile on her lips before she turned to face the woman. *"Gude mariye."*

Sara Ann grinned as she pivoted toward Jeff's booth and then looked back at Salina. "I thought I heard Christiana say she and Jeff are engaged. Is that true?"

Salina debated her response since it wasn't her news to tell.

Sara Ann placed her hand on her chest. "I promise I won't tell anyone."

Did Sara Ann think Salina would actually believe that? But she gave in. "It is true, but it's not our place to tell everyone. We should let Christiana tell the people she wants to tell."

"Oh, I agree." Sara Ann took a step toward her. "How come that handsome Mennonite hasn't been around lately? What's his name?" She touched her chin. "Oh yes. It's Will, right?"

"I deliver produce to his restaurant on Wednesdays now."

"How nice." Sara Ann's smile took on that devious quality again. "Is your boyfriend jealous of your relationship with Will? I mean, he is awfully attractive."

"Josiah has no reason to be jealous. He understands that I have only a business relationship with Will. Besides, Will has a girlfriend."

"Right." Sara Ann glanced around the Farm Stand. "You have a lot of ripe vegetables today. I'll have to pick up some of your spinach for *mei mamm*."

"Stop by later. Have a *gut* day." Salina started for the back of her booth, hoping Sara Ann would take the hint and leave.

"Do you think you'll get married next?" Sara Ann called after her.

Oh, not you too! "I guess we'll see."

"Haven't you been with your boyfriend for more than a year now?"

Would she just leave? Salina turned to face her. "Not everyone is in a rush to get married."

"Oh." Sara Ann's smile faded, and an exaggerated look of concern filled her face. "Are you two having problems?" She stepped closer. "You can tell me if you are. I'm a *gut* listener."

Salina leveled her gaze at her nosy neighbor. "Josiah and I are not having problems, but when we do, you'll be the first to know."

Sara Ann blinked and then smiled. "Okay. Well, I better get back to my booth. Bye!"

"You do that," Salina muttered under her breath as Sara Ann left. Then she straightened the items on her counter, doing her best to put both Josiah and Will out of her mind.

CHAPTER 26

On Friday evening, Salina sat in the family room while her father read from his favorite devotional book. Locking her fingers in a clasp, she closed her eyes and listened to the words, taking in the Lord's message. When he read a verse from 2 Corinthians, she held on to the verse, committing it to her memory.

"And our hope for you is firm, because we know that just as you share in our sufferings, so also you share in our comfort," *Dat* read.

Salina felt a warmth come over her—as if God were offering her a hug. He would listen to her fervent prayers and help her through this confusing season. He would lead her down the right path.

She opened her heart in silent prayer as *Dat* continued to read.

Please help Josiah and me have an honest conversation about our feelings, God. Grant me the right words to tell him how I feel without hurting him. Help us both understand and accept the futures you have for us.

When devotions were over, *Dat* announced it was time for bed and headed upstairs, giving Salina a moment alone with her mother.

"*Mamm*, could I please ask you something?"

"Of course." *Mamm* looked over at her from her favorite wing chair, identical to *Dat*'s.

"How did you know *Dat* was the one God had chosen for you to marry?"

Mamm seemed to ponder her response. "I suppose I just knew in my heart. When I first met him, I was blinded by the excitement of love. As we got to know each other, though, that love turned into something much deeper. I felt as if God had brought us together for a purpose. I was certain we were supposed to get married and raise a family. And then we did. We were blessed with Neil, and then you came along, completing our family. Meeting your *dat* was a blessing from God. I'm so grateful for my life and family."

Salina considered her mother's words, waiting for understanding. But it didn't come. She was just as confused as she'd been before she'd asked the question. She couldn't relate to the feelings *Mamm* had described because they didn't reflect how she felt about Josiah. And more than ever, she had to be honest—with everyone.

"What's on your mind, Salina? Are you still wondering about Josiah?"

"*Ya.* Ever since Christiana and Jeff got engaged, I keep thinking about my relationship with him. I know you and *Dat* feel he's the one God has chosen for me, but I'm certain more now than ever that he and I couldn't be together." Salina heaved a deep sigh of relief. It felt so good to get that truth off her chest.

When *Mamm* opened her mouth, Salina held up her hand. "Please, *Mamm*. Let me finish."

Mamm nodded. "All right."

"I know you believe Josiah is a *gut*, solid Christian man, and he is. And I know you think he'll be a *gut* provider for me and my future *kinner*. But I can't even imagine myself married to him, so how can he be the one God has chosen for me?"

Mamm frowned and shook her head. "I'm sorry to hear you say that, and I know your *dat* won't agree with what you're saying."

Salina shook her head. "No, he won't. But it's up to me to choose my husband."

"That's true. And more than one of *mei freinden* married men they were certain would make them *froh*, but now they're stuck in loveless marriages. But don't dismiss Josiah so quickly. As I told you before when we talked about this, if you break his heart and then realize you made a mistake, he might not give you a second chance."

Mamm's words sent a tremor through Salina, but she knew what she had to do. With God's help, she just had to find the confidence and the words to do it.

. . .

On Sunday morning, before the church service, Salina stood with the other women in the community in the Glick family's kitchen, watching Christiana. She was surrounded by youth group friends excited about her engagement to Jeff. Then Salina stepped out onto the back porch and looked across the yard.

Josiah stood near the barn, leaning on his crutches and talking to Jeff. She tried to imagine what they were discussing. The engagement? Or maybe their upcoming weeks at work?

Leanna came up beside Salina and touched her arm. "Penny for your thoughts?"

Salina turned toward her older cousin and smiled. "It's a relief the humidity has finally disappeared, isn't it? I love this time of year, when it's still warm during the day and cooler at night."

"I love it too." Leanna paused, and then said, "You've seemed like you're going through a tough time lately. I don't mean to pry, but I'm here if you need to talk. I'm always around."

"*Danki.* I really appreciate that. But I'm fine."

The clock chimed nine, and Salina and Leanna entered the barn. Salina sat down in the unmarried women's section between Christiana and Bethany. Leanna still sat in the married women's section even though she was a widow. Salina tried to imagine Christiana sitting there with her. Soon she'd leave her unmarried cousins, and it would feel so strange to sit in church without her nearby.

Salina began singing the opening hymn and turned her thoughts and prayers toward God. But when her father began the first sermon, she glanced at the unmarried men's section. Josiah was watching her. He smiled, and she returned the gesture. She took a deep breath and tried to imagine what she would say to him when she got him alone today. She couldn't wait any longer.

Please, God, she prayed, *give me the right words as I speak to Josiah today. Then, if with your guidance, we decide to end our dating relationship, help* Dat *understand so he won't try to punish me. Please warm his heart toward me and help him forgive me for not marrying Josiah.*

Then she sat up straighter and focused on her father's words.

. . .

"Do you want to go to Eli Blank's for the youth gathering this afternoon?" Josiah asked. The noon meal was over, and the congregation had begun climbing into their buggies to head home for a restful afternoon.

Salina took a deep breath. "Actually, I was wondering if we could talk."

"Oh." Josiah rubbed his elbow and looked toward the pasture. "Do you want to go sit on that bench over there?"

"That would be perfect." She glanced down at his leg and crutches. "Is it too far for you?"

"No. I'll be okay. I've become somewhat of an expert at traveling with these things."

Salina and Josiah made their way along the pasture fence as the warm afternoon sun shone down on them. She looked out at the Glick family's horses and took in their beautiful shades of tan and brown against the lush green grass. Then she focused on the farms in the distance and marveled at the rolling hills and beautiful patchwork of pastures and fields in the area.

"What do you want to talk about?" Josiah asked after he was settled on the bench and she'd joined him.

"Us." Her hands trembled, but she forced herself to look at him. "Our relationship."

He hesitated as he searched her eyes. Then he focused on the horses and said, "What's on your mind?"

Salina mustered all the courage she could, looking at the horses as well. "Ever since Christiana and Jeff got engaged, *mei dat* has been pressuring me to marry you, assuming you would be proposing soon." Out of the corner of her eye, she saw Josiah's shoulders and back stiffen. "That's why I need you to be completely honest with me. Do you want to marry me?" She held her breath as she turned to him and waited for his response.

Josiah looked at the ground and rubbed the back of his neck. "Salina, you and I have been *freinden* for a long time, and I care about you. We have a lot of fun together, and I appreciate that we get along so well."

"I feel the same way," she said, willing—even eager—to admit it.

He took a shaky breath. "But, honestly"—he paused once again, and then he grimaced—"I'm not ready to get married."

A weight lifted from her shoulders as she released the breath of air she'd been holding. "I'm not ready to get married either."

He huffed out a deep breath of his own. "I'm glad you agree."

They sat in silence for a moment, both staring at the horses again before Salina continued.

"But do you think you'll ever want to marry me, Josiah? That's what I really need to know. Where do you see our relationship going?"

He turned to look at her. "I'm . . . I'm not sure what to say."

"Please be honest."

He looked down at his lap and then back up at her again. "You're a dear *freind*, but . . . I don't think of you that way." Regret seemed to flicker over his face. "I'm sorry."

She choked as an unexpected sob escaped. Embarrassed, she looked down at the ground and pulled a tissue from her pocket.

"*Ach*, Salina." He took her hand in his. "I didn't mean to hurt you. That's the last thing I'd ever want to do."

"You didn't hurt me. And don't be sorry. I don't think of you that way either."

He didn't seem as surprised as he looked relieved.

"You don't?"

"*Ya*. I just feel like I'm such a disappointment to my parents. Yet I can't live a lie. And I'm so sorry I haven't been honest with you before."

"Shhh." He gave her hand a gentle squeeze. "I'm sorry I haven't been honest either. And you're not a disappointment. We've both been pressured by our parents. *Mei dat* keeps telling me I should propose to you, but I feel the same way you do." He shook his head. "It's so complicated, though. I've known you my whole life, and we have so much history. Just about every *gut* memory I have involves you in some way."

She nodded as more tears leaked from her eyes. "I feel the same way about you. You've been a part of every youth gathering, every birthday party, and every holiday since I was little." She gave a little laugh. "You were there the day I learned to ice skate on that pond behind our barn and I fell so many times that my legs and arms were black and blue."

He chuckled. "I remember that. I fell down trying to help you back up."

"*Ya*, our legs wound up twisted together like a pretzel."

They laughed, and he threaded his fingers in hers. "What would I do without you?"

"I don't know." She rested her cheek on his shoulder. "What would I do without you? You're one of my best *freinden*."

"And you're one of mine."

They were silent for a moment, and she stared out over the pasture as the truth came into view, clear as the blue sky above them. But Josiah said it first.

"Should we break up?" His voice was soft, but his question held more weight than she could express.

"I think we should," she whispered.

"I think so too." His voice was ragged. "I care about you, Salina, but I want to marry a *maedel* who captures my heart."

She looked up at him and nodded as her eyes misted again. "And I want to marry a man who captures mine."

"You deserve a love like that." He gave her a sad smile. "It's hard to believe we've both been feeling this way but were too afraid to admit it."

"Exactly." She sniffed and gave him a trembling smile.

"I just didn't want to hurt you. You're important to me."

She bumped her shoulder against his. "You're important to me too."

"I guess we'll break up, then."

She nodded, and then a new thought came to her. "Have you met someone else?"

Josiah looked out toward the horses again and shrugged. "Maybe. I don't know if she likes me."

"Tell me about her."

"Well, she's *schee*. She has brown hair like you but brown eyes. I repaired the roof on her father's *haus*."

"Have you asked her out?"

He gave Salina a look of disbelief. "Well, not yet. Up until a few minutes ago, I had a girlfriend."

Salina laughed, releasing some of the sadness she'd been carrying around for weeks. "You should ask her out."

"Okay. I will. It's just a little strange for my ex-girlfriend to encourage me to get to know another *maedel*."

They laughed.

"What about you?" Josiah gave her a nudge in the ribs with his elbow. "What's going on with you and Will?"

"What do you mean?"

Josiah rolled his eyes. "Please, Salina. It's been so obvious that you two like each other—and never so obvious as the day the youth group met at your *haus*. I just didn't know what to do about it, and since he has a girlfriend . . . Anyway, I'm surprised you didn't want to have this conversation weeks ago."

"Oh. But I don't think he's interested in me. We're just *freinden*."

He gave her another look of disbelief. "Salina, a blind man could tell he is."

"But he's still dating Caroline—and he's been with her for a long time."

Josiah shook his head. "I don't think he loves her, though. I had lunch with my crew at his restaurant one day, and she was there with him. He didn't act like he was in love with her."

Salina almost nodded, but she wouldn't betray Will's confidence by letting on she knew he struggled with his feelings for Caroline.

"But she loves him and does have a hold on him. Besides, *mei dat* would never accept him. You know how he feels about young people in our community marrying within the community. He'd never allow me to be with a Mennonite from Lititz."

Josiah gave her a warm smile. "I truly believe that if it's meant to be, God will find a way for you and Will."

She smiled. "I appreciate that."

Josiah gathered his crutches, pulled himself up, and nodded in the direction of the buggies. "Would you like to go to the youth gathering? We can hang out with our *freinden* as *freinden*."

"I'd like that. But let's not tell anyone about this yet. I have to tell my parents when the time is right—and when I get up the nerve."

"I agree. I might tell *mei schweschder* tonight, though. I know she'll stay quiet until the cat is out of the bag."

"Okay. And I'll do the same with my cousins. I trust them too."

As they headed to Josiah's buggy, Salina felt lighter. They'd finally been honest with each other, and it was such a relief to end their dating relationship.

. . .

"Let me get this straight," Bethany said as she sat with Salina and Christiana in the field beside the volleyball nets. "You and Josiah just broke up and then decided to come to the youth gathering as *freinden*."

"That's right." Salina bent her knees and then hugged her legs.

Christiana seemed to study Salina's face. "Are you sure you're okay?"

"I am. I'm relieved, actually. This has been burdening my heart for a while, so I'm glad we got it out in the open." Salina looked out to where Jeff played volleyball while Josiah sat on the sidelines nearby. "But remember not to tell anyone else. Josiah and I still have to tell our parents, and I don't know how soon that will be. We both have to find the right time."

"I thought for sure you and Josiah would be engaged next," Christiana said. "I'm a little stunned."

"And I'm sorry I haven't been honest with you all." *Especially you, Christiana.* "But I'm really okay with it. As I said, this is a relief." Salina stood and swiped her hands down her apron. "I need to burn off some energy. Why don't we play volleyball?"

Christiana and Bethany shared a look of disbelief before they stood.

Salina was grateful that her cousins had taken the news of her breakup well. But as she walked with them toward the volleyball game, she tried to ignore the anxiety building in her chest as she imagined telling her parents the news.

. . .

"*Danki* for bringing me home," Salina told Josiah as he guided his horse up her driveway later that evening.

"*Gern gschehne.*"

"I really do think you should ask that *maedel* out. And I want you to tell me how it goes."

He chuckled. "I will."

She touched his arm. "Have a *gut* night—and be safe going home."

"*Gut nacht.*"

She climbed out of the buggy and hurried up the back steps and into the house, where she found her parents sitting in the family room.

Mamm looked up from the novel she was reading. "How was the youth gathering?"

"It was *gut*." Salina stood in the doorway and fingered one of the ties to her prayer covering. She needed to tell them what happened with Josiah, and she needed to tell them now—if she could calm her nerves enough to do it.

Dat looked up from his own book and removed his reading glasses as he peered at her. "Is something on your mind, Salina?"

She opened her mouth but then closed it. "No. *Gut nacht.*"

Then she climbed the stairs to her room.

You're a coward, Salina.

She sighed as she reached her bedroom. She would tell her parents, but not tonight.

CHAPTER 27

L ater that evening Will laughed as Caroline's grandfather, Norman, shared another story, this one about growing up on a dairy farm and chasing escaped cows. Will had grown up on a dairy farm, too, so they had a lot in common.

"I never realized how fast they could run," Norman said as he sat in a chair across from Will and Caroline in his family room. At ninety-three, Norman had silver hair, green eyes still bright, and a warm, welcoming smile. His funny personality made him seem much younger than his true age, despite the wrinkles lining his cheeks and the corners of his eyes.

"How is the restaurant business, Will?" Caroline's grandmother asked. Alta was also in her early nineties, and just like Norman, her bright and spry personality seemed to be at odds with her silver hair, intelligent eyes, and the wrinkles on her face.

"It's *gut*, Alta. *Danki* for asking." Will lifted his glass of iced tea and took a sip.

"It's actually booming, *Mammi*, but Will is too humble to brag." Caroline slipped her hand into his and gave it a squeeze. "His parking lot is full at both lunchtime and suppertime every day."

She gave him a smile that told him she was proud of him,

and his stomach twisted with renewed disgrace. Her love for him showed in her eyes, but he couldn't fabricate the same feelings for her, especially when Salina's beautiful face still haunted his thoughts and dreams.

"Oh, you two remind me of Norman and me when we were your age," Alta said from her chair beside her husband. "We met when we were in our midtwenties. I'll never forget it. Norman came into *mei dat*'s store looking for chicken feed. I took one look at him and knew he was the man I was going to marry. It just took a while to convince him." She chuckled as she patted his arm. "He didn't ask me out for nearly a month, and then it took him a year to propose."

"I wasn't in a hurry. I figured we had all the time in the world." Norman gazed at Alta, and their eyes seemed to twinkle at each other.

Then Alta looked back at Will and Caroline. "I was so nervous on my wedding day. It was a beautiful November day— unusually warm and sunny. We had so much fun celebrating with our *freinden* and families. And that next fall we welcomed our firstborn. We had six more, and they were all *wunderbaar bopplin*. We've been so blessed in our long life together."

"It's been long for sure," Norman joked, and Alta swatted his arm as she laughed.

"Stop it," Alta told him before looking at Caroline and Will again. "You two have so much to look forward to. I pray you have the same happiness and love Norman and I have had."

"*Danki, Mammi*. Will says we'll get married when he has the money to build a *haus* for me." Caroline beamed at him. "Hopefully that will be soon."

Alta gave Will a pointed look. "Now, don't you wait too long, William. You need to propose to our Caroline soon. We're not getting any younger. We'd like to see her get married and start a family before we go on to see the Lord."

Caroline gave Will an *I told you so* look, and Will shifted on the sofa as heat crept up his neck.

"Ah. Well." Will stood. "Would anyone else like more iced tea?"

Norman chuckled as he handed Will his glass. "You're a sneaky one, huh?" he muttered.

Will forced a laugh as he took Alta's glass, too, and then he strode to the kitchen, where he leaned on the counter next to the sink and grimaced. He felt like a fraud, a heel, someone who didn't deserve Caroline's love. But how could he end their relationship now when he was already welcomed as a part of her family? It felt so wrong to lead her—all of them—on, but it would feel even worse to break her heart.

"You okay out here?"

He turned to see Caroline standing in the doorway.

"*Ya.*" Will cleared his throat and then took a pitcher of iced tea from the refrigerator. "Do you need a refill too?"

"Please." She moved closer and held out her glass as her expression grew serious. "I know I once said I can't wait forever, but the truth is I'll wait as long as I have to for you. You know that, right?"

He nodded and continued refilling the glasses.

She placed her hand on his arm. "I mean it, Will. I'm not trying to pressure you. I just look forward to our life together. It will be worth the wait."

Will smiled at her. "*Danki.*"

But I'm not sure I'm worth the wait.

· · ·

Will walked Caroline to the door and then kissed her cheek. "*Danki* for inviting me over to visit with your grandparents tonight. I always enjoy spending time with them."

"They love you just like I do." She touched his cheek. "I'll see you soon."

Will nodded and watched her go into the house. Then he climbed back into his buggy, his thoughts roaring through his mind like a summer storm, wrestling with guilt, confusion, and shame, as he headed toward his street.

He needed to reevaluate his life, figure out if he could truly have a future with Caroline. But once again he wondered how he could marry a woman he didn't love. How could they build a life together when he would most likely wind up resenting her? That wasn't fair to her!

As the horse trotted onto his street, Will's thoughts turned to Salina. He'd suggested that she have an honest conversation with Josiah, and if she did, he hoped it would go well.

He shook his head and snorted. He'd counseled Salina to be honest with Josiah, but he couldn't bring himself to be honest with Caroline. Who was he to give advice when he couldn't even follow it?

He began to whisper a prayer. "Lord, please show me what future you've chosen for me. And if that future isn't with Caroline, help me find the right words to say to her. Also, please help Salina find the strength to have an honest conversation with Josiah."

As his horse pulled the buggy up his driveway, a calm washed over him. God would direct him and Salina to the right path—wherever it might lead. He just had to be patient.

· · ·

"What do you think of this hunter green?" Christiana held up another bolt of material in the fabric store on Tuesday morning. Salina stood between Bethany and Leanna and watched their aunt and cousin Phoebe consider Christiana's choice. She was grateful her cousins had agreed not to tell anyone else about her breakup with Josiah until she'd told her parents. She had to stop putting that off, but she knew it would be painful.

"I like it." *Aenti* Lynn looked over at her nieces. "What do you think?"

"I think it really goes well with your hair," Bethany said.

Leanna nodded. "It's the perfect contrast."

"I agree." Salina gestured toward Phoebe. "That will look great on you too."

"I think we've found the right shade of green, then." Christiana gave a little squeal just as Salina spotted Caroline coming toward them. She stilled, and her shoulders tightened.

"Salina! Bethany! Christiana! Leanna! How funny to run into you all at once."

"Caroline," Christiana said as she turned to her mother and sister, "this is *mei mamm*, Lynn, and *mei schweschder*, Phoebe."

"So nice to meet you." Caroline shook their hands. "What are you all doing here today?"

"We've been looking for material for Christiana's wedding dresses." *Aenti* Lynn's smile widened, excitement shining in her eyes.

"You're engaged?" Caroline gave Christiana an awkward hug. "How *wunderbaar*." She inspected the material. "Is this what you've chosen?"

"*Ya*. What do you think?" Christiana held it up.

"Oh yes. Green is your color. I love it," Caroline sang. "I just can't wait until Will and I are planning our wedding."

Salina's stomach soured, and she hitched her purse higher on her shoulder as though she could just turn and escape.

"Are you engaged too?" *Aenti* Lynn asked.

Caroline gave a dramatic sigh. "Not yet, but hopefully soon. Will says he won't ask until he has enough money to build me a *haus*. I keep telling him I don't need one. We can just live in his apartment. But he says I deserve a home better than that. I've told him I'll wait as long as I need to, but I keep praying it will be sooner than later. After all, Will and I have been together more than three years now."

Salina felt as if the walls were closing in on her. And a needle of pain seemed to puncture her heart every time Caroline said Will's name. She had to get out of there before she screamed.

Salina turned to Bethany and then pointed toward a revolving display of sewing patterns. "Oh, look at those." Then she walked over and gave the display a harsh turn.

"Are you all right?" Bethany whispered as she joined her.

"No." Salina kept her eyes focused on the patterns she'd never buy. None of them were for Amish clothing.

"Will owns Zimmerman's Family Restaurant down the street," Caroline went on behind them. "He has the most *appeditlich* buffet. Oh! It's about lunchtime, isn't it? We should go have lunch there together. I'm sure we'll get the family discount."

Salina tensed as dread took over every part of her body, but what could she do?

Bethany placed a hand on her shoulder. "You look like you're about to cry."

Salina shrugged.

"Lunch sounds nice. What do you think, Christiana?" *Aenti* Lynn asked.

"I'd love it."

"*Ya*, we can celebrate finding the material for our dresses," Phoebe chimed in.

After Christiana made her purchase, they all walked down the block to Will's restaurant. Salina hung back and walked with Bethany while the others all listened to Caroline go on and on, telling them how Will had opened the restaurant a year ago and become so successful.

"It's okay," Bethany said. "She can't take away your friendship with Will."

But could she? If Will was promising to marry her, why was Salina wasting her time being his friend when her heart wanted more? She felt like a dolt. She was pinning her hopes and dreams on a man who had already committed himself to another woman.

They walked into the restaurant, and Danielle greeted them at the podium. "Hi. Would you all like a table together?"

Caroline lifted her chin as if she were part owner. "*Ya*, please. *Mei freinden* and I would like your best table."

Danielle gave a little laugh. "All right. Please follow me."

"Oh my. This place is busy," *Aenti* Lynn said as they passed tables full of customers enjoying their lunch.

Salina breathed in the delicious aroma of the food she saw as they passed the buffet—country fried steak, sweet potatoes, rolls. And was that apple pie on the dessert display? Despite wishing she were anywhere else, her stomach now gurgled with delight.

She scanned the dining room for Will, but she didn't find him.

Danielle stopped at a long table. "Here you go." She'd brought several menus with her. "You're welcome to enjoy the buffet, or you can order from the menu. It's up to you."

Aenti Lynn looked around their group. "I think I'd like to get the buffet. What about everyone else?"

They all nodded.

"Great. What can I get you to drink?" Danielle asked as they settled into their chairs. After she'd written their orders on her notepad, she looked at Caroline. "I'll let Will know"—she glanced at Salina before turning back to Caroline—"You're here."

"Great!" Caroline looked at *Aenti* Lynn and Phoebe as Danielle left. "I can't wait for you to meet him."

Salina wondered why Danielle looked at her that way. She was just a customer today.

Caroline was still talking, and when she took a breath, Bethany said, "I hope no one minds if I go ahead, but I'm hungry! Who's with me?" Then she gave Salina a pointed look.

"I'll come with you," Salina said.

At the buffet, they picked up plates and made their way down the line. Salina glanced back at Caroline.

"You still look like you're on the brink of tears," Bethany muttered.

"I'm okay." But she wasn't. She was still hungry, though. Weren't women supposed to lose weight under stress? Yet her appetite didn't seem to suffer—especially at Will's buffet.

They both made salads before returning to their table. The rest of the family stood at the beginning of the buffet line now, but Salina spotted Caroline talking to Will next to the kitchen doors. Her heart stopped. He looked so handsome in the blue plaid shirt she'd decided was her favorite because it brought out the blue in his eyes. He was smiling, obviously happy to see Caroline. Salina's heart sank.

Will cared for Caroline. He wasn't going to leave her. He was going to marry her as soon as he had enough money to build a house. And Salina felt torn down the middle as that reality smacked her hard across the face. Why had she ever hoped anything would change between her and Will after she and Josiah broke up? Not that Will knew about that yet.

Will's gaze drifted past Caroline, and his eyes focused on Salina. He gave her a warm smile and a nod that felt like it was special and meant just for her. But she quickly sat down with Bethany. She had to find a way to stop this attraction. Will wasn't hers. He belonged to Caroline, and it was time for Salina to once and for all face that fact.

Soon the rest of her family joined them. *Aenti* Lynn took a bite of the country fried steak and nodded. "Mmm. Oh, this is *appeditlich*."

"I agree." Christiana dabbed her mouth with a napkin. "Just fantastic."

Caroline returned, Will with her. Salina willed herself to stay calm.

"This is my boyfriend, Will Zimmerman." She made a wide gesture toward him. "Will, this is Lynn and Phoebe. They're Christiana's *mamm* and *schweschder*."

"Nice to meet you." Will shook their hands and then greeted everyone else at the table. "How are you all?"

"We're great because we're eating this amazing lunch," Leanna said, and everyone laughed.

Caroline sat down, and Will placed his hands on the back of her chair as he leaned forward.

Caroline looked up at him and grinned. "I was telling Will how I stopped in the fabric store and just happened to run into you all."

Will's gaze tangled with Salina's as he spoke. "I'm so glad you all came for lunch today."

Salina turned her attention to her sweet potatoes to avoid his intense stare.

"I'm glad we came too," Leanna said. "This food is so *gut*."

"That's because of the produce. I have the best supplier in town," Will said.

"Oh really?" *Aenti* Lynn asked.

"Salina supplies a *gut* portion of his produce," Christiana told her.

"No kidding," Phoebe said.

"That's right." Then Will told them about his first visit to the Farm Stand. "It was the best business decision I've ever made."

Salina continued to study her lunch. She couldn't bring herself to look at Will while he bragged about her. After all, they were just empty words.

Her hand stilled as she realized what she had to do. She needed to halt all contact with him, and the thought made her feel like choking. She would never be more than an acquaintance now.

"I'm going to check on my other customers," he said. "You all enjoy your meal. And it's on the *haus*."

"Oh, no, no. Nonsense," *Aenti* Lynn said, protesting. "You be sure to give us the check."

"I can't do that. You're all like family."

Salina looked up, and Will smiled at her. She bit her lower lip. How could he smile at her with such intensity when his girlfriend was sitting right there? How would Caroline feel if she knew Will had almost kissed her! They had been playing a dangerous game, and she wanted no part of it.

She almost gasped at her next thought. Maybe Will *was* interested in more than friendship with her. What had Bethany asked her? If Will was playing both sides?

She had to end this. It had already gone too far.

"*Danki*, Will," Christiana said. "We really appreciate it."

He gave them a little wave and then moved to the next table, where he chatted with the customers there.

"So now that you have the material for the dresses, what's next on your list of tasks?" Caroline asked Christiana.

"Well, besides making the dresses, *Mamm* and I need to talk about the menu, and I need to plan table decorations."

Salina stared down at her plate, her appetite dissolved. She took a drink of cold water, but it did nothing to mitigate the numbness she felt. She was so embarrassed as she considered the last few months.

She'd fallen for Will and given him a piece of her heart. But how could she have allowed herself to develop feelings for a man who already had a girlfriend, who never planned to leave her and might not be the ethical person she'd supposed him to be?

But she couldn't place all the blame on Will. How could she have emotionally cheated on Josiah and hurt Caroline? Her father would be so ashamed of her. And Neil would have met with her and discussed her emotional infidelity if he'd known about it.

Salina looked at Will and took in his handsome face and radiant smile. Tomorrow she'd deliver produce to him one last time, telling him how she felt, because being completely honest with him was the best thing to do. She'd learned that lesson when she'd talked to Josiah.

Then she would cut Will off. It was the only way to get over him and stop pining for another woman's boyfriend. And deep inside she was growing more and more angry with him. He'd been just as much a part of this mess as she'd been—a mess even worse than that office of his.

When they'd finished lunch, Salina followed her aunt, cousins, and Caroline to the front of the restaurant. Great. Will was talking to Danielle at the podium.

"*Danki* again for lunch," *Aenti* Lynn told him.

"*Gern gschehne.*" Then he turned to Salina as the others filed outside. "I'll leave you my order tonight."

"Fine. I'll be here tomorrow."

"I look forward to it." He smiled, but she couldn't return the gesture. She just nodded and headed outside, where Caroline stood talking to *Aenti* Lynn and her cousins.

One more time Salina took in Caroline's smile, and she felt even more certain that God was telling her to stop risking this woman's happiness. Tomorrow she'd put an end to this farce with Will.

Inwardly, she sighed. Even though she was angry with him, she still loved Will, and she prayed her heart would someday recover from the blow of losing him.

CHAPTER 28

"Here you go." Salina didn't smile as she handed Will her invoice the following morning.

"*Danki.* Let me just get my checkbook." He slipped into his office and grabbed it, then made out the check before returning to the kitchen.

"Here it is." When she took the check from him, she slipped it into her apron pocket without a word. Yet she seemed to want to say something to him.

"Are you okay?" Concern whipped through him when she didn't answer. He took a deep breath. "Did you talk to Josiah?"

She nodded. "I did."

So that was it. "And?"

"We broke up." Her words were matter-of-fact, without emotion.

He tried to ignore the happiness dancing through him, keeping his expression solemn. "Oh. Are you upset about it?"

She shook her head. "It was bound to happen. Neither of us was in love. And we were both ready to move on."

Yet she looked so sad. "I'm sorry."

She nodded again. Then he realized she also seemed . . . angry? No. Why would she be angry?

He took her hands in his. "I can't stand to see you this upset. I wish I could take away your pain."

She yanked her hands out of his and glared at him. "If you want to take away my pain, then let me tell you the whole truth."

He stilled.

"I have feelings for you, Will. I've been in love with you for a while now. I tried denying how I felt, and I even begged God to help me love Josiah the way I love you. But the more I prayed"—she took in a breath—"The more I realized I couldn't stop loving you. Thoughts of you are always lingering at the back of my mind, and you fill my dreams at night. You're the person I want to tell my secrets to, to share my joys with, and to comfort me in my sorrows. But we can't be together. Not only are you committed to Caroline, but you're not Amish."

She took a deep, ragged breath as tears rolled down her cheeks. "It's painful to watch you with Caroline because I keep longing to be the one you've chosen. It was torture to watch you together here yesterday. I want to be the one you choose. I want to be your girlfriend, but I can't."

Stunned, Will opened his mouth, but he couldn't form a response. Confusion stormed through him like a cyclone, swirling his thoughts into a jumbled mess.

"Besides, I'm . . . so angry," she continued, her hands balling into fists. "Angry that you've been paying attention to me, making me feel like you cared. As though I might have a chance with you. But you've always known you'd stay with Caroline, no matter what. Yet you've risked hurting her—and so have I!"

The anger seemed to disappear in a flash. Her eyes rounded, and she took a step back.

"I'm sorry. I have no right to be angry with you. This is all my fault, and I've said too much. I-I . . . I need to go." She started for the back door but then spun to face him. "I can't deliver to you anymore. Growing season is over, and I don't have enough stock to supply both your restaurant and the Farm Stand. I need to keep my booth open."

He shook his head as the words she'd nearly spat at him slammed into his heart. "Don't say that."

"Good-bye, Will." She wiped her wet cheeks, turned, and walked out.

Will placed his palms flat on a counter for support as his heart seemed to shatter. Salina had confessed her love for him, and he'd just stood there like a moron, too stunned to speak.

She was angry and hurt, but she loved him!

The door to the dining room opened with a whoosh, and Roger appeared. His expression clouded with concern. "What's wrong?"

"Salina just told me she and Josiah broke up. She seemed so sad, and when I told her I wanted to take away her pain, she said she loves me." He shook his head and told him everything else Salina had said.

Will dropped onto a stool. "But the main thing is she loves me." He let the words sink into his soul. "Now what do I do?"

"Do you love her?" Roger asked.

Will sighed. "I think I do."

Roger gestured widely. "Well, you better figure it out. You can't have both women, although neither of them would let that happen. Actually, Salina may have just made the choice for you."

Will swallowed against a nearly closed throat as his brother rattled the pans he'd started pulling out. Roger was right. He had to make a difficult choice—assuming Salina would ever give him a second chance if he chose her.

Help me, Lord.

Roger halted what he was doing and stared at Will. Then his expression softened and his shoulders sagged. "You know how I get on you about the mess in your office? I just don't want you to make that kind of mess in your life. You deserve better, and so do Salina and Caroline. Don't put off cleaning this up."

. . .

"How did the delivery go?" *Mamm* asked as Salina stepped into the family's kitchen.

"Fine. But I have a lot of work to do downstairs."

She moved past her mother, and after closing the basement door behind her, she hurried down the steps. Then she dropped onto the nearest stool, covered her face with her hands, and broke down.

Will had sounded so genuine when he said he wanted to take away her pain. But when she confessed her feelings for him, he'd just stood there. Humiliation sliced through her heart. How could she bare her soul like that? And then for him to just stare at her! Oh, she couldn't think of anything worse— except losing total control and berating him for something that was her fault! How could she have ever thought he'd hurt either her or Caroline deliberately? He wouldn't. He just had never realized she'd fallen for him, and once he knew, he didn't know how to let her down.

It was over. He never loved her. Believing he ever could had been a figment of her imagination, and now she had to find a way to move on without him.

Josiah had moved on too. She knew breaking up with him had been the right thing to do, but loneliness wrapped around her chest as she glanced around her kitchen, recalling all the times she'd packed orders for Will's restaurant and looked forward to the few minutes they'd spend together on Wednesday mornings. She'd no longer see his handsome face or talk to him. Their heartfelt conversations were now a part of her past.

But as much as it hurt, she'd made the right decision. It was time for her to be the dutiful bishop's daughter and deacon's sister—if that was possible. She'd probably never stop messing up, and she might never marry at all. But she had to stop running the risk of embarrassing her family, do everything in her power not to.

Suddenly fear of being alone for the rest of her life raised its ugly head, and cold crept up her insides. But she knew to the depth of her bones that it was better to be alone than to marry the wrong person. As her tears began to flow again, she whispered a prayer.

"Lord, I'm sorry it took me so long to realize how sinful I've really been. Please forgive me. But please also heal my heart. Will belongs with Caroline, but I've felt closer to him than to anyone else, including my cousins and my parents. Help me not to miss him for the rest of my life. I feel so lost and alone."

She paused to take a deep breath.

"Only you can help me live in a way that's pleasing to you—and to my parents. I know they only want what's best for me. And even if you never intend for me to marry, I know you'll be with me. Amen."

Then, hugging her arms to her chest, she sobbed with a sorrow difficult to bear.

• • •

Friday evening, Salina forked two meatballs and a sausage onto her bed of spaghetti before adding tomato sauce. She sliced the sausage and then took a bite.

"I have a question for you, Salina," *Dat* said.

Salina looked at his stony face and braced herself. *"Ya?"*

"Neil told me something today. Ellen heard a rumor that you and Josiah broke up after church last Sunday. Is that true?"

Salina met her mother's surprised expression and then nodded. "It's true."

Dat dropped his fork on his plate and glared at her. "Why didn't you tell us?"

Salina sat up straighter. "Because I knew you wouldn't approve."

Mamm and *Dat* exchanged a look. To Salina's surprise, her mother looked sad more than upset. She reached across the table and touched Salina's hand. "I'm sorry you didn't feel comfortable telling us."

"We had a right to know." *Dat* jabbed the tabletop with his finger as if to make his point. "And I hope Josiah tells his parents soon."

She hoped so too. Otherwise, they'd hear it from her father.

Salina suddenly felt courage she hadn't expected swelling inside her, and she stopped fidgeting. "I didn't want to argue about it with you once the decision was made, and I still don't. It was mutual. Josiah was just as unhappy as I was in our relationship, but we're still *freinden*. Everything is better this way. Now he's free to ask out a *maedel* he recently met and wants to date."

Dat studied her as she fingered her placemat. "Is this because of that Mennonite?"

She shook her head. "No."

"Don't lie to me, Salina. I know you and he like each other."

Salina looked out the window and then back at him. "I do care about Will, but he has a girlfriend, and I've cut off my relationship with him. I'm not even going to deliver to his restaurant anymore. Our friendship and our business relationship are both over. You don't have to worry about him."

Dat gave a curt nod. "*Gut*. You're not to see him or have anything to do with him. You're not to be his *freind*. Just stay away from him." Then he looked down at his plate and began eating.

Salina fought the urge to say she didn't need him telling her to do what she'd just committed to doing. But he didn't trust her now. And she'd meant it when she asked God to help her be a good daughter.

After supper Salina carried the plates and utensils to the counter while *Mamm* began filling one side of the sink with hot water.

"You know, Salina," *Mamm* began as she added soap, "you need to let your *dat* know what's going on in your life. He is the leader in our community, and he wants what's best for you."

Salina turned toward her mother. "I know. And with God's help, I'll find my way. Then I hope *Dat* will be able to trust me."

Mamm nodded. "I'm sure he will."

"*Danki.*"

Now Salina just needed God to show her what path he wanted her to take.

. . .

On Sunday afternoon after church, Salina stepped onto the porch at the *daadihaus* where her grandparents lived and looked out toward the barn. Her father was out there talking with

Neil and the other men in her family. She walked to the end of the porch and leaned on the railing, breathing in the cooler air that had descended on Lancaster County in the past week. It was a beautiful early October day, and as Salina took in the gorgeous flowers blooming in *Mammi*'s garden, the colorful marigolds, zinnias, chrysanthemums, and mums seemed to smile up at her. Were they mocking her sad mood?

The back door opened, and *Mammi* appeared. "Hi, Salina."

Salina gave her a half smile. "Hi."

Mammi sat down on the swing. "Why didn't you go to the youth gathering with the rest of your cousins?"

Salina shrugged as she turned and leaned back on the railing. "I just didn't feel like it."

"Sit with me and talk for a while." *Mammi* patted the porch swing beside her.

Salina sat down before pushing the swing into motion. "Your flowers are *schee*, *Mammi*."

"Danki."

They swung in silence for a few moments.

"Salina, you've always been my quiet one, but today you seem quieter than usual. And you seem awfully *bedauerlich*." *Mammi* placed her wrinkled hand on Salina's. "Would you please tell me what's wrong?"

Salina nodded as she tried to put her feelings into words. Then the dam inside her burst, and she began sharing everything burdening her heart. *"Mei dat* has been pressuring me to marry Josiah for some time. But Josiah and I were dating only because our parents insisted we were a match. When we were finally honest with each other, admitting we were only *freinden*, we broke up. That was two weeks ago."

She took a shaky breath. "We're both interested in other

people, but the man I care for is dating someone else. In fact, he's in a long-term relationship with her, and I know now that he'll never break up with her for me." Her voice wobbled. "He's an Old Order Mennonite too. I'm in love with him. No matter how hard I try, I can't get my heart to forget him. I've prayed and prayed . . ."

She looked down at her lap. "I miss him, *Mammi*. And I feel so lonely. Christiana is planning her wedding, and I'm here feeling sorry for myself—which is *not* how I want to feel." She fought tears. "And now that Christiana is making a family of her own . . . I'm *froh* for her, but I already miss her. I feel like I'm losing everyone. I've never felt this lonely before."

"*Ach, mei liewe.*" *Mammi* rubbed Salina's hand. "You're not alone. Your family loves you. *Ich liebe dich.*"

"*Danki.* I love you too. I just feel so lost and confused."

"Did you say he's Old Order Mennonite?"

Salina nodded. "He is. Will's the one who owns the restaurant where I was making deliveries. But I'm not making them anymore."

Mammi looked out toward the barns and patted Salina's arm. "One of my best *freinden* married an Old Order Mennonite man when she was around your age."

Salina's stomach did a somersault, but then reality set in. "But he wasn't dating someone else, was he?"

"No, he wasn't, but he fell in love with her, and he became Old Order Amish for her." *Mammi* smiled. "Just because Will is Old Order Mennonite doesn't mean you can't be together."

"But I'm not his first choice. He's dating someone else, and they've been together for three years. I was so wrong to even think he might choose me over her. His girlfriend deserves him more than I do, but I'm sure she could tell I'd developed feelings for Will. He . . . he had feelings for me, too, although not like he has for her. It was more like a great friendship. Anyway, it had to hurt her." Salina looked down at her lap again as regret clawed its way into her shoulders. "I'm so embarrassed by my behavior."

"You didn't mean to hurt her. You were just overwhelmed by your emotions. We don't choose who we love. It just happens. And if that person isn't the one we're supposed to spend the rest of our life with, God guides us to the person who is."

Salina shook her head. "Maybe I don't deserve love."

"Don't say that." *Mammi* took Salina's hand in hers. "God has the perfect plan for you. When it's time, he'll lead you to your life partner. You're *schee*, *schmaert*, and a shrewd business-woman. I'm so proud of what you've done with your garden. A Plain man who will appreciate you and love you for the rest of his life is out there. Just trust God in your moments of sadness. He's working for you in ways you could never imagine. I can feel it in here." *Mammi* touched her chest. "You just be patient."

"I'll try my best, *Mammi*." Salina rested her head on her grandmother's shoulder. She hoped *Mammi* was right, that God would send her a man who would love and cherish her. But it wouldn't be Will.

CHAPTER 29

Will nodded to some of the other members in his congregation as he walked out of church the following Sunday. "Will!"

He turned toward his older brother, who was waving at him as he stood beside his wife and daughter.

"Come over and spend the afternoon with us," Irvin said. "*Mamm*, *Dat*, and Roger are coming too."

"*Ya*, *Onkel* Will," Heather called. "Come visit with us."

Will nodded. "All right. I will."

"Yay!" Heather jumped up and down and cheered.

Will followed Irvin's buggy in his up the street and around the corner to the large, two-story brick home his brother had built for Karen before he married her seven years ago. It was a beautiful home, complete with three barns in the back, a large fenced-in pasture, and a huge garden where Karen grew tomatoes, cucumbers, and lettuce.

A garden.

Salina.

Will jammed his eyes shut and rubbed the bridge of his nose as soon as he parked his buggy. Thoughts of Salina had assaulted his mind ever since she'd broken off their friendship two and a half weeks ago. Her confession still haunted him.

She loved him! She wanted to be with him! If he closed his

eyes, he could hear her words over and over. His heart craved her, but how could they possibly be together? Yet he couldn't stop the memories of her beautiful smile, her adorable laugh, or her gorgeous eyes from filling his mind throughout the day. Most nights he dreamed he was in the kitchen at the restaurant talking and laughing with her. Other nights he dreamed they were sitting on a bench by a pond, holding hands and sharing their deepest secrets.

But each morning he woke up alone, longing for her companionship. And each day, he thought about what Roger had said, that he shouldn't let his life become the mess his office was. So—

"Will?"

His eyes snapped open as someone leaned into the buggy. "Hey, *Dat*."

His father gave him a strange expression. "Are you going to come inside with the rest of us?"

"*Ya*." Will climbed out of the buggy and unhitched it before putting his horse in the pasture. Then he walked inside, where the rest of his family was just sitting down to lunch at the large kitchen table. He settled beside Roger, and after prayer, he made a chicken salad sandwich.

"Where's Caroline?" *Mamm* asked from across the table.

"She's staying with her *krank aenti* in Western Pennsylvania. She hopes to be back in a couple of weeks." *That's when I'll tell her.*

"*Ach*, I'm so sorry to hear that," *Mamm* said. "I hope her *aenti* gets better sooner rather than later."

Will nodded and took another bite of his sandwich. He glanced at the end of the table, where Karen sat close to Irvin. His brother had his arm stretched over her shoulders. Heather asked her mother a question, and Karen leaned down close to her, smiling as she answered her.

One more time, Will imagined building a home for Caroline, having children with her, and spending the rest of his life with her. But he knew to the depth of his bones that he didn't want those things with her. She wasn't the one God had chosen for him, and he had to release her. He just didn't know how after all the time they'd invested in their relationship.

After lunch Will followed his brothers and father to the sun-room. Roger and Irvin sat down, but Will walked on out to the pasture. He leaned on the white split-rail fence and stared at the horses.

Dat came up beside him and leaned on the fence too. They stood in silence for several moments, Will waiting for the question sure to come.

Finally, *Dat* turned to him. "I've seen you upset before, but I've never seen you like this. I'm afraid to ask you what's wrong, but I'm also afraid to not ask."

Will snorted as he looked at him. "Why are you afraid to ask?"

"I guess I'm worried that you're going to tell me something really bad happened. Have you run into trouble with the res-taurant? Do you need money?"

"No." Will ran his fingers over the fence. "That's the one thing that's going right in my life right now."

"Then what's going wrong?"

Will gazed across the pasture, taking in the beautiful roll-ing hills and trees decorated with colorful fall leaves. "I've been living a lie."

"What do you mean?"

"I've been with Caroline for three years now, but when I think about my future, I don't envision spending it with her."

"Oh. I had no idea. Have you told her this?"

"No." Will nearly groaned as guilt grasped all the muscles in his chest like an invisible hand.

"Why not?"

"I haven't known what to say because anything I say will hurt her. I know she loves me. She tells me all the time, and I see it in her eyes."

"But you don't love her?"

Will hesitated. "I think I convinced myself I did. But then when she started mentioning marriage all the time, pressuring me to propose, I realized—" He swallowed back the shame he felt, letting Caroline believe their relationship was solid when it wasn't. "I think I have to break up with her and give her a chance to find someone who truly loves her and wants to marry her. And that's what I thought five minutes ago. But I made a promise. I told her I would marry her when I saved up enough money for a *haus*."

"But if you haven't proposed to her, you haven't truly made a promise. People change, and sometimes the Lord's plan for us can change. If you feel in your heart that Caroline isn't the one, God may be sending you a message." He paused. "*Sohn*, I think she's going to be hurt no matter what you do."

Will looked down at his shoes. "I know. It's just that she stood by me as I struggled to open the restaurant, and she still supports me. For a while I thought I owed it to her to stay by her side, but as I said, she's not the *maedel* I imagine when I think about my future."

"Now you're telling me the whole story. You've met someone else."

Will covered his eyes with one hand and sighed. "*Ya*, I have. And I feel terrible about it."

"Tell me about her."

Will let his hand fall to his side. "Her name is Salina, and she's Amish. She's the *maedel* who had been supplying most of the produce for my restaurant. She's *schee*, funny, and *schmaert*."

"And you're in love with her," *Dat* finished.

"*Ya*, I am. But I don't know what to do."

"*Ya*, you do." *Dat* gave him a knowing look. "You need to break up with Caroline and tell Salina how you feel."

"It's more complicated than that. Salina has stopped talking to me. She came to the restaurant and . . ." His throat seemed to thicken. "And she told me she loved me and wanted to be with me. I was so stunned and confused that I couldn't respond. When I didn't, she told me she couldn't deliver to my restaurant anymore, and I haven't seen her in more than two weeks."

"Why haven't you gone after her?"

Will felt desperation well up inside of him. "How can I be sure Salina is God's plan for me? How do I know I don't belong with Caroline?"

Dat sighed as he looked out toward the pasture. "I dated a *maedel* named Vera for a couple of years before I met your *mamm*. I was certain I was going to marry her, but we grew apart. Then my heart came alive when I saw your mother. I broke up with Vera, and I married your *mamm* about a year later."

"Was your family upset with your decision to marry *Mamm* instead?"

Dat looked confused. "Why would my family be upset?"

"Because they all expected you to marry Vera. I feel like everyone *expects* me to marry Caroline. Her family and our family talk about when we're married and have *kinner* all the time. If I break up with her, I'll be hurting everyone."

"The families will forgive you, and Caroline will move on with her life. Many of us don't marry our first loves."

Will nodded. But his doubt wouldn't go away.

"This is *your* life, William. This is *your* decision. It's not up to me whom you marry. It's up to you and God, and your *mamm* and I just want our *kinner* to be *froh*." *Dat* rested his hand on Will's shoulder. "You decide who will be your *fraa*. If God has put love in your heart for Salina, then you need to talk to her. Tell her how you feel. Then you need to decide if you want to be with her. If so, you both have another decision to make—if you're going to become Amish or she's going to become Mennonite."

"Her father is the bishop."

Dat grimaced. "Oh, then maybe you need to think about whether you want to become Amish. Is that where God is leading you?"

"The more I've thought about this in the last couple of weeks, the more I've begun to believe he is. But along with all my other confusion, I'm still not sure."

"You need to really think about that. But before you do anything else, including talking to Salina, you need to be honest with Caroline as soon as she returns. You owe her that."

Will took a deep breath. "I know you're right. And our talk has helped. I know what I have to do. *Danki, Dat.*"

Now he had to figure out what he was going to say to Caroline. First he had to gently apologize for leading her on for so many years. He prayed she would forgive him, and he hoped she'd find her true love, someone who would cherish her for the rest of her life. Surely such a lovely *maedel* would easily meet someone new and move on with her life.

But then he had to face his next issue. He had to find out if

Salina would even consider giving him a chance after all the mistakes he'd made.

And he had to ask for God's help.

Please, God, let both Caroline and Salina find it in their hearts to forgive me.

. . .

Salina looked up from her accounting log book as her cousins walked into the Farm Stand the following Friday morning.

"*Gude mariye*, Salina," Bethany sang with that bright smile of hers as she held up a cup of coffee and a chocolate donut. "It's your favorite—vanilla-flavored *kaffi*."

"*Danki.*" Salina took the cup and donut as her three cousins looked on. "What's going on?"

"We're here for an intervention." Leanna pulled a stool over and sat down.

Christiana stood beside her. "You haven't said much to us in two weeks, so we're here to check on you."

"That's right." Bethany wagged a finger at Salina. "You haven't joined us for *kaffi* and donuts in the mornings, and you haven't talked much at church. So here we are."

"What's going on?" Leanna asked.

"Nothing." Salina shrugged as she took a sip of coffee. "I've just been busy. I work in my garden, can my vegetables, help out with chores at home."

"Are you sure it's not Will?" Christiana asked. "You know we could all see you had feelings for him the day the youth group met at your *haus*."

"I didn't tell them!" Bethany said.

"I know you didn't," Salina told her. "But I also know if it was obvious to one of you, it was obvious to you all. No, it's not Will. I haven't seen him or heard from him." The words nearly broke her heart. In the deepest recesses of her mind, Salina had hoped that Will would realize he loved her, break up with Caroline, and tell Salina he was sorry and wanted a relationship with her. But she knew how selfish and prideful those thoughts were, so she'd buried them, telling herself Caroline was the one who had won Will's heart.

"I'm sorry." Bethany touched her shoulder. "I hoped it would turn out differently."

"It's fine." Salina picked up her donut. "I'm relying on God to get me through this. He'll heal my heart, and then I can move on." Then she took a bite.

"That's right." Leanna stood. "You need to forget Will. He isn't the one God intends for you. If he were, he would have come after you. You'll meet someone else."

"Come back to youth group with me," Bethany said. "You'll meet someone else. We have a combined event on Sunday. We're going to play volleyball over in Ronks, and plenty of Amish guys our age will be there."

Salina shrugged. "I'll think about it." She couldn't imagine meeting someone else when her heart still belonged to Will, but she couldn't admit that to her cousins. It was too awkward and uncomfortable. "So, Christiana, how are the wedding plans going?"

Christiana's expression brightened as if she'd never expected Salina to ask. "It's going well. I'm working on the dresses, and I think I have the table decorations figured out. I'm thinking about a small candle that matches the green in the dresses, along with some baby's breath and maybe a little basket with green mints. But I'm not sure."

Salina nodded and feigned interest, her heart breaking with each word Christiana spoke. Were Caroline and Will planning a fall ceremony too?

. . .

Will wiped his sweaty hands on the legs of his jeans before knocking on Caroline's front door. Waiting for her to return home from Western Pennsylvania had been torture—especially since her aunt had a relapse and Caroline had stayed an extra two weeks. God was in control, but Will had told him he didn't think he could wait much longer.

Salina had probably given up on him, but that didn't mean he wouldn't try to win her back. He just had to tell Caroline his decision first.

After a few moments, he heard footfalls in the hallway, and then the door opened, revealing Caroline through the glass storm door. She pushed it open and smiled. "Will. Hi. I'm so glad to see you after all these weeks!" She touched his arm, and he kissed her cheek.

"Thanks for letting me know as soon as you were back. How is your *aenti*?"

"She's doing much better. *Danki*." She beckoned him to come into the house.

He followed her into the kitchen, where he waved hello to her parents and sister. *"Wie geht's?"*

They all greeted him, and then he followed Caroline into the family room.

She pointed to the sofa. "Would you like to sit?"

"I thought we could talk outside. You'll just need a light sweater. It's not too cold, and it's such a nice Sunday afternoon."

"Oh. Okay. I'll just grab one." Caroline retrieved a gray button-down sweater from the hall closet and then led him to the back door.

Will's nerves felt as if they were standing on end as they sat down on the porch swing.

Caroline immediately threaded her fingers with his as she pushed the swing into motion. "I missed you while I was gone."

He angled his body toward her and tried to remember what he'd practiced on his way there. "Caroline, I've been doing a lot of thinking, and I need to talk you about some things."

"Oh." Her smile faded. "What do you need to talk about?"

He paused and cleared his throat as he gathered his thoughts. "You mean so much to me. You've been my best *freind* for years now, and you stood by me while I was struggling to open the restaurant. When I wanted to give up and just go back to working as a cook, you encouraged me. You were my rock when I was at my lowest."

A worried look flashed over her face, but he pushed on.

"You're sweet, kind, and loyal. You always see the best in people, and you're always positive no matter how tough a situation is."

"Will, what are you trying to say?" Her voice trembled.

He took her hands in his. "I think the world of you, and I'm so grateful that God led me to you. We've had some *wunderbaar* times together, and I will always cherish those memories." He took a deep breath and searched for the right words to continue as an awkward moment passed between them.

Caroline pulled her hands away. "Please tell me what you're thinking, Will. You're scaring me."

He looked out toward the farm that backed up to her family's property. "I don't know how to say this."

"Just say it." Her voice had fallen to a whisper.

"I don't want to hurt you. You're so special, and you should have all the happiness in the world." Now his words came out in a tumbled rush. "But I have to be honest with you. I know this is going to hurt you, and I'm sorry. But you need to know the truth." He paused and pinched the bridge of his nose. "You deserve someone who loves you completely and who will always keep you at the forefront of his mind."

"What do you mean?" She spoke so softly he almost hadn't heard her.

"I'm saying I don't think we should see each other anymore. I'm not the right man for you."

She clapped her hand over her mouth. "Are you breaking up with me?"

Will looked at her, and the tears streaming down her face nearly broke him in two. "I think it's for the best, and I'm so sorry. Almost more than anything, I don't want to hurt you. I've tried to make it work for a long time, but I just don't feel the way I used to. And I believe you'll find a man who will love you and cherish you the way you should be loved and cherished."

She wiped her eyes as her expression changed. Now she looked furious. "You said you'd marry me when you had enough money for a *haus*. You lied to me! You just told me that to shut me up."

He reached for her hand, and she swatted his away. "I wanted to believe it so badly. But now I get *You deserve someone who loves you without reservations, Caroline. You are so kind and generous, Caroline. But I don't believe I'm the man for you, Caroline.*" She nearly spat the words at him.

She was seething now. "This is about Salina, isn't it? You just said you don't feel the way you used to, and she's the only thing that's changed. You're leaving me for *her*. I knew you loved her. I could tell. I've been a moron making myself believe you loved *me*." She pointed to her chest.

"It's not Salina." He shook his head. "We're not *freinden* anymore. She stopped talking to me weeks ago."

"Right," she deadpanned. "You're probably going to go to her the minute you leave here." She stood and strode across the porch, putting her back to him.

He walked over to her, reaching for her shoulder but then pulling back his hand. "No, I'm not leaving you to be with her. I'm only telling you the truth. I need to let you go so you can find the right man to marry. I've been holding on to you for too long, and I'm so sorry. I hope you can forgive me someday."

She looked up at him with tears streaking her face. "Just go."

"Caroline, can you forgive me?"

"Will, just go." She looked back out toward the cows. "I want to be alone."

He bit his lip and then nodded. "I'll go. But believe me when I say I will always cherish my memories with you. *Danki* for being a part of my life."

He descended the steps and headed around the house to his waiting horse and buggy.

Guilt plagued him as he traveled down the driveway toward the road. He hoped Caroline would understand what he'd done someday. He hadn't wanted to hurt her, but to delay their breakup any longer would have been cruel. He'd wanted to let her down easy, but as he told her the truth, he could see more pain in her eyes than he'd expected. He'd been a fool.

His grief pressed down on him, and he asked God to bring Caroline peace and comfort.

CHAPTER 30

Will walked into his parents' living room later that evening, still in a daze.

"William!" *Dat* said. "We were hoping you'd come by."

As Will sank onto a chair, he glanced across the room and did a double take. Roger was sitting on the sofa, but he wasn't alone. He was holding hands with Danielle. When had Roger started dating her? Had he been so absorbed with his own problems that he hadn't noticed Roger and Danielle had moved from friendship to something more?

"Hi," they told him in unison. Roger grinned. Danielle smiled sheepishly.

"Hi," he said, a little stunned.

"Hi, Will. Would you like a piece of apple pie?" *Mamm* asked as she came in from the kitchen. "We just finished one, but I made two."

"*Ya*." Will stood. "I'll get it."

"Let me," *Mamm* said.

"*Danki*, but I'll come with you." Will followed *Mamm* into the kitchen, where she took some vanilla ice cream from the freezer and then began slicing a pie that smelled as if it had just come out of her warming oven.

"Where have you been?" *Mamm* asked.

"I went to see Caroline."

"She's back?" *Mamm* put a piece of the pie on a plate and added a scoop of ice cream before handing it to him.

"*Danki. Ya*, she's back."

"How is her *aenti*?"

"Better." He scooped a bite of pie into his mouth and enjoyed the taste. He may be a chef, but nothing beat *Mamm*'s apple pie.

"Why didn't you bring her with you?"

Will took another bite of pie and then swallowed. "Because we broke up." Then he shoved a bite of ice cream into his mouth and waited for her shocked reaction.

But *Mamm* just nodded. "It's about time."

Will sucked in a breath and started to choke. Coughing, he set the plate on the kitchen table.

"Calm down." *Mamm* rubbed his back and handed him a paper towel. "It's okay. I'm sorry for surprising you."

"I wasn't expecting that reaction." Will wiped at his eyes.

"I've just had a feeling you haven't been *froh* for a while now. You seemed like you couldn't breathe when Caroline was around. It was as if you couldn't be yourself with her."

Will tilted his head. "Really?"

"*Ya*, really."

He picked up the plate and took another bite of pie.

"Are you going to ask out that Amish *maedel* now?"

Will narrowed his eyes. "How did you know?" Then it hit him. "*Dat* told you."

"*Ya*, he did. We talk about you and your *bruders*. We worry about you all." *Mamm* smiled. "Salina sounds special."

"She is. But did *Dat* tell you her father is the bishop in their district? I keep thinking about how I feel about her, forgetting I don't think he'd ever approve of me. Salina says he tells the young people in the community they should marry within the community. He doesn't trust outsiders." He sighed as he looked down at the half-eaten pie. "Did *Dat* also tell you the last time we spoke, she confessed her feelings to me? She told me she loved me and wanted to be with me. I just froze and didn't respond to her because I was confused and shocked. I'm sure that hurt her."

He shook his head. "Now I need to tell her Caroline and I broke up and show her how much I care for her. But I don't know how. I also need to show her I'm ready to make her the priority in my life." He sat down on a chair with a thud and then looked at his mother. "Do you have a suggestion?"

"*Ya*. Make a grand gesture. Go see her. Talk to her. And after you talk to her, talk to her father. Show her whole family you love her." *Mamm*'s expression was full of optimism. "If it's meant to be, God will find a way. He always finds a way."

Will nodded as hope took root in his heart. Maybe he could convince Salina to give him another chance. He'd worry about her father and the rest of her family later.

Please give me an opportunity to talk to her, God.

. . .

Salina walked out of the grocery store with her mother Tuesday morning, and then they loaded their groceries into her father's buggy before climbing inside.

"Would you like to have lunch out?" *Mamm* asked as Salina guided the horse toward the road. "We didn't buy anything perishable except what would fit into the cooler we brought. Besides, the weather is so much cooler now."

"Sure. Where do you want to go?"

"How about there?" *Mamm* pointed to the sign for Zimmerman's Family Restaurant. "Of course, it's up to you."

Salina hesitated as her heart flipped. She'd have to face Will sometime. But was she ready? Maybe she just needed to get this over with. He might stay in the kitchen anyway. "Okay."

"Gut." Mamm rubbed her hands together. "I love a *gut* buffet."

"Ya, I do too." Salina steered the horse to a hitching post and tied it up before they walked into the restaurant.

"Hi, Salina," Minerva said as they approached the podium.

"Hi." Salina gestured toward her mother. "This is *mei mamm,* Mary."

"It's nice to meet you. We're excited to have the buffet today," *Mamm* said.

"Great. Follow me." Minerva led them to a nearby table. "Today's special is roast beef. We also have baked chicken and salmon." She took their drink orders before leaving.

"It smells fantastic," *Mamm* said as they made their way to the buffet.

"It always does."

Salina scanned the restaurant as they filled their plates. She spotted the other servers she knew, but she didn't see Will. That was probably a good thing, but part of her longed to see him. She still missed him and craved their special talks, but he'd chosen Caroline over her, and she had to accept that and move on. That's what she'd asked God to help her do, and maybe coming here today was part of his plan.

Once their plates were full and they each had a bowl of salad, Salina and her mother walked back to their table and sat down. After a silent prayer, they began to eat.

"This is delicious," *Mamm* said. "The best roast beef I've ever had."

"It is *gut*."

"And it's awfully busy here." *Mamm* took a bite of her salad as she scanned the dining room.

Salina forced herself not to look toward the kitchen, but her stomach tightened when she realized Minerva might have told Will she was here.

"You remember your *dat* saying Will is off-limits, Salina. You don't need to even think about him."

Salina's eyes snapped to her mother's. Had *Mamm* suggested they come here as some kind of test? "I understand."

"*Gut*."

But as much as Salina understood, she prayed for her heart's desire. *If it's your will, Lord, please bring Will back to me.*

. . .

"Will, someone is here I think you'll want to see."

Will turned as Minerva walked over to the counter where he was slicing the roast beef he'd just taken out of the oven. He wiped his hands on a cloth and looked at her. "Who is it?"

"Salina."

The name was like music to Will's ears, yet he froze even as his heart sped up, reaching a lurching gallop. "Salina. She's here in the restaurant now?"

Minerva nodded. "She's eating with her *mamm*." She pointed toward the dining room. "They're sitting near the front of the restaurant close to the podium."

"Oh." Will shook his head and looked down at the roast beef. "I have to get this ready to go out."

"Will." Minerva gave him a knowing look. "I know you miss her. It's been apparent every day since she stopped delivering to the restaurant. Go talk to her."

Roger walked over to Will. "Go on. I'll take care of the roast beef." His brother and staff all knew about his breakup with Caroline, and there was no more hiding his feelings for Salina.

Will stepped into the dining room, forcing himself to smile at customers as he scanned the front of the room for Salina. When his eyes found her, his body thrummed with excitement. This was his chance to make things right between them. He could tell her he loved her! This was the opportunity he'd asked God to give him.

But then he calmed down. After all, her mother was here too. He squared his shoulders and approached their table.

When Salina's gaze met his, she stilled, and her eyes widened. She looked beautiful in a rose-colored dress, and her eyes sparkled under the fluorescent lights. She blinked, but she remained silent. Was she happy to see him? He wasn't sure, but he wasn't going to walk away.

"Salina." He smiled as his pulse raced. "How nice to see you."

"Hi, Will." Salina took a sip from her glass of water without taking her eyes off him.

He turned to her mother. "Hi, Mary." He held out his hand. "It's nice to see you again."

"It's *gut* to see you." Mary shook his hand and then shared a look with Salina before she said, "The food here is *appeditlich*."

"*Danki*. Please enjoy your lunch on me."

"No." Mary shook her head. "That's not necessary. We'll pay for our meal. But thank you for the offer."

Will turned to Salina, and she looked down at her plate. He needed to talk to her alone so he could tell her what was in his heart. He wanted to tell her he loved her. But her mother sat there staring at him, judging him. At least her father wasn't there.

The silence between them stretched as conversations from surrounding tables seemed to grow louder.

Will looked at Mary. "If you need anything, please let me know. I hope you enjoy the rest of your lunch."

"*Danki.*" Mary gave him a smile that seemed forced.

Will moved to the buffet, where he busied himself with rearranging the salad bar, adding the additional lettuce and tomatoes Valerie had just brought out on a cart. He tried to focus on the task at hand, but his gaze kept moving to Salina's table. She was frowning as her mother spoke to her. Were they talking about him?

Then Mary got up from the table and walked toward the restrooms, giving him his chance. With his heart pounding against his rib cage, he quickly weaved through the knot of tables until he got to Salina's.

He dropped down into the seat beside her, and she jumped.

"What are you doing?" Her brow pinched as she glowered at him.

"I've missed you. How are you?"

"I can't talk to you." She looked behind him. "You have to go before *mei mamm* gets back. She'll be furious if she sees us talking. Just go."

Her words were like ice thrown in his face.

"Give me a minute. I need to tell you something." He took a deep breath. "The truth is—"

"Will!" Danielle rushed to the table. "Roger needs you in the kitchen right now."

He shook his head. "This isn't a *gut* time."

But Danielle's expression was serious. "He said the produce vendor showed up and he can't both cook and talk with him. He needs you to come—*now*." She looked at Salina. "Hi. I'm sorry to interrupt."

Will stood as Danielle walked away and then turned to Salina. "I have to go, but we need to talk sometime soon."

"Just go, Will." She looked behind him once again. "Please, just go."

As he hurried toward the kitchen, disappointment whipped through him, but he wasn't giving up. He'd find a way to win her over—and her parents and brother too. He'd find a way to not just capture Salina's heart but to also prove to them all that he and Salina were meant to be together.

· · ·

Will walked into his office and set the invoice from his new produce vendor on his desk just as Roger appeared in the doorway. "You okay?"

"*Ya*, I am."

"How did it go with Salina?"

"We didn't get a chance to talk." Will dropped into his chair. "I was interrupted by Danielle telling me you needed me. Also, Salina told me to leave."

Roger frowned and shook his head. "I'm sorry."

"It's okay. I'm not giving up. I'll find a way to get her back."

Roger smiled. "Attaboy."

Danielle appeared in the doorway. "We need more rolls ASAP." Then she disappeared as quickly as she'd come.

"I've got it," Will told his brother.

As he busied himself in the kitchen, a calm settled over his heart. With God's help, everything would work out—one way or another.

CHAPTER 31

Salina walked into the Coffee Corner Thursday morning and was greeted by the delicious aroma of macadamia nut coffee. "Smells *appeditlich*."

Jeff held up a cup as he sat between Christiana and Leanna at their usual table. "Bethany made my favorite, and that makes my day!"

Christiana bumped her shoulder against his. "He thinks Bethany made it just for him, but she didn't."

"Don't burst his bubble. Let him think I did." Bethany held up a cup as she stood at the counter. "Here you go, Salina."

"Danki." As Salina took a sip of the delicious brew, she felt something soft rub on her leg, followed by a meow and a peep. She looked down and found Daisy blinking up at her as the small, brown tabby kitten next to her peeped again. "Why, hello there." She leaned down and rubbed Daisy's head before petting the kitten.

"Oh, it's Daisy and Lily!" Bethany pulled out two bowls of cat food, along with a bowl of water. "I thought they'd show up for breakfast soon."

"This kitty is named Lily?" Salina asked as the cats scampered over to the bowls and began eating.

"Ya. Kent took the other two kittens to his kids, but he

kept Lily here as a second marketplace cat. She's keeping Daisy company."

Salina smiled. "How nice."

"You haven't met her?" Leanna asked.

"Not since . . . I found her with Daisy." Salina sat down beside her. "I guess I've been too focused on my booth." *And my heartache.*

"I still can't believe you and Will found Daisy after we'd searched for her all day long," Leanna said. "That was a miracle."

Salina's chest squeezed at the mention of Will's name. She missed him so much that her heart still felt as if it had been torn to shreds. Every day she hoped he would walk into her booth and say hello. He'd said they needed to talk, and at least her mother wouldn't be there.

But those hopes and dreams were a waste. Whatever he'd wanted to say, he must have changed his mind.

"Gude mariye," Sara Ann sang as she swept into the booth.

Salina was certain she heard either Leanna or Christiana groan under her breath.

"Do I smell macadamia nut *kaffi*?" Sara Ann asked as she joined Bethany at the counter.

"You sure do." Bethany poured her a cup. "Here you go."

"Danki." Sara Ann paid for it and then took a sip. "Your *kaffi* is the best, Bethany."

"Danki," Bethany said as she put the money in her cash register.

Sara Ann came toward their table, and Salina bit her lip. *Please keep walking. Please keep walking.*

But Sara Ann stopped and gave her an exaggerated look of concern. "Salina, did I hear that you and Josiah broke up?"

Salina gripped the edge of the table, sure Leanna and

Christiana were just as unhappy with this conversation. "*Ya*, that's true, but it was mutual. We're still *freinden*."

"Aww. That's a shame. You were such a cute couple. I remember seeing you together in your booth." Sara Ann's face brightened. "Have you seen that handsome Mennonite? What is his name?" She tapped her chin. "Is it Will?"

Salina took a deep breath through her nose. Why did Sara Ann play these games? She knew what his name was. "No, I haven't seen him. I'm not his supplier anymore. Why?"

"I just saw his ex-girlfriend at a quilting bee. Now, what is her name?" Sara Ann snapped her fingers. "That's right. Caroline Horst. I told her I had a booth at the marketplace, and she said—"

"Did you say his *ex*-girlfriend?" Salina enunciated the *ex* as her stomach seemed to plummet to the floor.

Sara Ann's smile was sunny. "*Ya*, that's right."

"They broke up?" Salina tried to wrap her mind around this news.

"*Ya*. She was upset, but she said she didn't intend to just stay home." Sara Ann glanced at the clock on the wall. "I need to get back to my booth." She gave them all a little wave. "I'll see you later. Have a *gut* day."

"You too," Christiana muttered.

Salina tried to steady her breathing. "Will and Caroline broke up. I can't believe it."

Bethany's eyes had lit up, and she sat down beside Salina. "Maybe you still have a chance with him."

"Maybe." Salina nodded as she allowed the news to settle in her bones. Will was single! But why hadn't he told her? Of course, this didn't mean he wanted to be with her. Still, a seed of hope took root in her heart.

Salina sipped her coffee and then looked at Christiana. She had to find something else to talk about before she drove herself crazy contemplating "what-ifs."

"How are your wedding plans going? It's coming up so fast. Next Thursday, so I'm surprised you're even here today."

Christiana smiled at Jeff. "We decided to finish out this week at our booths, and then we'll be closed next week."

"Did you get the last table decorations put together?" Salina asked. "You said you were almost done when we talked yesterday."

Christiana nodded. "Phoebe and I finished them last night. We're all set."

As they continued talking, Salina tried to wipe thoughts of Will from her mind. But they came back again and again.

Bethany jumped up when a young man who looked to be in his midtwenties walked into the booth beside an elderly gentleman. Salina realized it was Micah Zook and his grandfather Enos Zook.

"Micah. Enos," Bethany sang. *"Gude mariye."*

"Gude mariye," the older man echoed as they met her by the counter.

"Would you like your usual?" Bethany's smile brightened even more when she looked at Micah.

"She seems awfully *froh* to see them," Leanna muttered.

"Why?" Christiana asked.

Leanna shrugged. "I don't know for sure, but I think she might like Micah."

"Huh." Salina watched Bethany grin as Micah gave her their order. Maybe Leanna was right.

"So. Bethany might have a crush she's not telling us about," Christiana quipped.

If that were true, Salina hoped Bethany's feelings for Micah wouldn't end in heartache like her feelings for Will had. But now that he'd broken up with Caroline, did she have a chance with him?

. . .

Will pushed open the passenger side door on Austin's van Monday morning. "I shouldn't be too long."

"Take your time," Austin said.

Will glanced down the road toward the Petersheim property and drew in a deep breath. Today was the day. After many talks with God, he'd found his solution for convincing both Salina and her family of what he desperately wanted them to know—that he and Salina belonged together. First, he'd ask for Lamar's permission to join the Amish church and date his daughter. That decision had settled in his heart, and despite some lingering trepidation about facing Lamar, he felt great peace.

He'd asked Austin to park down the road so he could walk to Lamar's place of business from the back—and return to the van without running the risk of seeing Salina if Lamar rejected him.

Will hurried toward the building with the Lancaster County Cabinets sign, but his body shook with anxiety when he peered into the showroom and found it empty. Was Lamar away somewhere?

Then he heard the sound of a hammer pounding away in the workshop where he'd used the phone to call his driver the night he ate supper with Salina's family. Memories of their time in her garden came to mind, and remembered warmth wrapped around his heart. How he missed their talks. He missed her smile, her beautiful face, her voice.

Get it together, Will!

He quietly entered the workshop and found Lamar and Neil working on a set of cabinets.

Lord, give me strength!

Squaring his shoulders, Will forced a shaky smile and raised his voice loud enough for them to hear him. "Neil. Lamar. Hello. *Wie geht's?*"

The men stopped their work and turned. Neil glared at him, but Lamar just seemed surprised. "What are you doing here?" he said.

"I'd like to speak to you. In private." Will stood a little taller to boost his confidence as Neil glowered at him. "I promise we'll be only a few minutes." *Or less if you send me away!*

Lamar glanced at his son and then nodded. "Fine." He pointed to a nearby door. "Let's go outside."

"Danki."

Will followed Lamar, and once they were outside, the older man said, "What's this about?" The expression on his face gave Will no clue how this conversation would go, but he pushed on.

"Lamar, I'm in love with your *dochder*, and she means everything to me. When I first met her, I thought we could be *freinden*, but the more I got to know her, the more I felt a deeper connection to her than I've ever felt with anyone."

He took a breath as Lamar's expression remained the same, and then he pressed on. "You probably know I was dating someone else, but I've released her so she can find the man God wants for her. I believe Salina is the woman God has for me and that I'm the man he has for her. He's brought us together."

Lamar crossed his arms over his wide chest. "Is that so?"

"*Ya*. I want to date Salina, and with God's blessing and your blessing, eventually marry her." He held up his hand to stop Lamar from cutting in. "I know you tell the young people in your community they need to marry within their community, and so I'm also begging you to let me join your community. I'll become Amish, and I'll live the proper way an Amish man needs to live. Please. I'll do anything you ask."

Lamar brushed a hand down his long, graying beard and searched Will's eyes. "You're telling me you want to become Amish so you can date my Salina."

"*Ya*, I am. I've prayed about this, and I feel sure God has led me to this decision." Will folded his hands as if he were pleading. "I'll buy a *haus* and make a home here in Bird-in-Hand. Then I'll keep running my restaurant and take care of Salina. I feel certain this is God's plan." He paused and searched for the words to convince this man he was sincere. "Lamar, do you remember when you fell in love with Mary?"

Lamar flinched as if Will had caught him off guard. "Why do you ask?"

"Do you remember that intense love that just consumed every cell of your body? That feeling that you would move mountains to have her by your side?"

Lama nodded. "I do."

"That's how I feel about Salina. The worst day of my life was the day she stopped talking to me. Now I'll do anything to have her by my side. And it would be an honor to join your community."

A few moments passed between them, and Will was almost certain Lamar could hear his heartbeat banging like the hammer in his workshop behind him.

"You truly feel that God is calling you to the Amish church?" Lamar finally asked.

"I do. I believe it in my heart, and I can feel it in my bones."

"Do you truly love my Salina, and do you promise to do your best to make her *froh* and take care of her?"

"*Ya.* If she'll have me."

"Are your reasons for wanting to join the Amish church pure?"

"*Ya.*"

"Then you'll have to attend three baptism classes in the spring. After that you'll be a member. We'll honor your Mennonite baptism."

"I understand. *Danki.*"

To Will's surprise, Lamar gave his hand a firm shake. "You have my blessing. And I'll tell you the truth. *Mei dochder* has missed you."

"She has?"

"*Ya.* Her *mamm* and I didn't want to see it. Her *bruder* still doesn't. But it's true. I suggest you talk with her as soon as possible."

"I will. But you won't say anything to her until I do, will you?"

"No." He paused and looked out over the fields. "But I do need to tell her a few things myself."

Will didn't know what Lamar meant, but he felt as if he might collapse with relief. Now he had to tell his family the news and win back Salina's heart.

. . .

Later that evening Austin parked the van in Will's parents' driveway. "Do you want me to wait for you?"

"No, thanks. I'll walk home." He looked out at the clear sky. "It's a beautiful night."

"It's not very warm. You know it's November, right?"

"I know. I'll see you tomorrow." Will shook Austin's hand and then climbed out of the van and started up the driveway.

The back door opened just as his foot reached the top step. *Dat* peered through the storm door and then pushed it open. "What a surprise. What are you doing here?"

"I was hoping to talk to you and *Mamm* for a few minutes."

"Of course. Come in."

Will followed his father into the kitchen, where *Mamm* sat at the table writing on a notepad.

"We have a visitor, Shirley," *Dat* said.

"Oh." *Mamm* jumped up. "Let me put on a pot of *kaffi*."

"No, it's okay. Please sit." Will pulled off his coat and hung it on the back of a kitchen chair before sitting. "I want to talk to you both."

Dat frowned. "Uh-oh. This sounds serious."

"*Ya.*" Will cupped his hand to the back of his neck as he considered how to begin. Then he took a deep breath. "You both know I have feelings for an Amish *maedel* named Salina."

Mamm nodded. "You've told us."

"Well, I feel in my heart that God has led me to her."

"Okay." *Dat*'s eyes narrowed. "What are you getting at, Will?"

"I've told you that her father is the bishop of her community, and you know the only way we can be together is if one of us converts."

"And you want to be Amish for her." *Mamm* smiled.

"*Ya*, I do."

"If you're asking our permission, we support you. We just want our *kinner* to be *froh*. Right?" *Dat* turned to *Mamm*.

"Exactly, Gary."

"So, then, you'll support me if I move to Bird-in-Hand and become Amish?" Will asked.

"Of course we will," *Mamm* said.

"Thank goodness." Will felt the muscles in his back and shoulders relax. "I met with her father today, and he gave me permission to join the community."

Dat gasped. "You did?"

Will nodded.

"And what about Salina?" *Mamm* asked.

"He said I can date her. He even admitted she's missed me. Now I just have to win her back."

"I'm so *froh* for you." *Mamm* covered his hand with hers. "You just make sure you bring those grandchildren over to see me frequently."

Will held up his hands. "Hold on now. Let me see if Salina will even date me before we start talking about grandchildren."

His parents laughed, and he joined in. He was grateful for their unwavering support.

. . .

Will knocked on his brother's door after the three-block walk home through the crisp November night. After a few moments, the door opened and Roger peered at him. He looked confused.

"Why are you knocking on my door this late?" Roger asked.

"I just got home. I've been at *Mamm* and *Dat*'s. Do you have a minute?"

"Sure." Roger opened the storm door and motioned for Will to follow him up the stairs to his apartment, which was nearly identical to Will's below.

They sat across from each other in the family room with Will on the worn brown sofa and Roger in the matching recliner.

"What's going on?" Roger asked.

"Remember when I ran to the market this morning for a few spices?" Will asked. Roger nodded. "I ran into the guy who's marrying Salina's cousin Christiana. Jeff invited me to their wedding on Thursday. Would you mind if I leave the restaurant after the lunch rush so I can go?"

"Sure." Roger shrugged. "What's the emergency, though? Why couldn't you have asked me that tomorrow?"

"Because there's more. I didn't tell you where else I went this morning." Will explained his conversation with Lamar. "I'm sorry I didn't tell you, but I was afraid Salina's father would tell me no. Then I got to the restaurant, and it was so busy we didn't have a minute to talk alone before you and Danielle left together. I just talked to *Mamm* and *Dat*. They support me, but I wanted to check with you as well."

Roger studied him for a moment. "Is this what you truly want?"

"*Ya*, it is. During my walk home, I thought about how my life will change. I'll have to give up electricity in my new home and change the way I dress. The way I worship with my community will change too. But I'll still be the same man with the same beliefs I've always had. I have a sense of peace I haven't had in months. This feels like the right answer, and I believe it came from God."

Roger smiled. "It sounds like you've made up your mind. I'll support you as long as you don't give up the restaurant."

"I won't. We'll still be business partners. I can have a restaurant with electricity even when I'm Amish—just not in my home. But the produce might be supplied by *mei fraa*.

That is, if Salina will even consider me after what I've put her through."

"I think she will. Are you going to tell Irvin?"

"*Ya*, I will when I see him. Do you think he'll be supportive?"

"*Ya*, I do. He'll be relieved that you're finally planning to settle down."

Will smiled. He was grateful Roger understood and had his back. Now he had to convince Salina that they belonged together. As far as he knew, she didn't even know he and Caroline were no longer together, and he trusted her father to keep his promise not to tell her what he and Will discussed.

A smile curled his lips as an idea filled his mind. It would involve getting to the restaurant early Thursday and pulling out that Betty Crocker cookbook. He couldn't wait to get started.

CHAPTER 32

Salina stood with Bethany and Leanna in Christiana's kitchen as the women of their church district buzzed with excitement. The day had finally come. Christiana and Jeff were going to be married!

"Salina."

She turned to see Caroline Horst walking toward her.

"Hi." Salina was so shocked to see her she couldn't think of anything else to say.

"I know you're probably surprised to see me, but Christiana's *mamm* and *schweschder* came into the bookstore yesterday, and they invited me to come. I hope you don't mind."

"Of course not. How nice." Salina was more than surprised, but then Sara Ann said Caroline had no intention of hiding out at home. "How are you?"

"I'm okay." Caroline shrugged. "How are you?"

"About the same."

Caroline's expression turned hesitant, almost nervous. "Is Will here?"

"Will?" Salina shook her head, confused. "No. He's not here." She paused and then added, "I heard you broke up."

Now Caroline looked confused. "We did. He broke up with me. But I thought it was to be with you. He didn't tell you?"

"No. I heard the news from someone at the marketplace."

"That's strange," Caroline said. "I thought for sure—" She took a deep breath. "I won't lie. The breakup hurt, and I was angry too. But after the initial shock, I finally admitted to myself that Will and I had been struggling for a long time. It wasn't working between us. Besides, I'd never want to be anyone's second choice, so if he wanted to be with you—" She pointed to the line of women walking out of the kitchen. "Oh, look. It's time to go to the barn. I'll see you inside." She paused. "I hope you're okay."

Salina nodded. "Of course." But as she watched Caroline join the line, her mind spun with confusion. Then she shook her head slowly as all the pieces of the puzzle came together at last. Will had broken up with Caroline, but not so he could be with her. Otherwise he would have told her—and right away. The tiny glimmer of hope that had taken root in her heart when she learned he was single again fizzled. She had no chance with Will. She never had.

Salina's knees wobbled, and she grasped the edge of the counter behind her to steady herself.

Bethany and Leanna sidled up to her, Bethany looking the most concerned. "We saw you and Caroline talking. What's going on?"

"You look *krank*," Leanna said.

"I am—a little. Caroline just told me Will did break up with her, just like Simply Sara Ann said. And she thought he did it because he wanted to be with me. But if that were true, he'd have told me they're not together, which means he never cared for me like I hoped. I never had a chance with him, and I still don't."

Leanna touched her arm. "He could have been waiting for you to come to him. You did say you pushed him away at the restaurant when you were there with your *mamm*."

"We have to go." Bethany took Salina's arm and tugged her. "Come on. The ceremony is about to start. We can talk about this later."

Salina let Bethany steer her out of the kitchen and to the barn, where they sat together in the unmarried women's section. Caroline was sitting in the back with one of Phoebe's friends.

Salina did her best to focus on the wedding. She marveled at how beautiful Christiana and Phoebe looked sitting at the front of the barn in their matching hunter-green dresses and how handsome Jeff and his brother, Nick, looked in their black-and-white Sunday suits as they sat across from them.

But she couldn't dismiss what Leanna said. What if she had ruined everything by turning Will away that day in the restaurant? Maybe he wanted to tell her he'd ended his relationship with Caroline then. Yes, *Mamm* was there, but Salina could have arranged to meet him somewhere later.

She shoved away the thought. This wasn't the time to dwell on the mess in her life.

She turned back to the bride and groom, who seemed to be listening intently to her father's lecture concerning the apostle Paul's instructions for marriage included in 1 Corinthians and Ephesians. Then he instructed Christiana and Jeff on how to run a godly household before moving on to a sermon on the story of Sarah and Tobias from the intertestamental book of Tobit.

The sermon took forty-five minutes, and when it was over, *Dat* looked back and forth between Christiana and Jeff. "Now here are two in one faith—Christiana Joy Kurtz and Jeffrey Merle Stoltzfus."

He turned to the congregation. "Do any of you know any scriptural reason for the couple to not be married?" He waited for a beat and then looked at the couple again. "If it is your desire to be married, you may in the name of the Lord come forth."

Jeff took Christiana's hand in his, and they stood before *Dat* to recite their vows. Then her father read "A Prayer for Those about to Be Married" from an Amish prayer book called the *Christenpflict*.

Christiana and Jeff sat down for another sermon and another prayer, and Salina willed herself to keep concentrating on what was happening right in front of her. Even if Will wanted a relationship with her, she kept forgetting he was Mennonite and she was Amish. She had her community and her family, and God was in control. That was all that mattered.

After *Dat* recited the Lord's Prayer, the congregation stood, and the three-hour service ended with the singing of another hymn.

And then it was official—Christiana and Jeff were married! Salina thought she might choke on the lump forming in her throat. Her cousin—and best friend—was Jeff's wife! She was so happy for her.

The men began rearranging the benches, and Salina had just turned toward the kitchen to help set out the wedding dinner when she heard *Dat* call her name.

"Might I talk with you for a moment?" he said when he caught up to her.

"Sure, *Dat*," she said as they moved to a quiet corner. "What's on your mind?"

Dat frowned and glanced down at his feet, and Salina braced herself. Was he angry with her, about to lecture her in front of the entire congregation and visitors? How would she ever recover from that embarrassment?

"With all the wedding preparations, this is the first time I've been able to catch you. But I owe you an apology," he said, his voice low. "I've realized that you're right about a lot of things. Most of all, you're right that I tried to force you to live a life you didn't choose. I thought I was doing what was best for you when I encouraged—no, insisted—you date and marry Josiah, but I never really paid attention to how unhappy you were until after you broke up with him. I wanted you to have a *froh* and stable life, but I couldn't admit you had a right to find it on your own."

He sighed. "I preach about following God's plan, but I couldn't even allow *mei kind* to follow the one he had for her on her own. I hope you can forgive me."

Salina's mouth dropped open. She couldn't have been more astonished.

"I've also been much too hard on you," he continued, his face expressing more regret. "I didn't realize that I constantly compared you to Neil until you pointed it out. I'm sorry for that too. I love you with my whole heart, Salina, and I'm ashamed for letting you doubt that."

He paused, and his eyes misted. "I'm proud of both *mei kinner*. You're a strong and courageous *maedel*. I'm proud of how you run a successful business at the market. I'm proud of everything you do." His smile was warm. "I just want you to be *froh*, and I'll support you in any way I can."

Tears filled her own eyes. "It's so *gut* to hear you say that, *Dat*."

"Please forgive me," he said.

"Of course I do." She gave her father a quick hug. "*Danki*."

"Lamar," a man in the congregation called. "Could I talk to you for a moment?"

"I'll see you later, Salina." *Dat* gave her hand a gentle squeeze and left.

"Salina." Josiah took her father's place. "How are you?"

"I'm *gut*." She looked him up and down, taking in his crutches.

"Much better." He looked down. "I'm hoping to get rid of these things soon." He smiled and then turned to a young lady beside him. "I want to introduce you to someone. Salina, this is Ruthie—my girlfriend."

"Hi, Ruthie." Salina smiled at the pretty brunette as she shook her hand. "How nice to meet you. I've heard *gut* things about you." She winked at Josiah, and he gave her a bashful smile.

"I've heard *gut* things about you too." Ruthie smiled and then turned to Josiah. "I'm so glad to be here today, so I can meet Josiah's *freinden*."

"Ruthie! Can you help us serve the meal?" Lizzie, Josiah's sister, called her over.

"Excuse me. I'll see you both later," Ruthie said before joining the other women.

"She's lovely," Salina said as Ruthie walked away.

"She is." Josiah stepped closer. "How is Will?"

Salina shook her head. "I don't know. I think we've missed our chance to work things out, to even be *freinden*."

"Don't lose faith," Josiah said. "God is *gut*."

Salina nodded, but her hope was dwindling with every passing minute.

. . .

Will breathed deeply as he hurried up the Kurtz family's driveway toward the large barn where wedding guests were milling

about. He set his cooler on the ground and then smoothed his
hands over his jacket and adjusted his hat. He glanced around
for Salina or a familiar face that might be able to lead him to
her. When he spotted Bethany, he was excited.

"Will!" Bethany met his gaze and hurried over to him.
"What are you doing here?"

"Jeff invited me. Have you seen Salina?"

"*Ya.*" She pointed toward the pasture. "I think she went for a
walk out there. She said she had to clear her head."

"*Danki.*" He picked up the cooler and walked away.

"Hey, Will," she called, and he turned back toward her. "I'm
glad to see you." Her smile was genuine.

"*Danki.*" Maybe Bethany knew he had a chance with Salina.
Hope swelled in his chest as strode toward one of the most
important moments of his life.

. . .

Salina hugged her heavy sweater against her body as she looked
out over the pasture where the wedding guests' horses roamed.
She sighed as she lost herself in thoughts of Will. It was no use
trying not to. She could almost see his face and hear his voice.

Then she froze. Had she just heard his voice? Or was she
losing her mind?

"Salina!"

She turned to see Will walking toward her. When he reached
her, he set a medium-sized, blue-and-white cooler down at his
feet.

"What . . . what are you doing here?"

"Jeff invited me. I ran into him at the grocery store. May I
talk with you?" His eyes seemed to plead with her.

Salina looked toward the barn. "*Ya*. But make this quick. If *mei dat* sees me talking to you, he'll be upset."

"I've already talked to him, and he won't mind."

"What do you mean?" She searched his blue eyes. Oh, how she'd missed him!

"I mean he's given me permission to talk to you."

"He has?" She stared up at him, her heart beating so fast she could hardly breathe. "I don't understand. What do you want to say?"

Will looked down at the ground and kicked a rock with the toe of his black boot. Then he met her gaze again, some kind of determination in his eyes. "I want to tell you the truth. And the truth is that I liked you from the moment I met you at your booth. As I got to know you, that morphed into something more." He huffed out a breath. "I'm in love with you."

Her body trembled as she waited for him to go on.

"Salina, I knew I was falling in love with you, but I was afraid of what would happen if I broke up with Caroline. I was afraid both our families would be upset with me. It took me too long to realize that God was leading me to you. And as much as I tried to ignore my feelings for you, they just continued to grow into something deeper and more meaningful than I've ever felt for anyone."

"I-I don't understand," she said, her voice reedy. "First, that day I told you how I felt about you, you just stared at me and didn't say a word." She shook her head as tears stung her eyes. "I was so embarrassed because I poured my heart out to you, and you said nothing. I was convinced you didn't return my feelings."

"I'm so sorry about that." He took a step closer to her. "I just couldn't speak because I was shocked. I never expected you to say what you did, that you loved me. I should have told you then that I loved you, too, but I was still with Caroline, and I felt trapped."

He took her hands in his, and invisible sparks danced along her skin. "I believe God sent me to the marketplace to meet you because you're my future. You're the one he's chosen for me. If you'll give me a chance, I'll prove you're the most important person in my life. You're my destiny. You're the one I want to spend the rest of my life with."

Salina searched his eyes, looking for any sign of a lie. "Are you sure?"

"*Ya*, I'm sure, Salina. I've never been surer of anything."

"I know I pushed you away, but still, why didn't you tell me you and Caroline had broken up when you saw me in the restaurant with *mei mamm*? Caroline is here today, and she told me she thought you broke up with her to be with me."

"Yes and no. I broke up with her because our relationship was all wrong. But I also realized that truth because I met you. I wanted to tell you everything that day, but not only did you push me away, but Danielle interrupted us." He gave her hands a gentle squeeze. "I love you, and I've missed you. And I don't want to spend one more day away from you."

"But you're Mennonite, and I'm Amish. I can't leave the faith without hurting my family. How can we be together if we're not from the same community or even the same faith?" she asked, her voice ragged.

"I've already thought about that. Prayed about it too." He ran his finger down her cheek, and she leaned into his touch. "That's why I spoke to your *dat*. He said if I attend three baptism classes in the spring, I can join the church, and he'll honor my baptism."

She shook her head as happy tears filled her eyes. Then she gave a little laugh as the tears streamed down her cheeks. "This has to be a dream. I can't truly be hearing you want to join my community and that *mei dat* has already given you permission."

"You're not dreaming." He grinned. "But I'll pinch you if you'd like."

She laughed again.

"Oh, how I've missed that laugh." He glanced down at the cooler. "I almost forgot. I need your help with something."

"What?" She wiped away the tears.

"I need to know which one of these I should name for us." He opened the cooler.

"What are you talking about?"

"I'm adding one of these to the menu called Salina and Will's Pie." He pulled out a pie. "This is blackberry. I thought you might want this one named after us since it was the pie that brought us together."

He handed it to her and then pulled out another one. "Or we can have Salina and Will's Butterscotch Pie because this is my favorite recipe in the Betty Crocker cookbook you gave me." He handed her the butterscotch pie and then reached for one more.

"Will!" she exclaimed as she balanced the two pies in her hands.

"I also brought an apple pie because you're the apple of my eye." He held up a third creation.

"How many do you have in there?" She peered into the cooler.

"Six. Can you take this one too? I have three more."

She shook her head as the urge to laugh gripped her. "No. I can't."

Will pointed to a nearby bench. "Put them there, I suppose."

She set the first two pies down, then took the third from him.

"And here's a strawberry pie because your love is as sweet as strawberries. We also have—"

"Will, stop." She took the pie from him and set it back in the cooler. "You can choose what pie you want to name after us."

"Does that mean you will give me another chance?" He placed one palm on either side of her face. "Tell me you haven't given up on me."

"I haven't given up on you. You've had my heart for a long time." She sniffed as her tears overflowed once again. "*Ich liebe dich*, Will."

"I love you, too, Salina. I love you more than I've loved anyone in my life."

He leaned down, and when he brushed his lips over hers, a fire inside of her came to life and spread its warmth until she burned all over. Salina closed her eyes. She'd never felt like this.

When Will broke away, he pulled her into his arms, and she rested her head against his shoulder. She sensed her heart mending as she breathed in his familiar scent.

God had answered her prayers. Will had come back.

EPILOGUE

"How did you like the church service today?" Salina asked as she and Will walked out of her family's barn a month later.

"It was *gut*." He nodded and smoothed one hand down his white shirt and black vest, his other hand grasping the jacket slung over one shoulder. December had brought the cold. "How do I look?" he asked as he slipped the jacket on.

"Handsome." She smiled up at him. "I love seeing you dressed Amish."

"Do you?" He waggled his eyebrows, and she laughed. "Well, I just love being with you."

She leaned into him, seeking warmth beyond her winter wrap. "I love being with you too."

Salina had smiled so much during the past weeks that her cheeks were almost always sore. After Christiana's wedding, she'd set to work making clothes for Will. Soon he started dressing Amish, and Salina thought it somehow made him even more attractive.

He'd joined her family for supper more than once, and even her brother had accepted him into the family. Salina also met Will's family, and she felt accepted by them as well. He had also found a little house to rent from an Amish couple in their church district, and he was adjusting to the Amish life well.

Salina felt as if everything was falling into place—they'd even organized Will's office at the restaurant—and she'd never been happier.

"Hey, you two!" Bethany called from where she stood with a group of young people from their church. "Are you coming to the youth gathering with us? We're going to play Ping-Pong in Henry Bontrager's barn."

Salina looked up at Will. "Do you want to go? Or do you want to stay and visit with my family?"

Will hesitated. "What do you want to do?"

Salina glanced toward her house, and she spotted *Mammi* and *Daadi* walking up the steps to the back porch. "I think my grandparents would enjoy spending more time with you."

"Sounds *gut*." Will winked at her.

Salina turned toward Bethany. "You go have fun. We'll stay here."

Bethany shrugged. "Okay. I'll see you Thursday at the marketplace!"

"I meant to tell you that I saw Caroline at the restaurant yesterday," Will said when Bethany had gone. "She seems *froh*. She introduced me to her new boyfriend. And he even ordered a piece of Salina and Will's Blackberry Pie."

"No kidding! And how's your sister-in-law, Karen?"

"She's doing well, and the *boppli* is doing great too." His smile widened. "I told you they named him Irvin Jr, right?"

"You did, and that's *wunderbaar*!"

"So. I have a question," he said as they approached the back porch. "In the spring, will I get a discount on produce now that you're my girlfriend?"

She jammed her hands on her hips and feigned a glare. "Are you using me for my produce?"

"Maybe." He gave her a palm up before chuckling.

She threaded her fingers with his and looked into his face. "It's a *gut* thing I love you."

"It's a very *gut* thing. In fact, it's the best thing of all." He leaned down and kissed her, sending heat sizzling through her veins. "*Ich liebe dich*," he whispered against her lips.

"I love you, too, Will."

"Let's go make some hot chocolate. I have a great recipe."

He pulled her to his side, and just before they walked into the house, she smiled up at the clear blue sky and silently thanked God for bringing Will into her life.

Acknowledgments

As always, I'm thankful for my loving family, including my mother, Lola Goebelbecker; my husband, Joe; and my sons, Zac and Matt. I'm blessed to have such an awesome and amazing family that puts up with me when I'm stressed out on a book deadline.

Many, many thanks to Cindy Linthicum for helping to research this book and proofreading the draft. Your friendship is a blessing, Cindy! I look forward to shopping in Amish Country with you again very soon!

Thank you to my mother and my dear friends Becky Biddy and Susie Koenig, who graciously read the draft of this book to check for typos. I'm sure you had some giggles due to my hilarious mistakes!

I'm also grateful to my special Amish friend who patiently answers my endless stream of questions. Thank you also to my wonderful Mennonite friend who read the draft and offered pointers. Both of you are a blessing to me!

Thank you to my wonderful church family at Morning Star Lutheran in Matthews, North Carolina, for your encouragement, prayers, love, and friendship. You all mean so much to my family and me.

Thank you to Zac Weikal and the fabulous members of my Bakery Bunch! I'm so thankful for your friendship and your excitement about my books. You all are amazing!

To my agent, Natasha Kern—I can't thank you enough for your guidance, advice, and friendship. You are a tremendous blessing in my life.

Thank you to my amazing editor, Jocelyn Bailey, for your friendship and guidance. I appreciate how you push me to dig deeper with each book and improve my writing. I've learned so much from you, and I look forward to our future projects together. I also cherish our fun emails and text messages. You are a delight!

I'm grateful to editor Jean Bloom, who helped me polish and refine the story. Jean, you are a master at connecting the dots and filling in the gaps. I'm so thankful that we can continue to work together!

I'm grateful to each and every person at HarperCollins Christian Publishing who helped make this book a reality.

To my readers—thank you for choosing my novels. My books are a blessing in my life for many reasons, including the special friendships I've formed with my readers. Thank you for your email messages, Facebook notes, and letters.

Thank you most of all to God—for giving me the inspiration and the words to glorify you. I'm grateful and humbled that you've chosen this path for me.

DISCUSSION QUESTIONS

1. At the beginning of the story, both Will and Salina are convinced that they're trapped in relationships approved by their family and communities. As the story progresses, they both realize they're open to moving on to dating other people. What do you think helped them realize they deserved happiness?

2. Salina enjoys spending time with her three favorite cousins. Do you have a special family member with whom you like to spend time? If so, who is that family member, and why are you close to him or her?

3. Will discovered his love of cooking when he visited his uncle and worked in his restaurant. He'd gone to spend the summer there when he was confused about his place in the community and the church. Have you ever encountered a season when you were unsure in your faith or in your church? Or have you been hurt in some way? If so, how did you reconcile your confusion or hurt?

4. Salina's father doesn't approve of Salina's friendship with Will. Close to the end of the story, he changes his mind and allows Will to convert and date Salina. What do you think made him change his mind about Will?

5. Salina always felt she was compared to her older brother. Have you ever felt like you were judged against someone else? If so, how did you handle that?

6. Will decides to join the Amish community so he can start a life with Salina. What do you think of his decision to convert?

7. One reason Salina enjoys working in her garden is that it gives her time to pray and feel closer to God. Do you have a favorite activity that helps strengthen your faith?

8. Which character can you identify with the most? Which character seemed to carry the most emotional stake in the story? Salina, Will, or someone else?

9. Salina is devastated after she and Will have a falling out, and her cousins try to console her. Think of a time when you felt lost and alone. Where did you find your strength? What Bible verses helped?

10. What did you know about the Amish or Mennonites before reading this book? What did you learn?

ABOUT THE AUTHOR

A my Clipston is the award-winning and bestselling author of the Kauffman Amish Bakery, Hearts of Lancaster Grand Hotel, Amish Heirloom, Amish Homestead, and Amish Marketplace series. Her novels have hit multiple bestseller lists including CBD, CBA, and ECPA. Amy holds a degree in communication from Virginia Wesleyan University and works full-time for the City of Charlotte, NC. Amy lives in North Carolina with her husband, two sons, and five spoiled rotten cats.

Visit her online at amyclipston.com
Facebook: @AmyClipstonBooks
Twitter: @AmyClipston
Instagram: @amy_clipston
BookBub: @AmyClipston

Follow four cousins and their journey toward love and happiness while working at the local market!

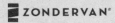